The Lake Trilogy

Troubled Waters

AnnaLisa Grant

For Kelly, Lisa B., Jenna, and Lisa S.
Your friendship makes my heart swell.

We must be willing to let go of the life we have planned,
so as to have the life that is waiting for us.
-Joseph Campbell

Chapter 1

I wake up and rub my eyes in another morning of disbelief, confusion, and elation. Every morning for the last two weeks I've woken with the first thought that finding Will's ring amongst my packed boxes was just a dream. But it wasn't. It's here, firmly affixed to the middle finger of my clenched fist, shining and reflecting the bit of light streaming in from the crack in the curtains. It rests on my hand next to Will's grandmother's ring. I look at the two rings next to each other and think how perfectly they go together.

My heart fills with joy as I recall the night we exchanged these rings. I think about the promise we made to each other to never give up on our love and our future together. I remember feeling so hopeful, so happy. I didn't know what Will, Luke and Claire were planning, but it felt like we were on top, conquering the giant. We were winning and nothing was going to change that.

Just as quickly as it soared, my heart drops as I'm plagued by the one question that I can't find an answer to: Why would Will take off the ring he swore to wear forever?

Fear fills my heart and my mind follows suit. I run scenarios through my head of the terrible and *unimaginable* things Gregory Meyer wouldn't hesitate to do to his own son. Has he sequestered Will to a place with 24-hour surveillance where Will has no contact with the outside world? Has Meyer threatened my family or me so much so that Will has had no choice but to abandon me? Did he have the ring pried from Will's cold, dead finger? The most terrifying thought of all is strangely not related to Will's demise. I'd be lying if I said I hadn't entertained the very real possibility that Will gave the ring back to me out of his own volition as a means of saying goodbye.

I can't do this anymore. The waiting and unknowing are slowly driving me insane. Clearly Will isn't going to show up at my door. If he were going to, he would have by now. There has to be a logical reason as to why Will would do the exact opposite of what he promised. I want to take it as a sign of something good, not something devastating and I need some reassurance.

It's time to tell Luke and Claire.

Luke and Claire have been exceptionally patient with me since Will's disappearance but I'm not sure how much longer that is going to last. I was compliant in helping to pack and unpack the house, even though I've been constantly distracted. Will's father having called off the search after less than a month was so incredibly distasteful that it made me physically ill. It wasn't enough to threaten everyone I love and force us out of town, but for him to move on so flippantly gave more evidence to the fact that ice is the only thing that runs through his veins.

I give Will's ring one last look before placing it back in the ring box and into my nightstand. Even though I'm not sure I'm ready to give up my secret, I know I can't wait any longer to tell my uncle- and aunt-turned-parents.

After a quick shower I grab the ring box and put it in my pocket. Then I'm downstairs preparing for whatever answers Luke and Claire may have, if any.

I'm beginning to feel really stupid. What if I was supposed to tell Luke and Claire as soon as I found the ring? What if there's some clue or answer or message from Will that I could have been clinging to these last few weeks but I missed it out of selfishness for wanting to keep the ring to myself? After all, they were working with Will on some master plan to take his father down before my world ended when Will dropped off the face of it. Maybe they're just waiting for me to say something.

"Ok, that's it. Classes start soon and you haven't even gone to see the campus yet," Luke says as I pick at my breakfast, lost in thought. Luke is gentle, but it's clear he's fed up with my zombie-like state.

"Uncle Luke, really, I…"

"No, Layla, you have to do this. No one is trying to keep you from dealing with Will's disappearance in your own way, but you have to start taking some steps to re-enter society."

"I know…it's just…hard," I choke out.

"Layla, your life cannot exist in the story of Will's disappearance. Will's disappearance is a chapter in the story of *your* life," Luke says taking me by the shoulders. "You have to turn the pages, start a new chapter."

"Has anyone heard anything at all?" I say, not knowing how to reply to his statement. I know he's right, but he doesn't know about me finding Will's ring a week after we moved here, which means there's clearly more to this story line than I'm aware of.

"Nothing new." I've watched Luke take on Claire's calm and gentle tone more and more. Like Claire, he seems to know just when to apply it. The look on my face gives me away as I think about Will's ring safely tucked away in my pocket. "What is it, Layla?" Luke asks, seeing through me.

"It's nothing," I lie, not sure how to tell him about the golden weight in my pocket.

"Layla…please don't start lying to me now." Luke is serious. "If you know something, you need to tell me."

"I was about to say the same thing to you." With a deep sigh I reach into my pocket and pull out the velvet box and place it on the kitchen counter.

"What's this?" Luke asks, furrowing his brow.

"Open it."

"Is this Will's ring?" Luke says as the box creeks open.

"Yes."

"Did Will give this back to you before he went to Hickory?"

"No. It was packed, alone, in a box underneath a mound of crumpled newspaper a week after we arrived here," I say. I can't help but smile a little looking at it.

"Why are you just showing it to me now?" Luke asks with disappointment.

"I…I don't know. I think I was waiting for something to happen…for Will to show up. But now…I'm thinking maybe you have some answers that I would have gotten had I shown you the ring two weeks ago. The three of you were planning something but you never let me know what. After a while I thought…maybe you were supposed to tell me something when I found it." I choke this out, not sure if I'm ready for whatever it is Luke is going to say.

Luke takes a long moment before he says anything, like he's searching for the right words that won't upset me. "Layla, I'm so sorry, but I don't know anything about the ring. Will never said anything to us about it." Luke's eyes are sad as he snaps the box shut. He can't give me an answer that will make the pain in my heart any less intense and that's difficult for him.

"You've got to know something! How does it show up in a box with my name on it? Will obviously meant for me to have it! Why? Why would he take it off? Why would he do this, Uncle Luke?" I land in a nearby chair, my face in my hands. "I just need some answers."

"I wish I knew what to tell you. I hate that you're going through so much pain." Luke pulls a chair up to face me and moves my hands so he can look at me. "Whatever the reason Will made sure you had this ring, it was rooted in his love for you."

"All I do is go back and forth between the best and worst my mind can come up with. At best, Will packed it so I would have it for safe keeping just in case his father discovered whatever it was you were planning. Will is going to be back for it, and me, any day now." I take a deep breath, calming myself like Claire taught me.

"And at worst?" Luke prompts.

"At worst…it's Will's way of saying good-bye. He finally realized that I'm not really worth all the trouble." I've run this picture through my head so many times that I don't cry anymore at the thought of Will ending our relationship.

"Layla don't…" Luke begins.

"I know…I know…I have to cling to the best. I can't give up hope that he didn't walk away from me, that he's alive. Even if he doesn't know who he is, he's alive, and that's all that matters." I fight back tears but there are too many and they begin to roll down my cheeks.

"We're never going to give up hope." Luke holds me tightly in his arms and I feel so safe. It's a feeling I've gotten used to. I could never have cried or shown emotion like this with Gram. Those years of being constantly reminded of how she blamed me for my parents' death are behind me. "I know it's hard. We're here for you when you're ready to talk."

"Thank you. I'm ok. Wherever Will is, I know he would want me to move forward; not on, but forward." I manage a small, thin-lipped smile and Luke echoes.

"You need to know that Claire and I are concerned about you. You don't talk about Will except to ask if there are any new developments, and now I know you found Will's ring and kept if from us for weeks. You've got to get out what you've been keeping inside, Layla."

"I know. There are moments when I feel like I'm going crazy. I don't have any answers so my mind exaggerates every scenario I think of. I want to talk…I just don't want to talk about Will in the past tense. I'll be ready to talk about him again soon. I promise." I sigh knowing that all I want to do right now is search every possible route between Davidson and

Hickory and find the love of my life and his mother. "I guess I could at least go pick up my books," I concede.

"That's my girl. Here are the keys. The address is already in the GPS. Go," he instructs as he kisses the top of my head. I love it when he does that.

The campus isn't far from where we live and is easy to find. The University is a major part of life in this town, so there are signs everywhere. I park near the admissions office and get a map of the campus along with my schedule. There's no one around to ask for help if I get lost, so I cross my fingers and make my way to the bookstore.

It's a beautiful campus. I notice the architecture and think that they've done an excellent job at mixing the new buildings with the old. I know how hard it is to mix the two. I hope I do a better job this time around.

As I open the door to the bookstore I catch a glimpse of a woman entering an adjacent building. I do a double take because from this distance the woman looks just like Will's mother, Eliana Meyer. She has long dark red hair and is stunningly beautiful even from this distance. Clearly I haven't been around people enough since we left North Carolina. I've been so out of touch that I'm afraid everyone I see will look like Will or his mother. I rub my eyes and shake it off as I continue through the door.

I buy my books and take them back to the car before I find the buildings where my classes will be. I'm fortunate that my classes seem to all be in one central location in two adjacent buildings. As I wrap up my self-guided tour of Florida State University, I notice there's a coffee shop right on campus. It looks like a pretty cool place that might have relatively cheap coffee and a dimly lit corner with my name on it so I make a mental note to check it out when classes start.

I've rounded out my tour, coming back full circle to the center of campus, when I see the woman again. It's eerie how much she looks like Will's mother. Without thinking I quicken my pace down the walkway and follow her to the College of Business building. I don't know why but I've got to get a better look at her. I reach the building and go inside but I've lost her. It's silent. Not even the sound of a single footstep. I contemplate for a brief moment the idea of opening each door in this hall but come to my senses and realize I need to go before campus security is after me.

I feel like such an idiot as I drive home. What was I going to say if I caught up with this doppelganger? "Hello. You look just like my missing boyfriend's mother, who is also missing by the way." Luke is right – I have to get out of this. I'll never give up hope, but I have to move forward. *When* Will comes back, he'll be so upset if he finds out I stunted myself in a place of desperate anticipation. He'll want to know what I've been doing, how I've grown, how I continued to get stronger. He always challenged me to do my best, so telling him I spent my days wishing and waiting will not be sufficient.

I walk into the kitchen with my stack of books and Luke helps me do my best not to let them topple to the floor when I put them on the table.

"I hope you're saving your money for the rest of my schooling. These books cost as much as this semester's tuition! My college fund is going to run dry sooner than later," I say picking up the one book that managed to escape and hit the floor. "And I still have to go back for one more that they didn't have in stock."

"I remember those days. It's worth every penny! What did you think of the campus? Claire and I stopped by the other day and thought it was beautiful," he says.

"It's really nice, and my schedule doesn't have me racing across campus from one building to the next. My first class doesn't start until nine so I'll have plenty of time to get there in the mornings." I hesitate to tell Luke about my Eliana sighting, but if I'm going to really make an effort to deal with this I need their help. They have more than proven that I can trust them with anything so I'm not going to start holding back now,

11

even if it points to me increasingly losing my mind. "I…saw something today…someone actually."

"Really? Someone from your high school in Orlando?" Luke raises his eyebrows in surprised excitement. I can tell he's hoping this is a step toward making new friends.

"Not exactly." I hesitate but suck it up and blurt it out. "I saw someone who looks *exactly* like Eliana Meyer. It was wild, Uncle Luke. I mean, if the, you know, the situation weren't what it is, I would *swear* it was her."

"That *is* wild. What happened?" he asks, sorting the tall stack of books into two columns.

"I tried to catch up with her but lost her. I don't know why I was trying. I guess I just wanted to get a better look at her. Anyway, I wanted to tell you in case I'm officially going crazy."

"You're not going crazy, Layla. We haven't really talked about this. No one knows where Will and Eliana are so your mind is looking for them everywhere. With Gregory calling off the search…" Luke looks at me curiously, waiting for my response.

"I know. It's just too hard to think about it like that. I can't give up hope," I say.

"Talking about the reality of the situation is not giving up hope," he says softly but sternly. "We're not going to pretend he never existed, Layla."

Luke's words take me back to our conversation about life with Gram. I wasn't allowed to talk about my parents. They were dead and we were going to live life as if they never existed. That was Gram's unspoken rule. I didn't realize until now that I was imposing that rule on myself and Luke and Claire. I have refused to talk about Will and, even now, am hesitant. For some reason I'm afraid to let the gush of emotions I've been holding in flow. But now, with my Eliana twin sighting, it's clear I can't do this anymore. Once my mind allows my heart to make this decision, there is immediately no reason to hold back. So I don't.

"I miss him so much!" I cry, letting the tears stream down my face uncontrollably. "He promised he'd be back. He promised he'd never leave me. Where is he?" I'm crying so hard that I'm hiccupping between words. "He hasn't contacted us in any way…that means he's hurt! He's out there and he's hurt and he can't get to a phone or anything!"

"Oh, Layla," Luke says taking me in his arms. "It's going to be ok. They're going to find him. Shhh…shhh." He strokes my hair in a smooth and comforting rhythm, easing my pain with every pass. "We aren't going to give up."

I sigh the sigh you take when you've just cried more than you thought possible. Luke has done a remarkable job at comforting me in a time when I felt hopeless. As I loosen my grip from around his middle, Luke looks at me and confirms my trust in him. No matter what happens, I know that I can trust him completely.

"See…that wasn't so bad, now, was it?" Luke grabs a napkin from the counter and gently wipes the tears that have streaked my face.

"That sucked."

"Yeah, I know." Luke and I chuckle as I regain my composure. "You gonna be ok?"

"I will be. I'll feel better when I know where he is," I say straightening my shirt and tucking some loose locks behind my ear.

"I think we'll all feel better." Luke tosses the napkin and leads me outside to where Claire is on the deck.

"Everything ok?" Claire asks. No doubt she heard my waling and is concerned. Luke gives her a nod and I see once again what a great team they make. She trusts him implicitly, which is why she didn't feel some motherly duty to come in and take on my crying. I love this about them.

"Everything is fine," I say.

"Well, since we're moving *forward*," Luke has told her about the ring as I assumed he would after I left. "Layla, did you see that there's a freshman reception next week? It'll be a good chance to start making

13

some friends before classes start." Claire is way more into my college experience than I am. She was clearly one of those students who went to every pep rally and football game. I bet she had the best spirit fingers around. The college experience is *very* important to her.

"Yeah, that sounds great," I say trying to appease her.

I would prefer to just go to class and come home each day. Much like when I first moved to Davidson, before I met Will, I have no desire to cultivate relationships. It means I might have to explain my life story at some point and I'm not about to do that. I can be the girl with the baggage, or I can pretend that my life is picture perfect. After thinking about it for a moment I decide that I don't like either of those options so I make a third. I'll keep to myself and avoid making too much conversation with anyone. I didn't get a chance to be the weird, reclusive girl at Heyward, so I'll give it a go here.

I go to the reception because I know it'll make Claire happy. It can't hurt. Maybe I'll find a study partner and it won't be a complete waste of time. I walk in and immediately feel out of place. Everyone seems to already know each other. At least at Heyward Prep I had my own little entourage to make me feel like I was part of something. My heart warms as I think about the days Will and I had with Gwen and Caroline, Chris and Tyler, and then saddens because I have no certainty that things will ever be like that again.

In the back of my mind I thought I might see someone from my high school in Orlando, but there are no familiar faces to be seen. God knows there's no way I'm seeing anyone from Heyward here. They wouldn't be caught dead at a state school.

I mingle and make less than small talk with people. When asked where I'm from my answer is a firm Davidson, North Carolina. I'm more connected to that town, even after being there just a year, than I ever was to Orlando. It's the place I discovered and learned so much about myself, the place I found a home with Luke and Claire, and the place I fell in love with and gave my heart to Will. Although exiled, I will always feel that Davidson is my home.

Two of the girls I meet are also psychology majors. We discover that we have a class together this semester and agree to form a study alliance. They seem like nice girls. I feel bad that I've already determined I'll never let them get close to me.

Having suffered long enough through feigned interest in other people, their majors and career goals, I decide I've done my due diligence in appeasing Claire and leave. Apparently everyone else is having a grand time at the reception because I'm the only one heading out of there.

The walk to my car is quiet. It would be just as quiet if Will were alive, but perhaps not as lonely. I thought I would spend my days here waiting, anticipating the moment until I could see my love again, touch his face…kiss his lips. Without that anticipation to keep me alive, each day I will be the walking dead.

I'm almost to my car when I hear someone else in the quiet of the night. My heart begins to race as I hear the quickened shuffle of feet behind me. I've just reached the tail of the Lexus when a hand grabs my shoulder and spins me around.

"Marcus!"

Chapter 2

Marcus is here and I'm happy to have a bit of home. I'm glad we were able to reconcile our friendship before I left. Between faking a romantic relationship for Will's father's sake, and his and Will's fight at Halloween, it had been an incredibly intense and stressful time. Seeing him now makes my heart happy, though, and I am excited to spend time with him, however short his visit may be.

"Hey, Layla!" Marcus says as our arms wrap around each other.

"What are you doing here? I thought you weren't coming to visit until fall!"

"Well, I'm not exactly visiting," he says.

"What do you mean?"

"I got to thinking…I don't have any family in Davidson – only some mediocre friends…and you're new here and could use a friend…so…I transferred!" Marcus seems so pleased with himself.

"Wow, Marcus! I…can't believe you did that!" And just like that, I'm happy and completely unnerved at the same time. I'm also now keenly aware that Marcus found me here on campus, which seems a bit too coincidental for me. Marcus made his feelings for me clear on more than one occasion, and even though I told him I loved Will, I'm not so sure he really gave up. With Will gone I'm nervous Marcus is going to try to rekindle what never had a spark in the first place. "Wow! Are you living on campus?" I stutter.

"Nah, I got a place nearby with some guys needing a fifth roommate. It was a stroke of luck that it all worked out in perfect timing."

"Why didn't you tell me you were coming?" A little warning would have been helpful. He has no idea what I've been going through, and just popping up like this isn't as helpful as he thinks it is. Had he told me I would have discouraged him, at least on the timing.

"I wanted to surprise you. Aren't you happy to see me?" He sounds annoyed that I haven't pulled out the pompoms to cheer for his arrival.

"No, I am…I'm happy to see you. I'm just surprised is all."

"Good. I knew you would be!" He smiles and grabs my hand, feeling that I'm still wearing Will's grandmother's engagement ring. "What's this?"

"It's a promise ring. Will gave it to me just before…" I can't bring myself to say the words out loud. Marcus scowls at the mention of Will's name.

"And you're still wearing it." It's not a question, but a chastisement.

"Yes. He's still out there, Marcus. I'm…I'm not ready to take it off," I say in a slight lie. I've given the impression that one day I will be ready to take it off, which is not the case. The only way this ring is leaving my hand is if it's pried off *my* cold, dead finger.

"Well, maybe that'll change soon." His tone is uncharacteristic of him, and I'm a little creeped out by it. It catches me off guard and I don't have an appropriate response to his inappropriate statement.

"Um…I need to get going. I've got the same cell, so, uh, give me a call. It's good to see you Marcus." I'm so caught off guard by him being here and his assumption of what may lie in store between us that my fight or flight is kicking in and I've got to get the hell out of here.

"Oh, ok. I thought maybe we could grab a coffee or something, but, uh, ok. I'll call you." He gives me a too-tight hug and I do my best to pull away naturally. "It's so great to see you, Layla. We've got a new life here and it's going to be great."

Excuse me, but we *do not have a life here. I have a life here. There is* no *"we".*

I smile and nod as I close the door to the car and do everything I can not to slam the gear into reverse and screech my tires out of there. The minutes home seems to last forever. I run through every encounter Marcus and I had together to figure out why in the world he would assume that a forward move like transferring to FSU would be well received. I never admitted to him that I liked being close to him when he was posing as my boyfriend for appearances sake. Even though it was nice, it was nothing like being with Will, and my feelings for Marcus were never romantic. I knew it then and I know it now. Marcus will never understand the difference.

I pull into the driveway of the house and check my phone for messages or texts from Luke or Claire. I've also been keeping in touch with Caroline, even though it's been a while since we connected. There are no messages from anyone, but three texts from Marcus.

Marcus Reynolds: So great to see u tonight. Can't wait to see u again!

Marcus Reynolds: U r not answering. R U OK? Or maybe u r driving.
If so, don't text and drive! ;-)

Marcus Reynolds: U should be home by now. Text me to let me know u r ok.

Great! Marcus has turned into a lovesick stalker puppy. I SO don't need this right now!

Layla Weston: I'm home now. I'll talk with u later. Goodnight.

Marcus Reynolds: Whew! U had me worried. I'll call you tomorrow!

I'm sure you will.

In the morning I recount last night's events to Luke and Claire and they're just as surprised as I was at Marcus' arrival.

"Why would he just up and leave Davidson?" Claire asks.

"I think he thinks we have some kind of future together now that Will is…." I silently applaud myself for being able to say Will's name so freely. I suppose Luke and Claire are doing the same thing since I've acted like his name is Voldemort.

"That's odd," Claire says, showing the same creeped-out feeling I had earlier. Only another girl would understand the uneasy feeling an unwanted suitor gives you. "Did you tell him that you're still holding out hope for Will's return?"

"Sort of. I really just wanted to get out of there. There's something different about him. The Marcus I knew wouldn't have just up and moved like that. Well, at least I never imagined that he would do something like that." Marcus' arrival has intensified my thoughts of Will. A swarm of memories invades my mind and I feel like I need some air.

I excuse myself to the back yard and find myself walking the long passageway of the dock to the lake for the first time since our arrival here. The path is lined with shrubs and trees with Spanish moss trailing down like vines and is very typically Floridian. It's thick in some parts and I have to brush branches and vines away as I move. When I arrive at the end of the dock I'm filled with mixed emotions. I'm elated and depressed at the same time. The manmade lake is nowhere near the size of Lake Davidson. Comparatively speaking, it's more like a massive pond.

I'm taken back to the first time Will and I sat at the end of the Lake Davidson dock together and I'm happy. I remember how nervous he was when he asked if I had seen the lake from the dock at night. I remember how it felt to feel the warmth of his body close to mine, and how he rescued me from an impending broken limb by taking my hand and guiding me up the flagstone to the house.

I feel the sting of tears in my eyes recalling the honesty of our conversations there, but I can't fight the tears anymore when I play back our graduation night. I trace my finger over my more-than-a-promise ring and recommit myself to the vow I made to Will. *I will never give up on us.*

I sit and stare out at the water, waiting to connect with this place as I did with its predecessor, praying to God that it happens soon because I don't think I will last another second here without the safety this connection will bring.

*****

My phone has been ringing off the hook all day. Marcus has literally called me seventeen times in six hours. Apparently *leave a message and I'll get back to you as soon as I can* doesn't really mean anything to him. When the day is just about over, and I decide it's too late for me to go out, I call him back.

"Layla! Are you ok? You haven't called me back all day!" Marcus sounds distressed. I've never heard him like this. He was usually so calm, cool, and collected.

"I'm fine, Marcus. I've just been busy today."

"Well, I'm just glad that you're ok. So, do you want to get that coffee?" he asks.

"You know, I'm super tired. It's been a long day. It feels like we're never going to get fully unpacked," I say, hoping to convey a reasonable excuse as to why I can't go out. I'm going to have to face him with the truth at some point. I won't be able to come up with excuses forever.

"Oh, yeah, I totally understand," he says hesitantly annoyed.

"Maybe another time?" I say as a peace offering.

"Definitely!"

"I'm sorry to cut it so short. I need to chill a little before I head to bed. Ok?"

"Chilling out sounds like a great plan. I'll talk to you soon then."

After echoing goodnights I take a shower and plop myself onto the couch in the Great Room with Luke and Claire. It's about 9:00 pm and I'm exhausted. Luke, Claire and I chit chat about the day and do our daily strategizing for the continued unpacking. When the doorbell rings we all mirror each other with puzzled looks. Luke dutifully gets up to answer the door since it's later than anyone should become an unexpected visitor.

I don't know why I'm surprised when Luke returns with Marcus at his side.

"Hello, Marcus," Claire says greeting him a bit more sternly than if he had called before he came. "Layla said you pulled quite a surprise by transferring to FSU. How's it going so far?"

"Hello, Mrs. Weston. It's going great. I got settled into my apartment a couple weeks ago and have been coordinating my classes. The last thing to do was to get reconnected with Layla. Now that I've done that, my life here is all set up!" He sounds like a little boy who just got the bicycle he's been asking for, almost giddy. Wait. If he's been here for two weeks, he arrived just a week after we did! "I know you were too tired to go out, so I thought I'd swing by. I hope you don't mind."

Actually, I mind very much.

"It's fine. Why don't we go out on the patio?" I get up and give Claire a wide-eyed looked, hoping to convey a "*Please* do not leave me out there too long with him. I really just need enough time to nip this in the bud."

Marcus follows me like the puppy he has transformed into and we take opposing seats on the patio. "Does that dock lead to a lake? We could go sit down there if you want," he says.

NO! "No, this is good. Besides, I don't think it's well lit." There's no way I'm going down there with him in the dark. "So, I think we should talk."

"Yeah, I think so, too." He clears his throat and I am filled with anxiety about what the next words out of his mouth are going to be. It's not the kind of throat-clearing one does as a means of actually clearing your throat. It's the kind that's a precursor to having something important to say. "First, I want to say again how sorry I am about Will. I know you really loved him." *Love him. I love him. It's not past tense.* "So I wanted to give you some time, you know, to get over him. That's why I've been here for a few weeks and didn't tell you."

"Get over him?" I challenge.

"Yeah. There's talk that Will's dad is going to have Will and his mom declared dead. You knew that, right?" Marcus says conversationally, as if he didn't just say *Will* and *dead* in the same sentence.

"They haven't found any bodies, Marcus. Until they do, Will and his mother are still alive as far as I'm concerned." I'm serious in my statement. I can't be wishy-washy; I have to be strong.

"Bodies or not..." Marcus' tone is off. I can't put my finger on it, but something isn't right.

"So, you're wanting...what?" I ask needing him to fill in the blanks. I want to hear it straight from him before I possibly tear into him for once again inserting himself into my life without my permission.

"Well..." He clears his throat again and straightens his posture. His puppy dog eyes are gone and in their place I see the fire of a determined man. "I care about you, Layla. I always have. And, not to be insensitive, but, now that Will is...gone...I hoped I could help you start over...with me." He reaches across the table and intentionally takes my left hand in his. "We could be great together, Layla. You just have to let go." He runs his thumb over my ring and I snatch my hand back.

"Marcus," I take a deep breath trying to compose myself. He has tainted any hope of us being friends and that makes me furious. He was another link to home and now he's ruined it. "I don't know what you thought was going to happen, but I don't feel the same way about you. I told you that back in Davidson. I'm sorry that you moved here under that assumption, but...you and me, we're never going to be more than friends." *If that.*

"Hmmm. Well, I beg to differ," he says confidently, his posture and tone changing. He's sitting back in his chair now, resting his ankle on his knee.

"Pardon me?"

"When we were back in Davidson, *pretending* to be together, it was more than just pretending with me…and I know it was the same with you, too." He leans across the table in a move to take control of the conversation physically. *Is he trying to intimidate me into being with him?* "Tell me you didn't like being close to me, and I'll leave."

I don't know why I don't just lie to him, but when I open my mouth the most foolish thing comes out.

"It was…*nice*. But you have to understand, Marcus, it wasn't the same for me. I *was* pretending, but it felt nice to be close to someone I thought I could trust when I couldn't be with Will." He's staring at me with piercing eyes and I feel a familiar uneasiness come over me. I can't place it because I've never felt this way around Marcus.

"You may say you were pretending, but I know. I won't make you say it, not yet at least." He sits back in his chair again, a disturbing air of confidence consuming him.

"Marcus, I think you need to leave. And don't call me or communicate with me for a while. I'm trying really hard to still want to be your friend, so you're going to have to give me some time here. Do you understand me?" I try to be solid in my delivery, the same way Claire can be when the situation calls for it.

"I understand," he says with a smirk.

"Are we clear?"

"Crystal."

"Then I think it's time for you to go. I'll communicate with you when I'm ready. Don't rush me, Marcus. Frankly, right now you're lucky I haven't called Luke to escort you out."

"There's no need to get hostile, Layla. I've had a lot of time to think about what you want and I'm confident that you'll come around." Marcus lets himself out while I stay on the patio, completely stunned by what just unfolded.

He's had time to think about what I want? What does that even mean?

"Are you ok?" Claire asks stepping out onto the patio from the porch with Luke a few moments later.

"Yeah, I guess. It's just so weird. I don't know what's come over him. He handled my rejection back home really well, but now, it's like he's a different person. You should have seen him. He was cocky and arrogant. And when I told him I didn't feel the same way about him, he actually said 'I beg to differ.' Can you believe that?"

"What did he say?" Luke asks slowly.

"He said, 'I beg to differ.' And then he tried to convince me that I preferred being with him while we were all show for Mr. Meyer," I explain.

"Hmmm." Luke's eyes are searching for something in his mind.

"Is that supposed to mean something?" I ask.

"It's just a strange response, don't you think?" Claire interjects.

"Definitely. And now I am sufficiently spent. I'm going to bed. I told him not to communicate with me, so…"

"We've got it covered," Luke reassures me. He's practiced at running interference for me.

I lay in bed thinking about how strange the last 48 hours have been. Seeing the Eliana Meyer clone was enough to freak me out, but then Marcus showing up? Him being here is more than I can handle right now. I wish he had told me he was coming. I would have told him that I didn't think it was a good idea. I would have told him that what I really need right now is to be in a place where I can start over, where nothing reminds me of the life I was forced to leave behind. But he's here now and I have a feeling there is nothing I could have said that would have kept him from coming here. I can only hope that he'll respect my wishes and give me time and space.

Chapter 3

I'm making it through my first week of classes pretty well, and despite my efforts against it, I'm making a few friends. It's a state school, so the majority of the students are like me. We've worked hard to get where we are, not having life handed to us on a silver platter. There are a few people who immediately put me at ease, but I still can't bring myself to take the wall down completely. It's not as heavily guarded as it once was, so I guess that's good.

The campus coffee shop is quickly becoming my favorite place to pass the time during my two hour layover between classes. It's here where I seem to be connecting with someone I might actually be brave enough to let in.

Finn is a barista on a work- study program. He's tall with short brown hair, brown eyes, and built like a football player. He's funny, charming, smart, and we have the same taste in men, so *that* not being an issue makes me feel safe. He's a music major and our little conversations about artists I've never heard of remind me of Will.

"Hey chai tea latte," he says as he comes through the shop to wipe tables. "How's your day going?"

"Hey barista guy," I tease in response. "Pretty good, how about you?"

"Great! Didn't anyone ever tell you that being a barista is the best job ever? I don't know why we're all wasting our money on a great education."

"Seriously!" We both laugh and I have another moment of feeling like Finn might be someone I can trust one day. My gut isn't screaming that I should turn and run, and that's a good sign.

"Did you listen to that Alex Clare album I suggested?" he asks as he stocks the counter next to me with stir straws and sweetener.

"Yeah, actually. I loved it! Thanks for the recommendation." I ponder telling him about having a *friend* back home who challenged me to broaden my musical horizons like he does, but decide it's too soon. The fact that I'm considering it is very telling, though.

"Well, I've got a whole list of artists you'll have to check out. Now that you trust my impeccable judgment your lessons have officially begun!" His reference to music lessons like Will and I used to have doesn't scare me like I thought it would have. It actually puts me at ease, allowing me to hold on to something that was so special between Will and me.

We laugh, but the laughter turns sour for me as I spot Marcus across the coffee shop. "Oh, no."

"What? That guy?" Finn says taking note of Marcus, too. "That guy has been in here every day this week. You didn't notice him before?"

"No, I didn't."

"Is he bothering you? You want me to have him kicked out?" Finn offers. "What's the deal?"

"No, don't kick him out. I'm not quite sure what will happen if you do." I sigh, wondering what to tell Finn about Marcus. I swore I wasn't going to tell anyone about my life before FSU, but my gut tells me there's something about Finn that I can trust, so I decide to divulge a snippet of my past life to him and still be in the clear since it won't have anything to do with Will. Besides, if Marcus is going to play stalker, I'm going to need some help here on campus. "He's a guy from back home. He was interested in me and I told him I didn't feel the same way. I moved down here with my uncle and aunt to, you know, go to school and kind of start over, and he followed me. I thought we were going to be great friends, but he's had some kind of psychotic break because he transferred schools and is now under the assumption that he and I are going to be together. I told him to back off and I would call him if and when I was ready to talk.

But…here he is, existing in a loop hole to my instructions, staring me down in your coffee shop. So…that's the deal."

"Whoa," Finn says in the slightest of surfer dude voices.

"I know, right? So now I'm going to go to class and I'm sure he's going to follow me." I sigh, frustrated at the inevitable confrontation in my near future.

"You want to duck out the back? There's an exit by the bathroom," Finn offers.

"Oh, Finn! You're a lifesaver!" I accept his offer and, as Finn covers me, I make my way to the bathrooms and then out the back door. I know it's a quick fix for today, but at least I'll get to class without having to look over my shoulder.

I spend the time in my English Lit class doing my best to pay attention. Knowing that Marcus is looming like a creeper out there somewhere is making that difficult though. It's a good thing Heyward insisted on all honors classes. Even though this is a second year class, most of what my professor has covered so far I did last year.

The hour and a half goes by relatively quickly and as I gather my books and make my way down stairs I realize that getting to class was the easy part. Leaving, however, is proving to be more difficult. As I exit the building Marcus is seated on the bench directly facing me. I stop in my tracks and our eyes meet. This has gone far enough. Determined, I follow my path down the steps and Marcus stands as I reach him.

"Marcus, what are you doing?" I demand.

"Why, Layla, I'm so glad you've decided to communicate with me," he says twisting my words to meet his selfish need.

"That is *not* what this is. I'm only *communicating* with you so I can tell you to stop following me. Don't you have classes of your own? If you had any hope of us being friends, you can forget it. You've gone too far, Marcus." I can feel my blood pressure rising from the anger bubbling up.

"I'm very disappointed to hear you say that, Layla. I had hoped this would be an easy journey for us, but I see you're going to make me work a bit harder. No worries. I can do that." His tone is unnervingly calm and my stomach twists into knots.

"What's come over you?" I ask in astonishment at his brazen statement.

"I just realized that I have more potential than I've been tapping into and I'm not going to waste it any longer. You want space? I can give you space…but not for too long, my dear. I've got some…loose ends to tie up. I'll be back soon." Marcus lightly pinches my chin before walking away and a shiver runs down my spine.

As I rush through the front door I call out for Luke and Claire. Marcus has taken this farther than I ever thought he would. After I explain the events of the day to them, a switch gets flipped and Luke goes into full on dad plus lawyer equals you-better-watch-out mode.

"I'll have his every move watched, his bank accounts monitored, and have him deleted from the university system. It will be like he never existed." He's talking and dialing and getting online all at the same time.

"What? You can do all that?" I ask in shock. I knew Luke had connections when he was with Meyer, Fincher and Marks, but I thought all that went away when we did.

"Layla, you have no idea what I'm capable of, but…perhaps it's time that you did," Luke says, smiling a satisfied grin.

There's something about his declaration that actually puts me at ease. It's a protective statement that it seems he's wanted to assert for a long time. I got that feeling from him when he and Claire said they had enough dirt on Gregory Meyer to take care him down, but when Mr. Meyer came at us with a threat to ultimately erase our identities if we didn't get out of Davidson and leave Will alone, I guess it was more than they could handle. But now…now that it's just Marcus, Luke has got to feel confident in his ability to protect me.

Luke is on the phone chatting feverishly with someone about *trailing*. "Reynolds. R-E-Y-N-O-L-D-S....November 11, 1990...No, today...*now*...I want his every move watched...Yes...48 hours then I want a full report...Good."

I stand there, my mouth agape, amazed at what I'm witnessing. "Layla, honey, why don't you sit down," Claire says, taking a break from searching files at her desk. "Luke," she calls. "It's time."

Luke stops mid-dial and breathes a heavy sigh. "Layla...hmmm...how do I even begin to tell you?"

"You told me not to lie to you. Just tell me the truth," I plead.

"Ok." Luke repositions himself on the small leather couch in their office to face me, much like he did the night in Asheville. "You're aware that I started my career at Meyer, Fincher and Marks as an intern. And I know that Claire gave you a general idea of some of my *responsibilities* for Gregory Meyer. Well...during that time I became acquainted with some less than desirable individuals: former FBI, CIA, and various ex-military. These men would prove to be great assets to Meyer. Do you remember when I told you that he never loses?" I nod. "These men are part of the reason he never loses."

"What...what does that mean?" I ask nervously. My wild imagination could put it together, but I'm afraid that what it creates will be wildly accurate.

"Meyer represented these men in cases in which they were no less than guilty. Tax evasion, assault, manslaughter, attempted murder. But he did what he does best and they all found themselves with Not Guilty verdicts. Rather than charging his standard fees, Gregory determined that his attorney fees would be paid through favors in their areas of expertise. They were kept on retainer, being paid a monthly stipend, since their services could be required of them at any given time. If they refused, they'd find themselves in the hot seat of a courtroom again."

"I don't understand. They can't be tried twice for the same crime. That's called, um, double jeopardy, right? Why would they go along with it?"

"Very good. They agreed because Meyer always holds at least one card up his sleeve. One refusal to carry out his directive and evidence of new charges, real or feigned, would magically appear before the District Attorney."

"So…what did these men *do* exactly?" I ask but I'm not sure I really want to know the answer.

"They're experts at going unseen, deciphering code, getting into places and systems the average citizen has restricted access to, and…intimidation for the purpose of gaining information." Luke speaks slowly, choosing his words carefully. He wants to be honest with me, but not scare me to death.

"I…I saw…*that*," I squeak out.

"You saw what, Layla?" Claire asks firmly.

"Um...last year…I saw Mr. Meyer overseeing some…intimidation. It was right there, out back, outside the law firm. These two guys were, well, they punched this guy in the gut until he lost his lunch."

"That would be Furtick and Taylor. They're the best at what they do, and Greg just cut them loose. He likes to bring in fresh muscle every few years just in case they start to get sloppy. I have a call into Furtick."

"What? Why would you want these guys involved in our lives?" I ask frantically.

"These guys are the best resource I have. They're ex-military and will know exactly what's needed to get the Marcus situation under control."

"I don't suppose Mr. Meyer represented them because of tax evasion," I say.

"No," he says with a bit of a chuckle. "But that's why we need them." Luke takes my hand in a comforting hold. "Are you ok, Layla? I know this is a lot of information to digest. Do you have any questions?"

"I don't want Marcus to get hurt. I just…I just want him to go back to Davidson."

"Marcus won't get hurt unless he puts himself in a position to get himself hurt. And, frankly, I don't care if that happens. My job is to protect you and I'll do that by whatever means is necessary," Luke declares. He's in protective-mode and I can't help but think he's enjoying a fatherly moment he never thought he'd have after Penny died.

"I understand." Luke gives me a hug and hurries himself back to the phone and computer. I hear the furious clacking of the keyboard and Luke's instructions being barked out over the phone. Claire returns to the desk and continues to sort through documents.

As I sit there my mind races, thinking about Will and what life would be like if he weren't missing. With him being at Princeton, would Marcus have braved a transfer to FSU to try to make something more of us? I can't shake that something happened to him after I left. His whole personality changed. Marcus had been so gentle and caring. Now he's someone altogether different. He's demanding and assumptive, and the fire in his eyes is frightening. I don't like that Luke is calling in the big guns on this, but I'm afraid that if he doesn't, Marcus is going to do something desperate.

Chapter 4

The coast seems clear over the next weeks of school with no sign of Marcus anywhere on campus. Just because I can't see him, it doesn't keep me from looking over my shoulder in between classes, though. By the end of the week I'm fully satisfied that Marcus is at least giving me the space I demanded. So, as I approach the counter, I enjoy ordering my chai tea latte from my budding friend Finn a little more comfortably.

"Hey! Where's your stalker?" Finn says with a wink as he hands me my drink.

"Oh, I ditched him. He was totally cramping my style." I tease only to keep myself from crying.

"That's good. Having a stalker is so nineties."

We smile and I move to find a table and get out of the way of the stream of students needing a caffeine fix to get them through the rest of their day. I sip my latte slowly while thumbing through the pages of magazine. I hesitate accepting this feeling of normalcy, but still, it's starting to settle in. The drama of getting rid of Marcus is unfolding but working out well. With him out of the way, I can refocus on my life here, making things as normal as possible while I hope for Will's return.

Walking into the house I toss my backpack in its usual spot on the big couch in the Great Room. I'm about to call out my Marcus-free day report when I hear something that sounds like someone sniffling. I search for the source and head to the kitchen where I find Luke and Claire looking solemn. I can see that it's Claire who has been crying by her red, puffy eyes and sniffing nose.

"What's wrong?" I ask, rushing to Claire's side.

"Layla, you should sit down," Luke says softly.

"Why? What's going on?"

"Layla…" Luke says slowly. "They found Will."

"What? That's great!" I say excitedly.

"No, it's not," Luke begins. "There was an accident."

The sound of Luke's voice is the last thing I remember.

*****

I wake up without opening my eyes. I'm in my bed and I can hear Luke and Claire's muffled voices.

"How much longer did Carol say she thought Layla would be out?" Luke asks quietly.

"She said that there's really no way to tell but considering her past experience, it could be a while. She said this type of shutting down is the mind's way of protecting itself. Carol was surprised when I told her how fast Layla went from hysterics to passing out," Claire says, seeming to relay a conversation she had with Caroline's mom. Having a psychiatrist friend has its perks.

"Is there anything we can do for her?" I can hear the sadness in Luke's voice.

"The best thing right now is to let her rest."

The voices stop and I try to remember every word that Luke said about the accident. It's getting blurry and I need to recapture it before the details are completely gone. If I can remember what he told me then I can piece together how it isn't true; how there's been a mistake.

Will and his mother were driving home from Hickory when something happened...Will lost control of the car. They hit...a tree...and the engine...it caught on fire. They were both knocked unconscious before the whole car went up in flames. There has to be something I'm forgetting. It can't be that cut and dry. Oil slick? No. Cow in the road? Yes, maybe that was it. Luke said they were on a back road off Interstate Forty. Something about it isn't sitting right with me. There's been a mistake. Or, if it's not a mistake, there's more to it. It couldn't be just a tragic accident. Not *another* tragic accident to add to the story of my life.

When I open my eyes the room is pitch black except for the bright red glow of the clock, which reads 11:45 pm. I get up and steady myself before I walk to the door and open it. My eyes are sore and swollen. It hurts to blink.

I walk carefully down the stairs and into the kitchen.

"Layla! Honey, how are you?" Luke rushes to my side from across the room in one fluid slide, trying to steady me although I'm balancing just fine now. He helps me onto the stool at the island counter and Claire brings me a glass of water.

"I'm fine," I say calmly.

"Would you like to talk, Layla?"

"How did you find out?" I answer, although the words were on the tip of my tongue before she asked.

"Will's father called," Claire answers.

"What did he say?"

"He told us what we told you. He thought…he thought you might want to know," she continues.

"That's very generous of him," I say with as much insincerity as I know how to convey. "Did he sound upset?"

"Yes," Claire answers slowly.

"How upset?"

"Very upset…in his own way." She knows where I'm going with my questioning.

"If they were on their way home from Hickory, why are we just finding out now? It's been over two months."

"Layla, you don't want all the details…" Luke starts.

"Yes. I do. Why are we just finding out now?" I reiterate.

Luke takes a deep breath, readying himself. "Their bodies were…unrecognizable. An investigator that Greg had on the case followed a lead that just now panned out. They were in the city morgue. They had to be identified through their dental records."

"Is he going to be investigated?"

"Who?" Luke asks.

"Gregory Meyer. Is Will's father going to be investigated?"

"Why would he be investigated, Layla?" Luke asks in his lawyer tone.

"Because…he had something to do with this," I reply very matter of fact.

"How do you know Greg was involved?" Luke asks.

"Will told me he had something planned so that we could be together. He also said that his father would rather see him dead than not fulfill his Meyer destiny. His father must have found out and retaliated," I say.

"Layla, Will's father was in Raleigh that day. This was an *accident*. It wasn't anyone's fault. The police think there was a deer in the road and Will overcompensated when he veered to miss it." Luke replies in a slow, concentrated tone. My composure is alarming to them.

"You can tell me what really happened." I demand. I can't get the image of the last time I was with Will out of my head. He had been restless and determined to make sure I knew how much he loved me. "I can handle it, Uncle Luke."

"Layla, there's nothing more to tell you."

"I don't care that he wasn't in town. You know as well as I do that he has the power to do something this awful," I protest.

"I'm so sorry, Layla, but…as much as I would love to pin Gregory Meyer to the wall on this, it's just a terrible and completely unfair accident. Will…is dead," Luke answers.

His words resonate in my head for what feels like several minutes. I study both of them, the expressions on their faces. They're eyes are dark and sad. They look worn and tired. There is nothing about them that says what they are telling me is anything but true. My head feels heavy, full, and I know. "You really don't believe Mr. Meyer had anything to do with the accident?"

"No. He had no involvement," Luke says. He's serious and I fight to believe him. I don't want to believe him.

"But…Will's ring…he said…he said we were going to be together. Oh, God. Will is…and his mother…" I can't breathe.

"Yes, honey. They're both gone." Claire wraps her arms around me, beginning to cry with me.

Somehow, when I believed Will's father was involved, it was almost bearable. I had someone to place the blame on, but now that it's *just an accident* there will never be justice. It will be *another* senseless tragedy in my life. My heart is going to beat out of my chest and now I really can't breathe. I rock back and forth and slide off the stool. Luke and Claire sit with me on the floor of the kitchen while I sob harder than I ever have before. I'm shaking and I think I might throw up.

It isn't fair! What did I do to deserve this? Why aren't I allowed to have peace and happiness in my life? Who did I wrong that I'm destined to be punished for the rest of my life?

"Oh, God! No, no, no, no! Make it stop! Oh, God!" I scream. I cry. Will promised that he would be here for me. He promised I could cry and scream with him and now he isn't here when I need him the most.

Was it all for nothing? Losing Mom and Dad…the years I spent with Gram, paying for my transgression…all the sneaking around, plotting and planning so Will and I could be together…everything we did to buck Gregory Meyer's Hitleresque system…whatever it was that Luke, Claire, and Will had planned for my and Will's future…it was all for nothing?

It's two o'clock in the morning when Luke insists we all go to bed. My body is worn out from crying for almost two hours straight and Luke has to carry me upstairs. My eyes are so swollen that I can barely hold them open. They pull the covers over me and all I can do is pray that I'll wake up in the morning to find that it was all a horrid nightmare. As they go downstairs I can hear Luke and Claire both sobbing and I know that this is really happening. It's no dream.

Will is dead…and so am I.

I do next to nothing over the next several days. Luke contacted my professors and told them what happened. They were all very accommodating in providing the assignments I would miss over the next week, although right now, I don't even see the point in going back to school. I have no drive, no motivation to do anything.

I sleep a lot, and when I'm not sleeping, I walk around like a zombie. We've been here for months and I've only walked the path to the dock once. It's not the same as the one I shared with Will. Now that he's gone, I don't know if I'll ever go back again. To sit in that artificial place will only make it hurt more.

Claire tries, but I can't eat either. I'm a mess, I haven't showered in days, and I don't care. Luke and Claire are more attentive to me than Gram was after my parents died, which is to say they're attentive at all. Gram blamed me and wanted to move on and act like they never existed. Not Claire. She asks me every day if I'm ready to talk and she tells me that I can cry, yell, scream or do anything I need to do to get through the pain. I never reply to her, but I appreciate that I don't have to.

Chapter 5

The memorial service for Will and his mother is today. We flew in last night and are staying with Caroline's family. We could have stayed at our old house since Luke and Claire haven't even put it on the market yet, but I just couldn't. There are too many memories of Will and me there that I just couldn't bear it. Besides, I think Claire wants Caroline's mom to observe me – make sure I'm not going to go off the deep end. Too late.

I initially didn't want to come because it makes me sick to my stomach to think of Will's father standing up there in front of everyone, lying about how much he loved his wife and son, and how much he'll miss them. I'm here because I care more about honoring Will than the charade his father will put on. I also have to show Mr. Meyer that I'm strong and resilient.

I wear a black pencil skirt and Will's favorite blue top. I twist my hair up, and clasp the necklace Will gave me around my neck. As I pull my hands from behind my neck the light hits my ring and the sparkle catches my eye. I stare at it for a few long moments like I have over the last several days. Will's words echo in my mind and I quickly remember the promise I made to him. I remember that night like it was yesterday. The speech he gave that day at graduation about seizing the opportunity of a lifetime in the lifetime of the opportunity. Will was my once in a lifetime opportunity. He was everything I wanted and his love was everything I worked so hard to finally deserve.

He may be gone, but I will never let him go. My heart will forever belong to Will Meyer.

As we arrive at the church, I'm greeted by Chris and Tyler, who sandwich me in a hug like big brothers. Gwen and Caroline are close behind them, arms extended. At some point all four of them have their arms wrapped around me and I feel so incredibly loved. I flash back to my grandparent's funeral and wish that I had allowed people to care for me like this then. I realize how much easier it may have made things.

The five of us sit together, with Chris and Tyler sitting on one side of me and Gwen and Caroline on the other. Tyler holds my hand and lets me squeeze it whenever I think I'm going to lose it. Will's father approaching the podium is one such time. I'll have to check with Ty at the end of the service to make sure he has all five fingers left.

"Thank you all for coming today. It is under sad and tragic circumstances that we are gathered here. But still, we celebrate. We celebrate the lives of two incredible individuals. Eliana and William were the two most important people in my life.

"Eliana was a good mother and a fine wife. Those of you who spent time with her know that she cared deeply for others and was always involved in one charity or another. She never failed to put others before herself and I loved and respected her for that.

"William was a brilliant young man with a bright future ahead of him. He had recently made some difficult changes so he could focus on what was really important in life, having just finalized his registration for classes at Princeton. He was strong-willed and stubborn…like his father. Perhaps that's why we butted heads so much. But William was a special young man. I loved my son and I will miss him and his mother very much."

Gregory Meyer's farce of a eulogy is cold and emotionless. It makes me sick to hear him say he respected his wife and loved his son. He doesn't know the first thing about love and respect. If he did he would never have done to us what he did, and right now I wouldn't be staring at an urn filled with the ashes of the only man I'll ever love. I watch him saunter back to his seat like he's walking back from the buffet at the country club and Tyler's hand takes a big hit to its circulation.

I look at the two urns placed decoratively on a table in the front of the room. All that's left of him is ash. I won't even be able to look at his body one more time to say goodbye. *Goodbye.* I wish I had held him longer, kissed him more passionately. Now it's too late. I'll never hear his voice, feel his arms around me, or his lips against mine again. I'll spend the rest of my life hoping I didn't waste a single second with him, and wondering what our life together might have been like if his father had allowed Will to love whoever he wanted.

An odd thought strikes me as I consider Will's mother: Will is lucky. It's a terrible thought, but it's true. Will lost his mother but he will never have to endure the pain that accompanies that loss. He won't go through his life feeling like a part of him is missing, living with the regrets of wasted time and senseless arguments. He can rest in peace having died next to the only other person in the world who loved him more than I did.

We walk through the receiving line to give our obligatory condolences to Mr. Meyer, not that he wants or needs them. He's probably glad they're out of his way. Now he can go on and be seen in the community as the grieving widower, mourning the loss not only of his wife but of his son as well. I politely shake his hand – even though it makes my skin crawl – and wonder how long until his new *bit of stuff* comes around to be Mrs. Meyer number five.

"Thank you, Layla. Believe it, or not, I'm sorry for you as well. We disagreed on your place in Will's life, but I know how you felt about him. I know it's a terrible loss for you." He almost sounds sincere, but I know that's not possible since sincerity comes from the heart, which Gregory Meyer does not possess.

"Thank you, Mr. Meyer," I force myself to say cordially.

"You can come back to Davidson now, you know. Since your relationship with Will is no longer an issue, you and your aunt and uncle are welcome back." He says it as if granting us permission, which I suppose he is. After all, he does unofficially own this town.

Luke steps in before I say or do something I'll regret. "That won't be necessary, Greg. We're all set up down there. And, well, you'll understand why I don't think our working relationship will withstand recent events." Luke extends his hand, "We're very sorry for your loss."

I step outside for some fresh air and stand across the street from the Village Green. I stare out, recalling that day over a year ago when I first met Will. Who would have thought that the boy I ran into that hot summer night would have changed my life so dramatically? I'm a better person because of him. I'm suddenly aware and afraid of what my life will be like without him. A world without Will Meyer is a tragedy and I'm not sure how I will exist in it.

"There's a reception at the Meyer's. Are you interested in going?" Claire asks softly as she puts her arm around my shoulder.

"No. I...I can't," I stammer.

"I thought you'd say that." Claire squeezes my shoulder and kisses my hair. "She's ready," she calls. I show her my puzzled face and she just smiles. Before I know it, Gwen and Caroline are by my side, whisking me away.

"Where are we going?" I ask as they shuffle me off.

"You'll see," Caroline says.

When we pull up to my old house I'm filled with sadness. I get out of the car and just stand there, frozen. "I don't think I can do this, guys."

"Yes, you can," Gwen says.

"There are so many memories here. So much heartache." I'm standing in the spot where I last saw Will. I remember how he held and kissed me before he left. I remember how full of hope I was when he drove away, so sure I was going to see him in just days...so sure he had the complication of us being together forever all worked out. This is also the same spot I said goodbye to my life here, to the ones I love. "Why are we here?" I ask, trying not to cry.

"C'mon." Caroline takes my hand and leads me through the side gate to the back of the house and down to the dock. Tears are welling up in my eyes and I'm really not sure if I can contain them.

"Caroline...I can't..."

"He deserves better than the crap his father spewed out. We're going to give Will the memorial he should have had." Caroline squeezes my hand and I follow her down the flagstone path. Chris and Tyler are already on the dock. They've got the red blanket Will used on our prom night date spread out with a framed picture of Will in the center. It's dusk and the candle next to the picture is glowing sweetly.

"Oh my gosh." I can't hold back the tears any longer and they begin to flow uncontrollably. I fall to my knees and surrender to the pain. All I can feel is the warmth of four bodies surrounding me, loving me. Our sobs join together in a chorus of mourning for the loss of the most incredible person we've ever known. When we have cried all the tears we can, we gather ourselves and sit in a circle around Will's picture.

"I'll start," Chris says. "Will was the best guy I knew. He was honest, hardworking, and a damn good football player. I miss you, bro." Short, sweet, and to the point. Anything else from Chris and it wouldn't have been sincere.

"Will always treated me with respect. Most guys looked at me and immediately thought I was just another dumb blonde. Not Will. He never assumed anything but the best about me. I never felt like I had to prove myself to him." Gwen stops before she gives herself over to the emotions welling up in her. I reach over and take her hand and she pushes out a tight-lipped smile.

"Will made life in this ridiculous bubble so much better. It was never about the number of commas and zeros in your bank account. He chose to be more than that. He cared about people. When we were little, I remember how genuinely kind he was. He never used anyone for his own selfish gain, and always thought of others before himself. My life is so much better for having known him." Caroline's speech is soft and sweet, like her. She knew better than the others about facing the Gregory Meyer test. I can't imagine having been adopted at six and spending two years proving yourself to that man, but she was able to do it because Will was steadfast in his acceptance of her even then. "Tyler?"

Tyler's head is in his hands and there are soft sobs coming from him. After me, I suppose this has hit Tyler the hardest. He and Will were best friends. They'd known each other since they were babies. They grew up together and had been inseparable. Knowing Will had to go to Princeton Ty worked his butt off trying to get in, too. It was near devastating when he didn't. He settled for Duke since it'd be easier for them to see each other any time Will came home to visit.

"Will wasn't just my friend...he was my brother. In this crappy, two-faced world we lived in, he had character and integrity. He didn't care if anyone agreed with him, or not. He's the one who showed me what it means to be a man...to stick up for what you believe...to protect your friends and the person you love most in the world. Will was everything I wanted to be. I'm gonna do my best to live up to the bar he set. I love you, man." Tyler can't contain it any longer and the sobs come again. I slide over and wrap my arms around him like he did for me that night in the Asheville vineyard.

"Shh...shh..." I hold him tight and stroke his hair. "It's ok...it's ok..."

"Layla, do you want to say anything?" Caroline asks after Ty has pulled himself together.

"Yes," I answer. *Breathe. Just Breathe.* "Will was the bright light at the end of a very long, very dark tunnel I had been in. A tunnel I never thought I'd get out of. He was everything you have all said, and more. Despite his upbringing Will was capable of this immense and immeasurable love. He taught me how to be loved and that I didn't have to be so strong all the time. He taught me how to trust again. He gave me things I thought I'd never have. Things like peace and comfort and assurance. I loved him more than I thought one person could love another and I will never stop loving him."

The others slide next to Tyler and me and we sit crying together until all that's left is the silence of night. We've given Will what he deserved: a memorial that spoke to who he really was, not some ideal that his father wanted to portray. For us, Will's memory will live on in the truths we have spoken tonight, and that's all that really matters.

"Thank you so much. I didn't think I was going to be able to do this, but I'm glad I did it. It was the memorial Will deserved," I say quietly, not wanting to disturb the peacefulness.

"It was also the closure you needed, Layla." Caroline rubs soft circles on my back.

"Yeah…I guess it was," I say.

I don't tell them about the ring or about how even though Will is dead, there's something in me that just can't let go of him yet. There's a reason he made sure I had that ring and I've got to find out what it is.

I made Luke promise that we would leave the day after the memorial – there's no way I can stick around this town with all its haunting memories – but when Caroline walks me out to the rental car I can't help but feel a twinge of regret in the decision.

"I really don't want to say goodbye to you again," I tell her.

"I know. I don't either. But we're both going back to school, so that should keep us occupied, right?" she says as she throws her arms around my neck.

"Yes, lots to keep us busy." I haven't told her about the situation with Marcus, which, after Will, is the thing currently occupying my mind – that and the fact that Luke has taken his fatherly duties to DEFCON 1. "Let's not get too busy to stay in touch, ok? You're a sister to me, Caroline. I don't know what I'd do if I didn't have you." I hold her tightly, not wanting to let go.

"I love you, too, Layla." Caroline hugs me fiercely and we have to force ourselves apart when Claire says we absolutely have to leave. "Text me when you land, ok?"

"Ok. I'll miss you." I force a smile and make myself get into the car.

Chapter 6

I don't know how, but I actually made it through a whole month of classes after Will's memorial. It's amazing what one can accomplish on autopilot. The few friends I'm making were not oblivious to my demeanor and showed the proper amount of concern when I told them that a dear friend had passed away. Had I told them it was my boyfriend, my love, my soul mate, it would have been a catastrophic case of sympathy, which I don't want or need. I suppose it's actually been really good that I've had school. If not for the busyness of classes and homework, I'm not sure where I'd be.

Walking into the house after a particularly boring day I stop cold as my eyes meet with the stranger sitting in the Great Room. Luke introduces him as Furtick, but I already know him as one of the thugs who beat the crap out of that poor guy outside the law firm.

"Miss Weston. It's nice to meet you," he says, standing to shake my hand. He's pretty cordial for a guy who roughs people up for a living, or hobby, or whatever you call it.

"Furtick," I say, mirroring his friendliness. He gives me just the smallest smile and somehow…I immediately like him. His smile is sincere and I can see in his eyes that he's more than what Mr. Meyer made him out to be, which I have found to usually be the case. The images of him outside the law firm that day disappear and all that I see is a man who came to our aid when Luke said we needed help.

"I need to talk with you about your patterns," he says, cutting to the chase.

"My patterns? I'm sorry, I don't understand."

"Furtick has been following you over the last four days. He's made some observations and has some suggestions that will keep you safe," Luke tells me.

"You've been following me?" I ask.

"Yes ma'am."

"I never saw you. I never even felt your stare."

"I'm very good at what I do, ma'am." Furtick smirks and I see the human, non-thug in him. He has a nice smile and beautiful brown eyes. I don't know what his past experience is to make him so good at what he does, or so useful to Gregory Meyer, but it doesn't matter, Luke trusts him, so I do, too. Moreover, my gut tells me he's the real deal.

"Yes, you are," I smile back. "Why, exactly is he following me?"

"We've been monitoring the situation with Marcus," Luke answers.

"I'm a bit confused. Marcus hasn't been around for over a month. I assumed he left town, came into his right mind, so what's the need to have him around?"

"We don't have confirmation that he's left Florida. His car is still here and there have been no flights registered under his name to anywhere, foreign or domestic. Also, he was never registered for any classes at the university." Furtick gives his report very matter-of-factly.

"Wait a minute. He said he transferred. You mean he dropped out of Davidson on some delusional whim, got into FSU, and never even registered for classes?" I can't even begin to understand this.

"I'm sorry, allow me to clarify. He was never a student at the college at all. There's no application on file," Furtick continues.

"This is so bizarre, Uncle Luke. I can't shake this feeling that something happened after we left. I mean...this just isn't like him. He's so polar opposite of the Marcus I knew."

"I agree, Layla. I've got someone working on that right now, but I think it's going to take a little time, so until then I need you to do whatever Furtick tells you. Can you do that?" I nod my head, still reeling from the craziness of the situation. "Are you doing ok?"

"Yeah, I'm good." I breathe deeply and try to separate the Marcus who was my friend and this new, Lex Luthor version. "Furtick, you said you had some suggestions for keeping me safe? I'm assuming that means you think he might come back."

"Well, Miss Weston, because we don't know where he is at the moment, we can't be too careful. So, first of all, I'll be following you at all times. This includes keeping an eye on you while you're at school. Don't worry – I'll continue to be a ghost. Secondly, I observed that you are consistently by yourself while on campus. Make friends, even if just for show. You need at least one person with you at all times. Should Mr. Reynolds approach you at school he may not make a scene if there are witnesses. Lastly, you're not to be out after dark."

"But you just said you would be following me at all times," I argue, even though I'm never out after dark anyway.

"It's much easier to keep a trail during the day, and alternate routes aren't as easily identified at night." Furtick stares at me for a moment. "You're *not* to be out after dark," he reiterates strongly. I nod in acquiescence.

"Is there anything else?" I ask him.

"Your phone. You're not to answer any unknown number. May I have it please?" Furtick says, stretching his arm out, palm up. I hand him my phone without question and he begins scrolling through the numbers. There are literally eight contacts so it takes him seconds to review. "Sir," he says to Luke as he shows him something on the screen.

"Layla, you've still got Will's number in here," Luke says with a soft, but disapproving tone. Why would Furtick even think to show that to Luke anyway? Luke must have given Furtick the whole story with all the sorted details.

"I know. I can't delete it…not yet. It would be…I would feel like I was erasing him from my life and I'm just not ready to do that. Please, Uncle Luke."

Luke hands the phone back to me and I give him a small smile of thanks.

"Is there anything else I need to know?" I ask Furtick.

"Yes. Despite what you may have seen, I'm not a violent man." Luke has obviously told him about me observing his handiwork.

"I believe you, Furtick. If Luke trusts you, I trust you." I stare him straight in the eye and hope he believes me, too.

As we wind down for the night, I help Claire make up the guest room for Furtick. It seems we'll be a family of four for a little while. I don't mind. There's something about him that is a welcomed addition. Perhaps it's that I already like him a lot, or maybe it's just the added safety he brings. Luke is a great defender but he's emotionally involved. Furtick, however, will be able to act on the situation based on his trained instinct alone.

As he unpacks his two bags I see that he's got just one small duffle bag for his clothes, but a larger bag with his *tools*, so to speak. As I attempt to catch a peek of his weapons of choice he gives me a not-so-subtle look. "It's better if you don't know what's in there," he says. His words are soft and caring so I respond in turn with a gentle squeeze of his arm and a smile that says *thank you*.

*****

Furtick has remained ghostly as promised, so I'm doing my part in trying to befriend a few girls in my Psych 101 class. Of the girls I met at the freshman reception just one is responding to my pathetic attempt at making friends. Dana is from Georgia and her southern accent reminds me of all that was good about living in Davidson. It's taken several days, but I've finally gotten close enough so that it doesn't seem weird for me to automatically walk with her after class.

"My parents are coming down for the weekend. Ya'll should come out with us! You and your aunt and uncle," she twangs.

"That'd be fun," I say. I'm working really hard at this. I don't really want to go out with Dana and her parents because the closer I get to her, the more I'm going to have to hide. But…I *do* like her, and maybe it won't be so bad to share my story with her one day. Plus, I'm under strict orders to make friends. If I don't make some effort here I have a feeling Furtick will have something to say about it. "Just let me know when."

"What's your number? I'll call you later when I find out what the plans are." Before I give her my number I quickly realize that I need to add her to my phone so I know it's her calling, so I suggest we swap phones and enter our information. As I'm typing away I think that Furtick is in a hidden corner watching and proud of me for being aware and making his job a little easier. "Later!" she says skipping away. As she leaves me at the entrance of the coffee shop I pause for a moment letting her southern sweetness linger in my ear.

I move quickly into the coffee shop, transitioning from one friend-in-progress to another. Finn is always here, whether he's working or not. I haven't been in since Will died so when I find him sitting at a table in the corner I usually call home he's visibly surprised at my presence.

"Excuse me. If you're here, who's going to make my drink?" I say. Being around Finn Reed is easy. I don't feel like I have to try with him and that makes my life right now just a little bit more bearable.

"Oh my gosh, you're alive! Are you ok? You've been totally MIA lately!"

"Sorry about that. A friend of mine passed away last month. It's been…really hard," I answer more truthfully than I had anticipated and surprise myself.

"Oh, gosh, Layla, I'm so sorry. I was afraid your stalker came back."

"No, he's not back, not that I'm aware of. That whole situation doesn't help me being on edge, though. No one knows where he is."

"He must have taken it pretty hard when you let him down," Finn suggests.

"Well, it's a little more complicated than me rejecting his advances. My boyfriend dated his sister and it didn't end well," I say without thinking.

"You didn't tell me you have a boyfriend. He obviously doesn't go here otherwise he'd never leave your side. Is he back home in NC?"

"Um…" *What have I done?* This is exactly what I didn't want. I didn't want to tell anyone about Will or his tragic and completely unfair death, and now I've opened up a can of worms. But…I suppose if I were going to tell anyone anything, it would be Finn. "It's kind of dramatic, but his father didn't want us together, so it ended."

"But you're still in love with him," Finn says, filling in the blank.

"Yeah," I say after a beat.

"And this guy is coming down here thinking he can replace him? He's an idiot. One look in your eyes and anyone can see your heart belongs to someone else." Finn's support is more helpful than I realized it would be.

"Thanks, Finn. I know I'll be able to move on one day. It's just going to take a while, and someone incredibly remarkable. But Marcus is really freaking me out."

"Oh, is that his name? Well, I've got your back. I'm serious, Layla. That guy gives me the creeps. You should have seen how he was looking at you. I'd feel better about putting you in an unmarked van with a guy waving brightly colored candy and a bloody sickle. I thought he was some love-struck newbie, but now that I know there's more to the story, you have to promise that you'll call me if anything happens." Finn is serious, his face taking on a new shape as he emphasizes his request.

"That's so nice of you, Finn. I promise I'll call if I need anything." For the second time in less than an hour I have added another contact to my phone. I scroll through the names and numbers and realize that Furtick added his information, bringing my measly eight contacts to a whopping eleven. I wonder for a moment where my shadow is hiding as I'm sure he's happy to see me following his instructions yet again.

As expected, Furtick requests my phone as soon as we walk through the door, takes it to run the numbers, and does background checks on my budding friendships. *If they only knew!*

"They're all clear," he says as he returns with my phone and Luke.

"Thanks, Furtick. Any news on what happened to Marcus after we left?" I ask. This missing piece is the thing that is making this the most difficult. I can't believe that the Marcus who surprised me in the parking lot is the same one I made peace with and said good-bye to in my living room in Davidson.

"No, nothing definitive yet," Luke says. "But the good news is that we have good reason to believe he's left Tallahassee. His roommates say that he hasn't been there in over three weeks. And there's been some activity on his bank card in North Carolina."

"That's good, right? That means he's gone," I say hopefully.

"Just because he's not here now, doesn't mean he's not coming back," Furtick assures me.

"That's right. So, get used to Furtick because he's going to continue being your shadow until we feel confident that Marcus is no longer a threat." Luke is firm in his instruction. I know that look in his eyes. There's more to what's going on that he isn't telling me. He knows something but doesn't think I can handle it yet.

"If you think that's best," I reply. I'm keenly aware in moments like this that there is a protective nature to Luke, and while he has had Claire to take care of, there's a fatherly protection that is so second-nature to him that, even in the midst of the threat Marcus is posing, I think he's enjoying.

"I do," Luke confirms.

Things have been so crazy that I haven't checked my email in weeks. As the screen flickers on, my heart fills with joy when I see an email from Caroline. It's dated over a week ago so I open it and find myself sinking into a place of joy. I settle in my chair, resting my chin in my hand, and read.

From: Caroline Jackson

To: Layla Weston

Subject: Hey Stranger!

Hi Layla!

I hadn't heard from you in a while so I thought I'd shoot you an email. Being in California I have no clue when to call! This time zone thing is messing me up!

Classes are good here. The interior design program here is really competitive, but I think I'm going to be ok. I really love it! I can't wait to get my prerequisite courses out of the way!

What about you? How are you doing? I've been worried about you. With Will gone and you being in Florida, I worry that you don't have anyone to talk to. I wish I could be there for you. We should set up a time when we can talk and it's not the middle of the night for one of us! Promise me you'll at least email me back so I know you're ok!

On to the gossip! Gwen and Chris got to Clemson and started dating! Tyler is settled in at Duke and (FYI) mad at you for not calling him back. And your friend Marcus Reynolds went crazy! Tyler said his dad told him that he and Will's dad had some big blowout at the law firm. Tyler's dad had to call the police. I don't think Mr. Meyer pressed charges, but no one has seen Marcus since. I know, right?!?!

What happened to the days of hiking, movie night, and Chinese food? I guess we're all growing up! I love and miss you so much! Please reply soon so I know you're ok.

Love,

Caroline

Oh, my gosh! I was right! Something did happen. But why on earth would Marcus and Will's dad have a huge, blowout argument?

I click reply and respond to Caroline with immediate apologies.

From: Layla Weston
To: Caroline Jackson
Subject: Sorry I've been MIA!

Hi Caroline,

I'm so sorry that I've been such a terrible friend! Things have been really crazy and busy here. But I promise to be better about staying in touch.

Classes are good here. I've made a couple of friends. One girl, Dana, reminds me of you, which is comforting. I can't believe Gwen and Chris! Wonder how long that's been brewing?!?! And I'll be sure to call Tyler soon. If you talk to him before I do, please tell him I'm sorry.

I'm doing ok since that last time I saw you…I guess. It's hard, but I just take it one day at a time. I can't really talk about him yet. I don't like the idea of talking about him in the past tense. So, if I'm tight lipped about it, I'm sorry.

I was thinking that maybe you guys could all come down around Thanksgiving. I know you'll have family things, but maybe you can come after for a long weekend? I really want to see all of you. Not being with you feels like a part of me is missing.

Thanks for not giving up on me. I love and miss you so much, too!
Love,
Layla

I say as little as I can about missing Will, and nothing about the excruciating pain that constantly exists in my heart every second of the day. She's dealing with losing Will, too, and it just doesn't seem fair to blather on about him to her, especially via email.

I certainly don't say anything about Marcus. I don't want her to worry any more than she already does. Now that I have a little bit of information that could be helpful to Luke, I'll pass it along and maybe we'll find ourselves one step closer to knowing what's going on with Marcus.

That night I dream about Will. I haven't dreamt of him in quite some time so even in my dream I cry tears of joy just seeing his face. This dream starts out as by far the best one I've ever had. In it my mind replays our day of nothing. Every detail is the same. We watch the same movies, read the same books, and play the same game carrying dialogue between two books. And as if in slow motion, I replay the passion we shared that day as well. I feel his hand on the skin of my back and his lips on mine. I recall how we pulled closer to each other, feeling like the line between where I ended and he began was gone. My heart swells with love for this man that I'll never get to hold again.

But just as I'm relishing in the warmth of remembering the passion Will showed me, my mind flips the page and we're face to face with Marcus in the coffee shop. I had forgotten that our day of nothing concluded with asking Marcus to be our ally. Only this time, Marcus swings across the table and knocks Will to the ground, grabs my arm, and drags me from the shop. I force myself to wake because I don't want to see this play out. I turn the light on and take a few deep breaths to calm myself.

It was just a dream. It was just a dream. I tell myself over and over again. As I regain my peace I am thankful for Luke and his plan of action in bringing Furtick on. I don't know how long he'll be with us, but I'm grateful for every second that he's here, and I hope that the work he's doing for us is somehow redemptive for the terrible things Mr. Meyer made him do.

Chapter 7

My phone rings and I see that it's Dana. She's been cleared so I answer it freely.

"Hey sugar!" she chirps.

"Hi, Dana. What's up?" I ask.

"Some of us are getting together to study for our test next week. It's the big one and I figured we could all use some help. You in?" she explains.

"Sure! When and where?"

"Well, I know it's short notice, but I'm on my way to campus to meet up with everyone now. Can you come? Please?" Her sugary sweet delivery makes me want to do whatever she asks, but the sun is quickly setting and I'm not sure if I'll be able to work it out.

"Um…let me check with my uncle and I'll text you." Gosh, that sounds like I have to ask him permission to do anything. I do, but Dana doesn't need that impression. "I mean, I just don't know what they have going on tonight."

"Ok. Just let me know! Later!"

I walk through the house calling out for Luke and Furtick. When they don't answer, I call out for Claire. No answer. Furtick's car is here so I keep looking. When I reach the back of the house I see that both Luke and Furtick are on their phones on the porch. It's still daylight, and things have been going fine with no sign of Marcus anywhere, so I text Dana that I'm on my way. I also text Luke and let him know exactly where I'm going and what I'm doing. He'll get it when he gets off the phone and send Furtick after me I'm sure.

I grab my keys and backpack and am meeting Dana and some of the other people in my class in the library inside of 30 minutes. At this time of day there's no one on the road, and parking on campus is choice.

I find everyone settling into a huge table made up of four tables in the library. Everyone agrees to turn their phones off or on silent so we won't be distracted. We toss them in the middle of the table so no one can covertly check email and get to work.

After three hours of cramming, we all decide that enough is enough. If we don't know it now, we never will, although we're all pretty confident that we'll do just fine. We gather our phones, say our goodbyes, and split off into different directions based on which lot we parked in. I'm halfway down the stairs when I have to go back for the sweater I brought for the chilly library. I send Dana on her way, as I don't want to hold her up any longer because of my absent-mindedness. I scan the room expecting to see Furtick in an unassuming location. There's no one around so there's no reason for him to stay hidden, but I don't see him and suppose he's just keeping with protocol.

As I make my way back to the door the woman who could be Eliana Meyer's twin is leaving, exiting the building at the far end of the room. Something in me won't let me miss my chance again. She walks quickly but I'm able to keep up this time. She's making her way to the parking lot. I want to call out to her, but shouting "hey" will just sound menacing.

"Excuse me! Excuse me?" I call but she doesn't turn around. In fact, she walks faster. She's fumbling with her keys. "Hello? Miss? I'm so sorry…I don't mean to scare you. This is going to sound crazy," I say as I approach her, out of breath. Still ignoring my calls she reaches her car and drops her keys. I catch her shoulder as she stands from picking them up. She stops, facing the car and then turns around slowly. "Oh, my…it's you."

We're both out of breath and shock mirrors our faces. This can't be happening.

"I'm sorry. You have me mistaken for someone else," the woman says. She's nervous but I know that over-pronunciated, over-rehearsed cadence.

57

"No, I haven't. You're Eliana Meyer. What the hell is going on here?" I demand.

"I don't know what you're talking about. Please, let go of me. You're hurting me." Her face is pained and I realize that I have just attacked a woman in the parking lot who has the misfortune to more than just resemble a dead woman.

"I'm...sorry. I...I'm sorry." I let her go. She gets in her car and speeds away.

I walk back to my car feeling incredibly confused. Maybe Luke is right and my mind is telling me it's time to really start dealing with Will's death, but the resemblance is more than uncanny. She's a *clone* of Eliana Meyer. I have to see her again.

I exit the parking lot just minutes behind her and find her in traffic faster than I could have hoped. I weave in between cars, driving more dangerously than I ever have. I'm right beside her, looking as many times as I can and still be safe, but it's dark and hard to really see. She speeds up and for a minute I think I'm going to lose her as she threads herself between other cars. I can't give up.

As I race to catch up to her I realize that I'm on a familiar path. This is the exact route I take to get home. Following behind her she turns into our neighborhood and I can't believe my luck! Even if I don't get another face-to-face with her tonight, I'll at least know where she lives. This will allow me to confront her in the daylight and get an even better look at her.

Before I know it she's pulling into our driveway where Luke, Claire and Furtick are standing. *What is going on?*

"Luke, what is going on here?" I demand as I exit furiously from the car.

"Where the hell have you been? Are you confused about what *you are not to go out after dark* means?" Furtick is pissed and I'm confused. Why didn't Luke send him? I told him exactly where I was going to be. "We've been calling and calling and you haven't answered. I didn't think I needed to sync the GPS on your phone to track you, but it looks like I'm going to have to do that!"

"I texted Luke and told him where I was! But that's beside the point! Someone needs to tell me what's going on here!" I'm yelling now. I've never yelled at Luke or Claire before and it's a little unnerving for all of us.

"Layla, just calm down," Claire says, trying to use her angelic tone to subconsciously calm me. I wish it were working but there is too much happening for me to even consider regaining my composure.

The woman approaches slowly. The light from the porch gives me my clearest view of her yet. I stare at and study her face.

"Hello, Layla." She says my name and I know that I have not gone crazy. This is Eliana Meyer.

"Now that you know this, you should know everything," Luke says. No sooner do the words leave his mouth than the front door opens and my world stops as Will emerges.

I'm taken back and not sure if I can hold myself up to stand. My head is spinning and everything starts to go dark. A rush of emotions floods me. I'm angry, confused, and elated all at once. How could this be? I'm staring at a ghost. But...he's not a ghost. He's real.

I realize that this is one of those moments in life when the best thing to do is stop and think, but I can't do that. I'm about to faint and I know it. I immediately wish I were standing on softer ground, but before I collapse I hear his voice...his strong, smooth voice. And as Will steps forward to catch me he simply and sweetly says, "Hey, baby."

*****

I wake up but don't open my eyes. I can hear voices, but most of them are muffled...they aren't in the room with me. The room is dark except for the light flowing from the kitchen. I move my hand from my stomach and feel the soft chenille of the couch in the Great Room. When I open my eyes I see that I'm covered by the blanket I took after Gramps died. It's warm and I feel comforted under it. My head hurts as I recall the strangest dream. Will is alive…and here. I feel a smile spread across my face. I don't want to let go of this feeling.

I hear the voices in the kitchen more clearly now that I'm a bit more awake. Luke is saying something about giving me space, followed by Claire asking someone to understand if it takes me some time to come around. There's a third voice that makes my whole body tingle and question whether I'm dreaming or not. I get up slowly and move toward the kitchen. As the room comes into full view I am rewarded with the gift that I was not dreaming.

Standing in the middle of the kitchen, looking just as he did the last day I saw him, is my Will. He's here, he's real. I feel like I might faint again and when I brace myself against the wall I catch everyone's attention.

"Layla, honey…come, sit," Claire insists. "Let me get you a glass of water." I'm having déjà vu from the night Luke told me Will was dead. I'm sitting at the kitchen table with five sets of eyes on me. I lock eyes with Furtick and think that maybe he's not as mad at me anymore. If he is, I can count on him to tell me later.

"Can someone please tell me what's going on?" I say softly, staring at Will.

"Well…there's the obvious," Luke says indicating to Will and his mother. "But I'm sure you're asking for, and certainly deserve, an explanation. Will?" Luke defers to Will to explain how he and his mother are standing in front of me, alive and well. Will sits to the right of me at

the head of the table and I smell the scent that I came to know only as *Will.*

"Layla…" Will says my name and I start to tear up. I never thought I'd hear my name said in the way only Will Meyer can say it again. "I'm so sorry that I lied to you. There were days I thought that I might as well have really died because it killed me knowing that you were in so much pain." He takes my hand and smoothes his thumb across the top and goose bumps raise across my body. "I've missed you so much." I relish in the touch of his skin against mine. I close my eyes and let my senses take over. I feel every pass of his thumb. I hear the soft sound as it sweeps across my skin. I breathe in his scent.

"I've missed you, too," I say, finally allowing myself to look into his blue eyes. I grasp his hand, feeling the realness of him. "You're here. You're really here." I grasp his hand tighter, feeling his pulse beat at his wrist proving his life. "But, I don't understand. What…what happened?"

"After my father's House Call, Luke, Claire and I knew something had to be done. Your refusal to back down was going to set him off and we knew that his next move would be severe. As you know, it was. We tossed around some different ideas. I kept going back to us running away together, but, besides the fact that Luke said that would happen over his dead body, he and Claire were level-headed enough to know that we'd end up running forever. That wasn't the life I wanted to give you.

"At first Mom and I were just going to be gone, disappear into thin air. We knew he'd put on a show for the media by calling the big dogs out with a manhunt. We also knew it wouldn't last long. So, we thought we could just ride it out for a few months. Luke and Claire were keeping me up to date with you, so I didn't feel like I had completely lost you.

"My father had Furtick watching your family even after he called off the search…even after he wanted us declared dead. It was then that we realized, until he had two bodies, he was never going to believe we were really gone." Will takes a deep breath and composes himself. It's difficult for him to explain the story of how he came to break my heart for the purpose of keeping it. "I've said before that my father would rather see me dead than let me live my own life, and it finally occurred to me that that wasn't an over dramatization. It was true and became the only option. The only way mom and I would ever truly be free is if we were dead." He sighs and rubs my hand again. "Are you ok? Do you want me to stop? Do you want to ask me anything?"

"I don't understand why you didn't tell me," I say directly to the room. "I could have helped."

"I knew my father would come to your house to look for me when mom and I didn't come back from Hickory. Your *greatest* help was your genuine response," Will says. I know he's right. I remember standing on the trail in Asheville with his father. Even though Will and I technically weren't together, he saw right through me and knew there was more to our relationship.

"Whose idea was the car accident?" I ask. Silence fills the room. No one wants to answer because they know, after the horrific tragedy of losing both my parents in a car accident, how much this, more than any other detail, crushed me.

"It was mine," Luke finally says.

"Why?"

"Honestly? It was the easiest accident to fake. When we began talking about the logistics it started coming together that Will and Eliana could reasonably be traveling to or from her family in Hickory. Gregory wouldn't go within a hundred miles of that place so we knew it was our best bet. Layla, it was the hardest decision we made, but it provided the easiest way to pull it off." Luke's response is pained. I can tell it hurts him to explain a conscious decision that caused me the pain not only of losing Will, but that resurfaced the agony associated with my parents' death. Now I know the sobbing he and Claire shared with me was for their genuine anguish over what they were doing to me.

"What about Eliana...tonight at the library?"

"If you had obeyed orders, you wouldn't have seen her and found out this way," Furtick says breaking his silence.

"Really? And what exactly was the plan for ending my agony?" I ask with obvious annoyance. Furtick is still pissed at me, but I can't worry about that now. We'll smooth things over later when I'm satisfied my questions have been answered.

"Eliana has been taking classes and we didn't want to risk you running into her. She wasn't supposed to be there the day you got your books. And *you* were not supposed to be on campus tonight. We've gone to great lengths to make sure your schedules did not intersect," Luke answers.

"Why was Will here?"

"Eliana called when you accosted her in the parking lot. She saw your determination and didn't know what to do. I told her to come straight here, and then I called Will and told him to come. It was time to tell you the truth," Luke tells me.

"I still don't understand why you didn't tell me right away?"

"That was my decision," Will answers. "I knew what we were doing was going to be tragic. And I didn't know if you would want to move on. I was missing after all. So…I wanted to give you time. You could have gotten here and met some great guy and…" Will's speech is sad. I can't believe he would think that I'd move on just like that.

"And that's why you packed up the ring and gave it back to me?"

"Yes. I didn't tell Luke or Claire I was doing that. It just didn't seem right for me to have it if you were going to move on." Will hangs his head in sadness at the idea that I would move on.

I stand and leave the room, leaving confused faces behind me. When I return I place the open black velvet ring box on the table.

"I made a promise to you Will. I said that I would never give up on us." I take my left hand and place it on the table so he can see that I'm still wearing my ring. Will takes the ring from the box and puts it back on his finger where it belongs. We smile at each other and the fog in my head begins to clear.

"We knew that Gregory isn't stupid. He had everything about us monitored from the moment we took the deal," Luke adds.

"You said your father had Furtick following us?" Will nods at my inquiry. "You were already following me, us," I say to Furtick, furrowing my brow at the irony.

"Taylor and I were assigned to your family."

"Greg should treat his henchmen a little better. I knew Furtick was about to be released from Meyer's service. He swaps his guys out after several years, opting for fresher, more desperate *clients*. I called Furtick when we took Meyer's deal and he was more than on board to help us," Luke says.

"You had this planned before we even left Davidson?" Luke nods and I shake my head in an attempt to keep everything straight. "How did you know he would send Furtick to follow us?" I ask.

"Meyer doesn't do any of the grunt work himself. He doesn't have or want access to the technology necessary to do the type of monitoring he requires, and he certainly isn't going to sit his ass in a car for days to watch someone. It's how he covers himself. If his fingerprints aren't anywhere, literally or electronically, he can make a firm case that he had no knowledge of what was going on. So, he uses the best. Furtick is the best." Luke's answer makes so much sense. Why would Gregory Meyer do anything himself when he can get someone else to do all the dirty work for him?

"So you lied to Mr. Meyer? You were never really following us, never really tagging all of our moves? You knew about Will and Eliana and you didn't tell him?" I ask Furtick directly.

"Yes, ma'am. Your uncle has been very good to me throughout the years. When he asked for my help I was more than willing." Furtick's answer is gentle, yet commanding. He stands firm in his decision to uphold loyalty to Luke and betray Gregory Meyer. "All the intel I've ever given Meyer has been more than accurate. He had no reason to believe anything I reported would be otherwise."

I'm shocked at the precision with which they've executed this whole plan. It seems that no detail was left unattended. This thought leaves my head spinning. This was more than just escaping the evil that is Gregory Meyer. This was a calculated move with perfect timing and perfect players. I'm overwhelmed as I realize that this was for me. Luke and Claire did all this because they know how much I love, and could never live without, Will.

"Do you think Mr. Meyer had something to do with Marcus coming here?" I ask feeling momentarily satisfied with my understanding of how we've been able to transition with relative ease…until now, that is.

"We didn't know at first. I wouldn't have put it past him. But after finding out that he and Marcus had a very public disagreement, I doubt he had anything to do with it. He would never have a public argument like that just to divert attention. That's not his style."

"Oh," I say, thinking of something else I want to ask about the accident. "What about the…bodies?" I'm trying to piece this together completely. It would have been helpful had they told me all this while I was in a better state of mind. I think my head is still spinning from my fainting. Of course, I'm the one asking all the questions and demanding all the answers.

"It pays to be friends with a medical examiner who despises Gregory Meyer for screwing up so many of his cases. There are a lot of Jane and John Doe bodies down there. We found two who were similar in height and build, and set fire to Will's car," Claire adds. I don't know why, but somehow hearing the words *set fire to Will's car* doesn't sound as bad when Claire says it.

"I see." I'm thinking of what to say next. There have to be more details that I don't know yet, and I don't want to leave this conversation until my need to know is fully satisfied. "So how long have you been here?"

"Do you remember the night of graduation?" Will asks as if that's a night I could ever forget. That's the night we exchanged rings and made our first vows. I nod and squeeze his hand. "When I said to goodbye to you…I went home, got mom, and we were on the road that night. We really did go up to see my mom's family. We didn't tell them what was happening, just that we didn't know when we'd see them again. They assumed it had to do with my dad, which isn't new."

"It was the worst day of his life, Layla." Eliana has been silent this whole time, but speaks now because she is the only one who can testify to Will's condition during the hours, days, and months since we've been apart. "He cried all the way here. He hated that you were going to think he was gone. He knew the pain it would cause you and it was unbearable for him."

I look at Will and he has tears streaming down his face. I see how hard it is for him that the decisions he made caused me the pain it did. But he's right. The only way out from under his father's thumb was to do something drastic. If he ever found out that Will and Eliana pulled the wool over his eyes, there would be more than hell to pay.

"Wait. How are you walking around here as Will and Eliana Meyer? I know Furtick has been your father's only eyes and ears, but isn't that still pretty risky?" Fear fills my heart at the thought of the ramifications of this carelessness.

"We had their names changed," Claire explains.

"You what? How?" My face is starting to hurt from all the confused squinting I've been doing.

"I know a guy," Luke says with a smirk and motions with his head to Furtick.

"Of course you do," I say, mirroring Luke's smirk. Ever since things escalated with Marcus, I've been learning not to underestimate my uncle.

"Would you like to tell her what you chose, Will?" Claire says.

He pauses nervously before speaking. "If it's not ok, we can have them changed again, really."

"I don't care what your name is, Will. I care that it's still *you*. Just tell me," I say.

"Well, I thought a lot about it and decided on a name that would keep you with me. Even if you decided you were moving on, there was no way I ever could." Will sighs and closes his eyes for a moment of strength. "My mom chose your mom's name, Elisabeth Holland. And I...I took your dad's first name, so, John. Is...that ok...with you?" I start to cry and Will immediately thinks he's upset me. "We can change them. It's ok, Layla. I'm so sorry."

"No! Don't change them. I love them!" I'm sobbing now. All my worlds have just collided and I can't keep my emotions hidden any longer. Everything I thought was lost has been found. I have my family and the love of my life right here. Now that Marcus is gone, nothing is going to stop me from living the life that I have worked so hard to finally earn.

I can't contain myself. I stand and move onto Will's lap and throw my arms around his neck, crying harder into his shoulder. I thought I'd never feel his strong arms around me again. I press my head to his chest and listen to his heart beating. It's the sweetest sound and I've missed it so.

"Layla." Luke calls softly and I force myself to release Will and turn to him. "Please, don't be angry with us." Luke's tone is the same sorrowful one he used the night I overheard him and Claire in the kitchen.

"I'm not angry, Uncle Luke," I say as I move to hug him. "I don't know what to say. You did all of this so that Will and I could be together. I'm...I'm so grateful." I burst into tears again and Claire and Will join our embrace.

I never thought that I would be the kind of girl that was worthy of such commitment and sacrifice, but I'm standing here in a room full of people who have done just that. Luke and Claire sacrificed the careers they worked so hard for. Will and his mother sacrificed their lives, their whole identities. And Furtick…the man would take a bullet for me and he barely knows me. My heart is full to overflowing.

Chapter 8

I collect myself as our emotional moment is interrupted by an obvious throat-clearing from Furtick.

"Yes, Furtick," Luke responds.

"I'm sorry to break things up, but we still have the matter of Mr. Reynolds." He's strong and straight to the point. I wonder how he felt watching us. He doesn't strike me as the kind of guy that gets emotional.

"What do you mean? I thought you said he had gone back to Davidson?" Will asks Luke. There's concern in his voice. Telling him about the situation with Marcus has been the last thing on my mind, but it seems that he's been made more than just aware.

"That's what we thought, but I just got a text from Taylor that he's disappeared. No movement at his home for two days. When he investigated further, he found the apartment empty."

"How is that possible?" Luke says with obvious annoyance.

"Don't worry, sir. Taylor will rectify the situation."

"So what do we do? What if he comes back? He can't see Will or Eliana," I say as I'm regaining my normal breathing pattern after so much crying. Although it seems I'm about to enter a new level of hyperventilating. "No, no, no, no. I can't, I can't go back to hiding. Not here, not now that I've just got you back. Your father will kill you if he finds out. He'll kill you both!" I start to shake and Will helps me into a seat.

"Layla, no one is going to find out, but I need you to pull it together. We didn't come this far for it to fall apart now. Just ride this out with us a little while longer," Claire's calming tone does its job and I begin to feel better immediately. I love that she has that effect on me.

"Let's just take a break here. Will, get the lantern in the garage and take Layla out on the dock while Furtick and I discuss some options."

Luke's is a welcome directive. Being alone with Will is just the medicine I need.

As Will and I walk the length of the dock out to the water my mind floods with memories of our time on Lake Davidson. It was there that he professed his feelings for me and there that I knew I had fallen in love with him. I want so much for the craziness with Marcus to disappear so that Will and I can begin a new life together here.

Will has a firm grasp on my hand and is carrying the lantern with his other hand. This leaves me to brush the palms and Spanish moss from our path. My stomach is doing flips like the first time Will and I walked the flagstone path to the lake together. I remember so clearly that being the night I became completely enthralled with Will. That was the night I truly started to live again.

"Here we are," Will says softly, inviting me to sit with him. It's so much like when we sat together back home. We take our shoes off and scoot as close as we can together, and as Will slips his arm around me I have to fight to keep myself from crying again.

"Here we are," I echo.

"I missed you so much, Layla," Will says softly. "I was so afraid I was going to lose you."

"You could never lose me, Will. In life and death, I'm yours forever." I turn my body so I can face him, taking his hand in mine. I run my finger across my father's wedding band. "Did you really think I would move on?"

"Layla," he sighs. "I knew I was taking a risk by disappearing and an even bigger one by faking my death. My father could have found out and I would have faced a worse fate. The scariest part was knowing that you could choose to move on. For all intents and purposes I was gone, dead. You had every right to move on with your life. I couldn't expect you to hold on forever." Will brushes my face with his thumb and I close my eyes relishing in his touch.

"It's only been a few months, Will," I say.

"I know…you weren't supposed to find out yet. We were going to wait until Christmas to see where you were." Will hasn't released my face from his caress.

"I told you I wasn't going anywhere, remember?" I smile.

"I'm so glad you didn't." Will pulls me to him and kisses me. It's exactly as I remember, only better. His kiss is strong and sweet and full of all the love he has for me. He holds my face in his hands, keeping me locked in this place of bliss.

"Oh, Will. I thought I'd never see you again." I break from our kiss and hold him tighter than I ever have. "Um…I don't want to bombard you, but there's still so much I don't know."

"You can ask anything, Layla. I've missed not sharing my life with you. It's been torture," he says, tucking a loose lock of hair behind my ear.

"Well…what have you been doing?" I ask.

Will gives a little chuckle at the simple curiosity of my question before answering. "Mom and I got settled in a great apartment not far from here. We had to lay low for a while, so Luke had everything set up for us. It was crazy! We walked in and the place was furnished, with a fully stocked kitchen, and even clothes in the closets. Luke and Claire are two of the most incredible people. We could never have done this without them." He shakes his head in amazement.

I understand exactly what he's saying. We agreed early on that if he and I were ever going to make it, we would have to make Luke and Claire our allies. When they took on that role without hesitating, I knew that we were in good hands.

"I agree. I don't know where I'd be if I didn't have them." We smile as we celebrate Luke and Claire's greatness. "Go on. I want to hear more!"

Will laughs again at my cuteness and continues. "I got mom registered for classes, which was really exciting. She always wanted to get her degree, but Dad put the kibosh on that from day one. Be careful when you ask her about it, though. She'll start talking and won't stop. It's really wonderful, actually." He smiles as he thinks about how happy his mother finally is. "Then, Luke got me connected with some contractors and we built the dock…for you."

"You built this?" I'm amazed.

"Well, not by myself. It takes a specialty crew to build out into the water, but I oversaw the project and got my hands as dirty as I could. With every board and every nail, I thought of you. I thought about all the time we spent on the lake back home. I thought of how it became a special place for you to think and clear your head. I thought about the night I gave you this ring." He takes my hand and we gaze at my beautiful promise ring as it twinkles in the light from the lantern and the moon. "I thought about all those things, and I wanted to create a place for you here that might give you at least a little of that."

"Thank you. You did an amazing job. I'm so proud of you…and I'm more than impressed." I kiss him once to show my thanks.

"I love you, Layla." Oh how I have longed to hear those words again. I watch his lips form the words and my heart flutters.

"Say it again."

Will takes my face in his hands and stares his ocean eyes into mine. "I love you."

"One more time?" I smile.

"I. Love. You." Will kisses my cheeks in between each word, and then ends with a soft, sweet kiss on my lips.

"I love you, Will." It feels good to say it directly to him, and not in some quiet declaration in hopes that he'll return, or as I did most recently, to the memory of him.

Our sweet moment is cut short by the sound of Luke's voice. "Will! Layla! We found him!" he shouts.

We race back to the house to hear Furtick finishing a phone conversation.

"Right…Where? Who is she? Ok, keep me posted…yes, stay on him." Furtick looks to us as he wraps up the conversation and ends the call. "Taylor has found Mr. Reynolds. He's been staying with a young lady in Charlotte. No information on who she is yet, but we'll get it."

"I want eyes on him at all times. Tell Taylor to bring in Cline. He is *not* to lose him again." Luke is both pissed and relieved at the same time. Claire stops his pacing and calms him, helping him to focus on the positive that has just transpired.

"As long as we know where he is at all times, we're good," she says, stroking Luke's shoulders.

"So I guess Furtick will be leaving us then, huh?" I say with a little sadness.

"Like hell he's leaving," Luke replies.

"If we know where Marcus is then there's nothing to worry about, right?" I ask.

"I'm not ready to let go of the extra protection. Marcus is too unpredictable." Luke is solid in his statement. If he thinks we need to keep Furtick then I'm not going to argue. I like Furtick and have actually really enjoyed having him here. "You and Eliana will need to make some physical changes," he says to Will and his mother, moving on to another topic.

"What kind of changes?" Eliana asks.

"How do you feel about shorter hair and a slightly different color?" Claire suggests.

"I don't mind at all. It is much hotter here so shorter hair will be a welcome change. I'm more concerned about William." Eliana's trained compliance is helpful in this situation.

"I'll do whatever I need to. I can grow it out and color it, or shave it for all I care. I'm open to anything." Will says, pulling me close to his side. He's unwavering in his commitment to me, and after all he has done, there is no way I could ever doubt his love for me.

"There's another matter we need to address, Layla. You have to be aware of how you refer to Will and Eliana. Here and *only* here are you allowed to call them Will or Eliana. As soon as we step outside of this house, you must *always* refer to them as John and Elisabeth." Luke stares at me until I respond.

"I think I can do that."

"You have to more than think, Layla. There is no alternative, especially if you're going to be seen with either of them on campus. Have you told anyone about your life in Davidson?"

"No, not really. I mean, I did say something to this guy, my friend, Finn. I only said something because he saw Marcus stalking me in the coffee shop. Am I in trouble?" No one said not to say anything about my life before FSU.

"It's ok, honey. Luke is just a little on edge right now," Claire interjects. "What did you tell him?"

"The truth, mostly. I told him that Marcus hated my boyfriend because he dated Marcus' sister and it didn't end well, that I had to break up with my boyfriend because his father didn't approve of us dating, and also that I moved here to start over. Was that ok?" I direct my information to Claire since she is providing the most comfort at the moment.

"That's perfect. You did great." Claire smiles, making me feel less like I'm in trouble.

"Wait. Luke, you said Marcus had shown up here. Why is Layla using the word *stalking*?" Apparently Will got the abridged version of the Marcus situation and not the whole story like I had once thought. There's a fire in his eyes. He's not happy about this and his blood is beginning to boil. I've seen this look before and it's not good.

"I didn't want to worry you. I thought we would have it sorted out before we revealed you and Eliana. But…it's bigger than I thought." Luke answers Will's fiery comment as coolly as possible.

"What does *that* mean?" Will asks with a quizzical look.

"Right now I'm just working on theories and I need some time to get the facts. For now, there's nothing to really worry about. We know where Marcus is, and as long as we know that, there's no threat. But I need you both to be patient. Can you do that?" He directs his question to me and I'm only slightly insulted. This whole thing with Marcus started because I couldn't leave well enough alone. I *had* to march myself down to the bookstore to unearth the story behind the story from Will. I can't help but wonder if I had kept my query to myself if things wouldn't have turned out differently. Or if Will and I had just been patient, waiting until we graduated like Claire said...if Will Meyer might still exist. There's no changing the past. The only thing we can do now is press on.

"Yes, Uncle Luke, we can do that." I give him a small smile and he returns it, letting me know his stress is dissipating at my willingness to be obedient. I look at Eliana and sigh. "Well, I guess it's time to get you to the salon."

Chapter 9

It's a rare morning in the Weston house. Luke and Claire are running errands and Will is at school. I'd be at school as well, but my instructors are at a conference so classes were cancelled. It's my light day, so that means no classes at all today. This leaves just Furtick and me in the house...alone. It's strange. He's always with me, but not *with* me. There he sits, at the kitchen table, with his laptop and a stack of files.

Furtick is handsome by anyone's standards. He's still physically fit from his military years so I have every confidence in his ability to protect me and the ones I love. His face is strong, and he's always so focused, but I've seen his eyes soften sometimes when he's watching me interact with Luke and Claire or Will.

I remember what Luke said about why Mr. Meyer *employed* certain men as his henchman, as Luke put it. It makes me wonder what Furtick did. What skills were so useful to Gregory Meyer? Considering he was in need of Mr. Meyer's assistance, I wonder if he ended up with an honorable or dishonorable discharge.

"You want to know what I did," Furtick says, not even turning around.

"What?" I ask, realizing that my curiosity has burned a hole in his back.

"You want to know what I did, how I got connected with Meyer." He's not asking me, but making an observation. I suppose I was going to ask at some point, but there hasn't been a clear opportunity. I've truly been so appreciative of all he's done, and how he's handled the whole situation, that any thoughts I've had about asking have been dismissed. I want to know for the pure curiousness of it because his answer isn't going change how I feel about him. I don't care what he did because that isn't the Furtick that I know. The Furtick I know is strong and quietly caring, not the thug his former boss would pigeonhole him to be.

"Yes. I'd like to know, but you don't have to tell me," I say.

Furtick turns around and I see a look on his face that is foreign. There's timidity to his presence. His eyes shift as if searching for the right words. He's struggling to find the right path to take in telling his story. Where to begin? His eyes lock on mine and they're filled with fear, afraid that what he is about to tell me will alter how I feel about him, how I trust him. I understand this feeling more than he'll ever know. I see the pain in his eyes and I want to cry. He's let his guard down and his humanity is leaking.

"Whatever it is, it's ok," I say in soft reassurance. "There's nothing you can say that will change what I think about you, Furtick."

"You may need to reconsider that statement after you've heard what I'm about to tell you."

It takes him another moment or two before he's able to articulate his story.

"My plan in life had always been to be a career Marine. My high school sweetheart didn't exactly love the idea, but she loved me, so she was supportive. We got married right out of high school and I went to Basic Training three weeks later. Heather went to college while I was stationed at Camp Lejeune and things were amazing for the first three years. I was home every chance they gave me so we made it work.

"A few years later when Heather told me she was pregnant I was thrilled. The timing was perfect. She finished her degree and graduated two months before Anna was born. I actually got to be there for her birth," Furtick smiles recalling that day. It was obviously the best of his days.

"But I went back to Base and things got hard. Even though I was home as much as I had been before, and then some, Heather resented me for not being there all the time. I don't blame her. She had just worked her ass off to earn her degree and now she was alone with a baby and trying to build a career. I wanted her on Base with me, but there wasn't any family housing available so I got permission to move off Base. She moved and

77

we found a great little house not far from Base. While it seemed like the solution to our problem, all it did was separate her from her family and friends. I was working a lot and she was at home, alone, with Anna.

"After five years of putting up with more than she should have, Heather filed for divorce and moved back to Charlotte to live with her parents. It was hard, but I understood. I kept visiting as often as I could. I wasn't going to miss out on watching Anna grow up. Heather never kept her from me, for which I was grateful." Furtick takes a moment to collect himself, letting out a big sigh.

"After a while Heather started dating. She had her share of hits and misses...mostly misses. I thought she would have remarried by then but, when Anna was seventeen, Heather started seeing this guy, Tim, who was kind of jerk, but ok, I guess. His friends, on the other hand, were total douchebags. Sorry," he says apologizing for his language. I shake my head and raise my eyebrows to let him know I'm not bothered by his description. "I was in town for the weekend and Anna came to stay with me at my parents' house like she always did. It was really great. I loved every second I spent with her. She was the only thing that brought me pure joy." He pauses relishing a moment that is the epitome of that joy.

"I knew my daughter and could tell that something was off so I asked her how things were going, just to check in. After some pursuance on my part she broke down. It took ten minutes to get her calmed down enough to tell me what happened." Furtick braces himself. "One of the douchebags forced himself on her. She...she said that Tim had his friends over for a cook out, and...uh...Anna went to change her clothes after she spilled soda on her shirt. This dou-, uh, guy, followed her into her room. If Heather hadn't come looking for her, calling her name through the house, the bastard would have raped her. He got close enough as it was."

"And you couldn't let him get away with that," I say. It's not a question, but a matter of fact. A man like Furtick doesn't let injustice stand.

"No," he says, echoing the firmness of my statement. "I followed him for three days before the perfect moment was given to me. I beat the – well, he spent a week in the hospital on life support before they pulled the plug and he died."

"Why were you arrested? Isn't what you did considered defense of a third party?" I allow a moment of pride as I recall a legal conversation with Luke last year. He let me ask him whatever came to mind and then gave me the legality of it. It was actually a pretty fun game and I'm a little surprised that I remember this term because there were so many. I'm impressed that anyone passes the Bar exam.

"Yes and no. The problem was that I followed him for three days. The argument was that it was premeditated. The beating was, but him dying wasn't necessarily part of the plan. Had I caught him in the act and killed him it would have been an act of passion in defense of a third party."

"I don't understand where Gregory Meyer comes in. Wouldn't you be tried in a military court?"

"Not necessarily. If the guy had been military, yeah. They have their own legal system and it can be kind of hairy. So I had a friend who suggested I seek some outside counsel since the guy was civilian. When you Google 'most successful attorneys in North Carolina' Gregory Meyer's name is front and center. After I told him my story, he said he'd take care of it. It took two weeks and my case was expedited and I was honorably discharged."

"And that's when Mr. Meyer told you his fee."

"Yes. When I had to explain to Heather why I wasn't working a *normal* job, she was furious with me. She convinced Anna that I was some thug and she hasn't spoken to me since."

I can't imagine. He goes after the guy who attacks his daughter and the mom turns against him? But it's all clear to me now why he took this job of protecting me. He's making up with me what he couldn't do for Anna.

"Thank you, Furtick."

"Wes." My quizzical look asks him the question that he answers. "My name is Wes. I want you to know that I'm more than a cold ex-marine."

"I don't think you're cold at all. I think you have one of the biggest hearts of anyone I've ever known. I know why Luke trusts you. It's because you're like him. You would do anything to protect the ones you love most." Furtick gives me just the smallest smile, but it's still the biggest one he's given me. I understand him better now and this makes me want him to stay forever.

I know it was difficult for him to tell me something so heart wrenching. I remember how I felt the night I told Will every detail of my parents' death, and about the months and years that followed. It's funny. When all you want to do is move on and forget, life brings you someone with whom you can entrust all of your secrets, everything you thought you wanted to leave behind. That person ends up holding those secrets with you, because you really can't leave everything behind. There are things that we must carry with us because they are a very important part of our life story. Without them, we don't make sense.

I don't know how many people know Wes Furtick's story, but I am honored to help him carry it.

*****

I can't sleep. You'd think that with Will being here, being alive, that the past month would have brought me my sweetest dreams, but for some reason I've not been sleeping well. Maybe it's the fear of Gregory Meyer finding out that he was duped, but more of what he'll *do* if that happens. Now that I know Will and his mother are alive, I don't like them being out of my site. They live in a great apartment eight and a half minutes from here, which is eight minutes too far for my liking. I haven't been there yet because Will is here every morning to pick me up for class, and every moment after that until Claire kicks him out to go home and sleep.

I feel only slightly better since Eliana has had her hair shortened and lightened, but a shaggier hairstyle for Will doesn't exactly disguise him. They're both working on their tans, so that'll help...I guess. I'm so close to convincing Will to color his hair. I think I'll have won him over in a couple of weeks.

I grab my phone and scroll through my contacts. It's 1:00 am here, so that makes it...uh...10:00 pm in California. I decide to text Caroline and see if she's up. Even if she isn't, it'll feel good to reach out to her.

Layla Weston: Hey! Are you still up?
Caroline Jackson: Hey!

Her response comes almost immediately and I feel a smile spread across my face.

Layla Weston: I can't sleep. Just wanted to tell you that I was thinking about you. Sorry I've been a crappy friend.

Caroline Jackson: You haven't been a crappy friend! I'm glad you texted. Big things happening here. I met someone!

Layla Weston: OMG! Really! That's great! How long?

Caroline Jackson: Just a few months, but it feels promising. I'll keep you posted!

Layla Weston: Definitely! Big things happening here, too. But I can't tell you via text. Are you coming to visit after Thanksgiving?

Caroline Jackson: Oh the suspense! I'm working on that. G, T, and C want to road trip down and then we can all fly back to school from FL. Just working on Mom and Dad's OK.

Layla Weston: Great! Keep me posted! I can't wait for you to come!!

Caroline Jackson: Me too! Break's over. Gotta hit the books again. I

love and miss you! Can't wait to see you!

Layla Weston: Love and miss you, too! Night!

With that, I'm lulled into a peaceful place. Caroline has that effect on me. I'm banking on somehow convincing Luke and Claire that we can tell Caroline and the others about the whole charade, but the more thought I give it, I'm certain Furtick will take the most convincing. I can't imagine them coming to visit and not telling them. It's not like *John* and *Elisabeth* could be here and our friends not know they're Will and his mother. Well, I extended the invitation before Will came back from the dead, so I can't take it back now.

I fall asleep and dream of random, bizarre things, waking with my alarm six hours later. As I stretch and recall my dream I have an overwhelming sense of normalcy. Isn't this what everyone dreams about, weird, completely unrealistic scenarios where you're dancing with giant butterflies in a meadow of marshmallow flowers?

Like clockwork, the doorbell chimes as my foot leaves the last step of the stairs. Will kisses me once as he steps through the door. He is firmly planted by my side no later than 8:00 am every day as he was in those final days when we lived in Davidson. On Saturday and Sunday, he waits patiently for me to wake and come down to meet him. I haven't told him this, but I set my alarm for 8 am on the weekends. He thinks my internal alarm clock wakes me, but I don't want him to wait too long. The earlier I'm up, the more time I get to spend with him.

Eliana has early classes, so she's already at school. We'll see her later for lunch and then she'll either go to the library to study or come to the house. It's been so much fun watching her immerse herself into college life. She's focused and doing really well in her classes, and has made some really nice friends. They can't mix a martini, but know which bars have $2 draft beers on which night.

Furtick is only charged with following me in case Marcus comes back so everyone else can come and go as they please. So far, Taylor and Cline have kept close tabs on him. He's still with some girl in Charlotte and hasn't returned to his place in Davidson. Having such firm tabs on him means that the last month has been the most relaxed I've had since the night he accosted me in the parking lot at school. I'm hoping this girl he's been staying with is the reason he's staying in Charlotte, and that he's moved on from his delusions about what he thinks we have together.

Furtick enters from his side of the house adjusting his gun holster over his fitted white t-shirt, gun included. Once he layers one of his signature plaid button-ups, you can't even tell it's there. He nods at Will as he does every day, and gives me a straight-faced wink.

Wesley Furtick and I have an interesting relationship. He loves me like a sister and I annoy him as such. We argue over my tenacious tendencies with him winning because, really, it doesn't matter what I want. My family's safety is of supreme priority. Even though we fight, I love him dearly and can't imagine our lives without him. Now that I carry his story with him, our relationship is even more wonderfully complicated, but I wouldn't have it any other way.

After breakfast and a quick review of my Psych 101 reading assignment, we're out the door and headed for campus. I always find it amazing that Will and I can weave in and out of traffic, merge onto the highway, and take unplanned short-cuts, and Furtick never loses us. I can only imagine the choice words he has for Will when he plays the *let's see if we can lose Furtick* game.

Will and I have found a quiet, yet public, place to spend our time in between classes. Furtick didn't want it too secluded so he could still keep a close eye on me. There is so much to catch up on, so much time that I just want to spend staring at Will, touching his face, taking him in.

There's been so much of my boring, everyday life that I want to share with Will. There have been so many times I've seen, heard, or experienced something and picked up my phone to text Will only to be disappointed with the reminder that there was no Will to text.

Today, though, instead of our usual spot, we decide to pop into the coffee shop. Finn's eyes light up as he sees me. When he realizes that I'm not alone, he raises an eyebrow in surprise.

"Hey, Layla! Where have you been? I've missed my chai tea latte girl!" He's excited and animated and Will isn't quite sure what to make of him. I haven't really talked about my budding friendship with Finn and his familiarity with me causes Will to tighten his gasp on my hand.

"Hey Finn! How's my favorite barista guy?" I say, giving him a half hug over the counter with my free arm. Will stiffens his arm so my range of motion is restricted.

"I'm good, but cut the crap…who's your guy?" Finn has the same subtlety as Gwen, which is probably why I like him so much.

"I'm John…the boyfriend." Will says firmly. He has yet to know that Finn is the least of his worries. This is the first time I've heard him call himself *John*. It's strange but I must get used to it since I'm supposed to call him this anytime we step foot outside the house.

"Boyfriend? That explains your MIA status over the last few weeks. You must be something pretty special. She's been through a lot. Don't hurt her." Finn gives Will a strong look of brotherly intimidation.

"I know. I'll take good care of her." Will smiles. Finn softens his face, satisfied with Will's response, and Will loosens his vise grip on my hand.

"How does stalker boy feel about this?" he asks as he begins to make my drink.

"Stalker boy doesn't know. He hasn't been around, but if you see him, please promise you'll call me."

"Anything for you, Layla. It's nice to meet you John." Finn smiles genuinely and I think Will is put at ease. "Now what can I make for *you*?"

Chapter 10

I've stopped sweating profusely the second I step out the door, which means its fall in Florida. It's a bit chillier than I was used to during my time here, but that's because we're farther north. It's ok since I still have my real cold-weather clothes from Davidson. They're in the attic, so I'll have to rummage through them soon. In the meantime, Will and his mother continue to mention how warm it is. It's comical, really. Will and I had the same conversations about how cold I thought it was this time of year in North Carolina.

"I need to talk with you about something," Will says helping me sit at the end of the dock. It feels good to have a place here with him. And it really is *our* place. No one ever comes down here. It's like our own private island, and right now the temperature this late evening is divine. The breeze coming off the water is just enough to bring a sweet coolness to the 70 degree weather.

"Are you ok?" I ask.

"I'm great. But…that's what I want to talk with you about. I want to make sure that you're great, too."

"Of course I am. I'm wonderful! Why wouldn't I be?" I take Will's hand in mine and touch his ring, so perfectly placed on his hand.

"I'm not dense enough to think that what I did to you didn't damage you in some way. I just want to give you the opportunity to be every shade of honest with me. Set aside everything else and say what you may have been keeping inside. I don't want us to keep secrets or our feelings from each other." Will's voice is sad and I don't like it. His tone makes my heart break. I have to relieve him of this burden.

"Well, since you brought it up. There is something I haven't said." Will braces himself, waiting for a tongue lashing of sorts. "I haven't said thank you yet."

"What?" Will creases his face, making a little V between his brows. This is the last thing he expected me to say.

"Thank you." I take his face in my hands and kiss him sweetly. "Thank you for loving me so much that you would literally do anything for us to be together. Thank you for showing me that I wasn't imagining the depth of our love. Thank you for risking everything to be with me, a girl so unworthy of everything you give. But most of all, thank you for bringing *this* back to me." I kiss him again and this time he lays me on the dock, not letting go of me for a single second.

Will's hand runs down my side and rests on the back of my leg as he lifts it to meet his hip. My fingers rake through his hair and tears of elation sting my eyes. I've waited so long to feel this influx of emotions, uncertain if I ever would again. I'm doing my best to savor every second because I know Will is going to retreat any second now. When it seems like we've been kissing forever, he releases my lips and my leg and brushes the hair from my eyes, not leaving his place over me. I gave up arguing with him about his overly chivalrous behavior when it comes to our make-out sessions a long time ago. I came to actually cherish the moment. Will shows more restraint than the average guy. Each time he forces himself to break away, he proves that he is anything but average.

"You…are…" he begins.

"…completely in love with you," I finish. "Was it devastating thinking you were gone forever? Yes. Did all of that go away the second I saw you in front of me? Absolutely. I love you Will and I would endure all of it again if it meant being here with you like this."

"I love you. I'm the luckiest guy in the world that I get to call you mine." He smiles and traces my face with his fingers. I close my eyes and delight in every surge of pleasure that it brings.

"*We're* lucky," I say, raking my fingers through his now-longer hair. "Like Luke and Claire. I would tell you not to forget to be here by six tomorrow night for their anniversary dinner, but you spend fourteen hours a day here!" I laugh and Will kisses me before taking my hand and sitting me up.

"That's right! I'm just buying my time until I can spend the other ten hours with you. I still think about the morning I got to wake up with you in my arms. Seeing your face as soon as my eyes opened was a gift like no other. It's what kept me going those months we were apart." Will holds his gaze on me and I'm entranced by the sparkle of his blue eyes in the dimming light of dusk. I touch my ring and remember all the promises we made…promises that I know will come to fruition one day.

I sigh heavily thinking about the craziness I'm facing with Marcus, wishing he would just go away forever. Even though we know where he is, it doesn't seem like we can really, truly relax. If Marcus starts to move, we'll be on lockdown with even more strict protection from Furtick. I trust Luke and know that he's doing everything to get it resolved so I don't want to waste the time I have with Will worrying about any of that. It's just so frustrating knowing that my life in Tallahassee was supposed to be free from anything that would threaten me. My *life* is my relationship with Will, but Marcus is ruining everything.

"C'mon. We have work to do for dinner tomorrow night," I say clearing my head and pulling Will up to stand. Marcus' whereabouts are known and he's not anywhere near here, so I'm going to live my new life with Will just as he's intended.

"*We* have work? I thought I was just supposed to show up and look good," Will takes me by the waist and gives me a tickle.

"You do that anyway. I'm helping you diversify your giftings, now let's go!" I give him a quick kiss before taking him by the hand and leading him back to the house.

*****

The anniversary party for Luke and Claire is going perfectly. Eliana and I make a great team in the kitchen. The biggest challenge is keeping Claire out of the way, which has become Luke and Will's job. Despite the few times we have to force Claire out, we manage to make and surprise Luke and Claire with all of their favorite dishes and they love them.

As we sit down to eat Luke toasts Claire's grace and beauty, which makes Claire cry. Then Claire toasts Luke's strength and charm, which also makes Claire cry.

Will and I can't help but feel closer in this moment. He holds me tight and whispers *that's how I love you, only more* when Luke finishes his touching tribute to his bride. We want so much to have what Luke and Claire have. Their deep-rooted friendship lays the foundation for everything. But more than that, they have a passion for each other that grows every day. They've celebrated incredible achievements and mourned great sadness, too. I am inspired by their love.

Furtick opted not to join us even though we all invited him at one point or another. He spent the evening in his room with the dinner plate I made for him. I don't know what else he would be doing, so I assume he spent the evening working. This is confirmed when he comes in reviewing a file as we're all in the kitchen tidying up from the night's festivities.

"Can I see it again, Aunt Claire?" Luke added to the necklace I gave her for Christmas. The charms aren't specific to anything like the ones I gave her that represent the three of us, but they complement the set beautifully. "The whole thing is just so pretty!"

"Yes, Luke! You did an excellent job! It was quite thoughtful of you," Eliana says. She doesn't chime in too often. I wonder if she's self-conscience about her over rehearsed speech. I suppose it would take some time to get back to a place where one even knew how to speak conversationally, relaxed. I'm glad she seems to be getting a little more comfortable.

"Hey Furtick!" I say excitedly. I'm still on such a high from the night that I can't contain myself. The joy in the room is palpable...there's no way I couldn't be happy right now. "We missed you tonight. How was your dinner?"

"Dinner was excellent, Miss Weston. Thank you." His demeanor is entirely opposite of mine.

"What happened?" I ask changing my tone to meet his.

"Nothing really. We've just identified the young woman Mr. Reynolds has been staying with. Turns out it's just his sister, Holly."

I take it back. There *is* a way I could be unhappy, and Holly Reynolds is it.

I look at Will. He's almost expressionless. He doesn't seem to be relieved, sad, angry...he's blank. That's ok because I'm be feeling everything for the both of us. A casket of emotions has just been exhumed and my mind is swimming.

"Will you excuse me, please?" I exit the kitchen and make my way to the porch and out to the patio. *Whoa.* I take a few deep breaths as I try to sort through everything that is rushing through my head.

Was she in Charlotte this whole time? Had Will known where she was would he have pursued a relationship with her with the same passion he did me? Would her parents have been fighting to keep her and Will safe the way Luke and Claire are? Now that he knows where she is, does that bring back any of those feelings he had for her before she was exiled by his father? What would that mean for me? I know exactly what that would mean: I wouldn't have Will.

"Layla? Baby? Are you ok?" Will asks finding me on the patio.

"Yeah, I'm ok. I just...so he's with Holly...in Charlotte," I sputter out.

"Yeah...that's good. It means we still know where he is, and Taylor and Cline can watch him more closely now that they know who he's with." Will tucks my hair behind my ear then lifts my chin up. "What's wrong?"

"Nothing," I lie. How can I tell him about the surge of insecurity that has just overtaken me?

"Layla, we just had this conversation. You can't keep things from me. Please, tell me."

It takes me a minute to push my insecurities aside long enough to be willing to accept whatever Will's response is. "Knowing where she is…where she's been this whole time…does it make you wish you could go back? I mean, if you knew she was in Charlotte, so close, would you have gone to be with her?" I'm not sure what response I'm looking for. Maybe it goes back to the conversation he just referenced. I want him to be honest about all of his feelings, even if they make me sad.

"Layla, honey, please…"

"Will, you just said we couldn't keep things from each other."

He sighs. "When I was looking for her, had I known she was in Charlotte I probably would have gone to find her somehow."

"Of course you would have." I look down contemplating where my life would be if he had chased her but quickly dismiss it because I literally cannot stomach the thought.

"But I didn't know you then." He lifts my chin so my eyes have no choice but to lock with his. "Do you know when I started falling for you? When our eyes met after inspecting the icy mess of my Coke on the sidewalk outside the coffee shop. I looked into those ridiculously beautiful eyes and saw your honesty, purity, integrity, the love you are capable of…you had something that I wanted to be a part of. At that moment, it didn't matter if Holly, or any other girl, ever existed. I couldn't eat…I barely slept. I counted the moments until I could see you again. I was so grateful Luke had already hired me to work on the basement job with him. Otherwise I would have had to wait until school started and I don't know that I could have waited that long.

"I'm indebted to Marcus for not giving up Holly's information when I begged him for it. It made me move on. It meant that my heart was available and open when you came into my life. So I only care that Marcus is with Holly in Charlotte because it gives us an upper hand in keeping tabs on him, which means that we can live our lives.

"You walked into my life and made me see why it never worked out with anyone else. I love you, Layla, and one day I'm going to marry you and spend the rest of my life making sure you never doubt that for a second."

I fall into Will's arms filled with both relief and joy. "I love you so much. I don't think you'll ever know how you've changed my life. I thought I'd never have anything so wonderful as you. All you have to do is ask, and I promise to say yes. I'll say yes to spending my life making sure you know how much I love you and how eternally happy you make me."

Will holds me for a long time in the tightest embrace. This is my sweet spot, the place I know that I'm loved, accepted, taken care of. If I ever doubt that, all I have to do is find myself here and it will all become clear again.

Will and I spend the rest of the evening in the Great Room watching TV, catching up on episodes we've missed, going back to the first season of new shows we've recently started watching. *Gosh, what did people do before DVR and Netflix?*

It's just the type of relaxed time that calms my heart and brings me back into the blissful place of normalcy that we have existed in since Marcus' location was discovered and his every move monitored. But even though we live in this normalcy, I can't ignore that it exists because of Luke's protective team. I wonder how long it'll be like this. Will Furtick ever enter a room without me thinking he's there to deliver devastating news? How long will Furtick be a part of our family? In all honesty, I've come to love Furtick so much that I hope he never leaves.

I push this uneasiness aside because I'm fully aware that the alternatives are not an option. I couldn't live in fear of not knowing where

Marcus is, but worse than that, I couldn't live without Will. So I will do whatever it is I need to do to make sure Will and I live a long and happy life together.

I wake up and realize I'm still on the couch, covered by a blanket, alone. I'm not cradled in Will's arms, nestled in my favorite place as I was before I fell asleep. I stretch and squirm, and as I turn on my side I see a mass of blankets stretched out on the floor next to me. There he is, my love, always the gentleman. He asked Luke's permission the only time we literally slept together on the couch on prom night. Since this was not a prearranged event, he did the honorable thing and tore himself away to sleep next to, but not with, me. I sigh at his perpetual sweetness a little too loudly and he stirs.

"Good morning, sunshine," I say. As the words leave my mouth I'm keenly aware that I did not brush my teeth last night. I quickly pull the blanket up enough to cover my mouth and nose so as not to send him back into an unconscious state with my morning breath. "How's your back from sleeping in the floor? That was very sweet of you."

He takes his turn to stretch and squirm and smiles as he rubs his eyes. "Morning, babe. Don't worry about me. I'm great. Being here with you first thing makes any discomfort more than worth it." He reaches up and moves the blanket from my face so he can give my chin a tug. "I will, however, need to go home to shower and change. I've got a great day planned for us."

"You do?" I say with a huge grin.

"Yes! It's been far too long since I've treated you like the princess you are, so I'm going to remedy that today." He smiles and raises an eyebrow and I know I needn't try to ask questions because not a one will be answered.

"Just tell me what to wear and I'm there!" I say sitting up. My stomach growls loudly and we both laugh. "I guess I should eat something, huh? Oh, where's your mom?"

"She went home last night. She's enjoying her independence. She loves coming and going as she pleases. She's good about telling me where she is though. She knows I worry," he says with a smile.

"Yes, I can understand that. I'm glad she's embracing her freedom."

With that we make our way to the kitchen where Claire is whipping up some pancakes. After thoroughly stuffing ourselves Will goes home for a shower and I head upstairs for mine.

I'm excited about spending some real time with him today, even though I know Furtick will be close behind. We never have any private time unless we're on the dock or have a mostly empty house to ourselves, which is close to never. It's very similar to the way life was back home.

I let the water rush over me and my mind wanders, thinking only about all things Will. My heart skips a beat and my stomach flips the more I think about every kiss, every touch he has gifted me with. I would have already given myself completely to Will were he not so honorable. I'm amazed at his restraint, but I appreciate it, really. I've just recently come into this world where my feelings are considered, and I'm free to express them, so sometimes I'm not sure how to show my own restraint. Will knows that and would never take advantage of me. My virtue being one of his top priorities is one of the things I love so much about him.

Will said to dress for being outdoors, so I dress casually in jeans and a sweater set and comfortable, yet cute, shoes. I've just finished pulling part of my hair back when my phone buzzes letting me know I either have new emails or texts. I'm hoping there's an email there from Caroline spilling the beans about her new boyfriend, or confirming their visit, but when I pull up the text I see that it is from Marcus.

Marcus Reynolds: I'm growing impatient, Layla.

Marcus Reynolds: I've made all the arrangements I need to here. I expect to have your undivided attention when I return.

Heart attack. *What do I do? Do I respond? Do I ignore him?* No. I do the only thing there is to do. I rush downstairs to tell Luke and Furtick. With each step I'm praying that Will isn't there yet. I don't want him to know, not yet at least. I don't want whatever he has planned today to be ruined. He's so excited about it. I just couldn't do that do him. It's not like I'm keeping it from him. I am going to tell him…just not right away.

There's no sign of Will yet so I start calling for Luke and Furtick. It doesn't take long for them to appear at the ready.

"He texted me," I say extending my phone out for them both to see. Furtick snatches it from my hand and he and Luke review the messages. Furtick pulls his phone out and as he's walking away I can hear that he's talking with Taylor.

"That's it, you're not leaving the house except to go to classes," Luke says firmly.

"Will and I have plans today…" I begin.

"I'm sorry, Layla, but you and Will can spend the day here. I can't risk something happening to you. I won't lose you." Luke embraces me showing both his vulnerability and steadfastness. Every time Luke says something like that or looks at me with desperate eyes I know that he's thinking of Penny. Defending Claire and me is like breathing for Luke. I would never take that away from him, but I can't live like this.

"Taylor and Cline still have eyes on Mr. Reynolds and his sister, so he hasn't left Charlotte yet. There's no way to know when he'll make his move. He'll most likely drive, but we're monitoring all flights just in case." Furtick is typing furiously away at my phone.

"What are you doing? You're not replying to him, are you?" I'm totally freaked out right now.

"No, not at all. I'm syncing our phones. Any emails, messages or calls you receive, I'll have access to them," he replies as he hands my phone back to me.

"I get personal stuff on there!" I protest, immediately regretting my whiney tone.

"You could get a personal text from the President but it won't matter. I only care about the communication you receive from Mr. Reynolds. You've got to take this seriously, Layla." Furtick's eyes are set on me. This is the first time he's called me by my given name. This is turning personal for him. Perhaps he finally sees us as the family that I see him.

"Ok...sorry," I say sheepishly. I forget sometimes just how hard everyone is working to keep me safe. I feel bad that I've disrespected that with my whining. Furtick gives me his signature wink and I know it's ok.

"Uncle Luke, about today...Marcus isn't anywhere near here...and I just really need this time with Will. I need to have time with Will where *all this* isn't happening," I say waving my phone in the air. "Wasn't that the point of everything all of you did? So Will and I could have a life together? Being sequestered to the house is not living." I pause, studying my uncle's face, praying that he hears how desperate I am to have just one normal day with Will. "Please. I won't refuse Furtick's follow." I look at Luke with desperate eyes, hoping he sees how important this is to me. I don't want my day with Will to be tainted. I want it to be the perfect day he's planned it to be.

Luke stares at me for a long time. I can see the wheels turning behind his eyes and know that there is so much more at stake for him here. He lost Penny so tragically. There was nothing he could do to stop her death, but now that I'm here he'll be damned if he doesn't do everything he can to make sure I don't go anywhere. I love him for this. It's the protection I had from my father until the second he died. It's the protection I missed during my time with Gram and Gramps.

There's a knock at the door. It's the same quick knock Will gives just before he opens the door to the house that has become just as much his home as it is ours. Will's arrival is the ding on the proverbial timer forcing Luke to make a decision. He looks to Furtick who gives him a slight nod indicating that he'll be just as much my shadow today as he is every other day.

"Ok…but, I don't care that Marcus is still in Charlotte…Furtick *has* to follow as usual." I hug him and tell him thank you over and over again. "I don't know what I'd do if anything happened to you, Layla. I love you so much," he whispers.

"I love you too. I could never fully thank you for all you've done for me."

Luke looks at me and I have to fight back tears. I am so overwhelmed by the enormity of his love. There was a time I thought being loved the way my father loved me was over. But right now, being here in Luke's arms, I feel like my heart could burst.

I have just enough time to get to a bathroom and pull myself together before Will sees me in my upset state. When I emerge he's in the kitchen waiting patiently for me, handsome as ever.

"Hey babe, you look beautiful," he says kissing my cheek.

"Thank you. You're always so sweet. I'm ready for Will and Layla's Day of Fun! Our shadow will be with us, but it's still going to be a great day. I promise." I say.

"No worries. I'm on board with whatever is best in keeping you safe."

Will takes my hand and leads me to the front of the house and to his car. He gets me settled in the front seat and as I watch him cross in front of the car I flashback to our first date. He rakes his fingers through his hair and I feel the same warmth come over as I did that night. His very presence elicits a feeling in me that I never knew existed. To say I love Will seems like such a subpar expression. What I feel for Will is so much deeper. I would *give* anything, *do* anything for him. I would sacrifice my life to be with him, and there is nothing that could ever change that.

"I found out about this place from your friend Finn. The real blooming months aren't until January through April, but Finn said it's still really beautiful. He's a pretty cool guy," Will says pulling into the Maclay

Gardens State park. "Oh, and, uh, I'm not worried about Finn." So he's found out Finn plays for the other team. I wonder if Finn harmlessly flirted with him and the thought of that makes me giggle.

"This is lovely. Thank you, Will!" I kiss him as I exit the car and he closes the door behind me. We find the brick path and Will takes my hand as we walk. It feels so good, normal, to be here with him like this. "How is your mom? She doesn't talk much," I ask, working to make normal conversation. Will is much better at normal conversation than I am, but I'm learning.

"She's good. She's feeling a weird mix of emotions. She loves school, and she's getting used to the weather here," he chuckles. "Oddly enough she misses my dad. She's broken down with me a few times, and sometimes I hear her crying at night."

"Oh, Will. I guess I never thought of that." I give his hand a little squeeze.

"She feels bad sometimes that we left the way we did. It takes a lot of conversation to remind her of what our life was like with him, and what our life is like now. After over a decade of training by him, it's going to take some time for her to find herself again."

"I can imagine," I say.

Will's gait slows a bit and his face betrays him.

"What is it, Will?"

"If I asked you...what my dad was like...at the funeral...would you tell me?" he asks.

"Um...I'm not sure you want my input. My interpretation of your father's demeanor at...on that day is a bit jaded. But...I'll tell you if you'd like," I say.

"Yes, please," he says quietly. He doesn't look at me. He just continues to walk slowly, holding my hand. It's almost as if he's forcing himself to know for sure what he's suspected his whole life: that his father couldn't have cared less about him and his mother.

I'm hesitant. I don't really know how to tell Will his father's eulogy was riddled with lies and misrepresentations. I want to be honest with him but I don't want to hurt him. But since we've promised not to hold back our thoughts or feelings, I'll tell him what he wants to know.

"Well, I never saw him cry, which bothered me a lot. Tyler let me squeeze his hand when I felt upset. Needless to say he had to ice his hand by the end of the service." We both smile knowing what an incredible friend Tyler had been. "He talked about what a *fine* wife and mother your mom was, always helping others. This was probably the most accurate thing he said."

"What did he say about me?" Will's quiet tone makes my heart sad. This is something he must have been thinking about for a long time. If my parent's lost me the way Mr. Meyer *lost* Will, my father would have had to be committed. They never would have made it through a funeral. Will doesn't have this assurance. Nothing in his life told him his father truly loved him. I can't imagine what that would feel like.

"Well…he said that you were a brilliant young man, stubborn like him, that you had recently made choices for a better life, and that you had finalized things for your studies at Princeton." I stop talking to check on Will. He's calm, looking straight ahead, but his grip on my hand has tightened. "He also said that he loved both you and your mom very much."

Will stops in his tracks, releases my hand, and falls to his knees, throwing his head into his hands. I hear the soft sobs of a man dealing with the scars left by the cold stabs of his father. All Will ever wanted was for his father to love and accept him, but Will grew up knowing that he was just a pawn in the game Gregory Meyer makes out of everyone's life.

"He never, not once, told me he loved me," he says through his tears. "You know, it used to be my wish when I blew out the candles on my birthday cake. I'd close my eyes and wish with everything that I could that my daddy would tell me he loved me, but I was never going to be good enough for him."

"Oh, Will, baby. It's wasn't you, you know that." Tears sting my eyes as I huddle on the ground with him. I can't help but imagine little Will, squinting his little eyes closed so tight, and wishing more than anything else for his father's love. My hatred for Gregory Meyer just went to infinity. "He's the most evil man on the planet and he doesn't deserve you. If he couldn't see all the love you had to give, then he missed out. One day he's going to see that he's all alone, and when he dies, no one will be there to pay their respects because no one truly respects him. I'd say he'll be filled with regret but you have to have a heart for that. How you came from that man I'll never know."

We sit on the walkway under the shade of a tree, me holding my love as he releases a lifetime of pain. Will continues to cry softly, healing scars one by one with each tear. I wonder what Furtick is thinking, watching us like this. I'd say it's too emotional for him, but perhaps it is Wes that's watching in this moment and not Furtick, the ex-marine.

"I'm sorry. I didn't know it would affect me like that," he says wiping his face. His breathing is steady now and he's regaining his sense of self. "I appreciate you being honest with me."

"Of course, Will. I will always be honest with you." I repeatedly run my fingers through Will's hair to comfort him. It's gotten so long since we left Davidson.

"It's crazy, but I didn't have any trouble with leaving, with not saying good-bye to him. I don't know why I'm so emotional now."

"Sometimes it's not the good-bye that hurts, but the flashbacks that follow," I say smoothing his hair. "Believe me, I know it can be hard to look back. But it's ok. I'm here and we'll get through it. We've handled so much already. We can get through anything." I smile and watch Will's face change.

I see how much Will loves me and is glad that I'm here. Even though in this moment I'm here for him completely, I can't help but feel fed by the joyous morphing of his demeanor. Knowing that I can help bring someone from a place of despair to one of happiness is an incredible gift to me. For so long I thought all I did was bring misery, but I know now that my life is worth more and has more potential than I ever thought. At the core of it is my love with Will that gives me the most solid foundation I could have ever hoped for.

Chapter 11

Will and I walk hand in hand through the gardens, quiet for some time. In between taking in the extraordinary colors and scents of flowers, I wonder what he's thinking. I consider his pain. I knew life with his father had been difficult, but I hadn't thought about the damage that was being done. I assumed, because he spoke so passionately about his mother, that her love – what she was allowed to show him – had been enough, that he didn't long for his father's love because he knew his father was incapable of love.

I know now that Will is not as invincible as I had once thought.

I know that he wasn't able to just cut off the natural desire a child has for the love and acceptance that can only come from a parent.

I know just how broken his heart is…and I understand.

When I moved in with Gram and Gramps I thought they would love me the way Mom and Dad did. Gramps did, or at least he tried. But like Eliana, there was only so much he was allowed to show before Gram said it was enough. It didn't matter what I said or did, I was never going to be good enough for her.

I tear up at the thought of our shared pain. It's the kind of pain that can only be understood by someone who has experienced it, too. As I think about Will, hunched over, crying, the picture of him as a little boy is all I can see. I imagine him crying himself to sleep at night, his little body shaking with the sadness brought on by the rejection of his father. I try hard not to cry, but I can't help it and tears begin to stream down my face.

"Layla, baby, what's wrong?" Will asks, pulling me to him. His arms are around me before I can even think about how to articulate my sadness for him. "I didn't mean to upset you by bringing up the funeral. I'm so sorry!"

"No, no…it's not that at all. Sometimes I get a little overwhelmed," I say. I don't want to rehash all the pain, especially for Will's sake. "Can we talk about something? Anything?" Focusing on something else will be calming and a welcome distraction.

I take in the scenery, working hard to focus my eyes and stop the tears from coming. I can't name any of the foliage but there are exquisite blues and reds and yellows. There are shapes of flowers I didn't know existed, and I'm struck by the genius creation of it all. I begin to calm as I concentrate my attention on the here, the now.

"Of course," he says wiping the tears from my face. "What would you like to talk about?"

"Did I tell you that I invited everyone to visit after Thanksgiving?" I say, feeling eons better at just the thought of having our friends together again.

"Everyone? Who, Layla?" Will's voice is filled with trepidation. It doesn't sound like he's going to be on board with telling our closest friends about his non-dead status.

"Caroline, Gwen, Chris, and Tyler," I reply softly…nervously.

"Layla…" Will beings.

"We can't tell them, can we?" I say.

"I'm sorry. I know how much it would mean to you to have us all back together again – it would mean a lot to me, too – but…we just can't risk it. I'm so sorry, babe." Will tucks a loose lock of hair behind my ear and brushes my face with his fingers.

"It's ok. I understand. I invited them before you came back though, so, if they come I guess you'll have to lay low. Sorry." I'm sad that he doesn't think we can trust them, but then it's not about trust. It's about safety. If Chris or Tyler ever accidentally said anything, their fathers would make a beeline for Mr. Meyer's office and all hell would break loose. Actually, it'd be worse than that. He'd be humiliated that he had been fooled and that would carry a far stiffer punishment. We'd all wish we were dead by the time he was done with us.

"Well, maybe you can tell Caroline," he says sweetly.

"Really?" I'm excited, but wonder why Caroline has been granted this extreme privilege.

"Yeah…um…her parents know. That's why Claire called Caroline's mom the day…well, the day Luke and Claire told you." That makes total sense. Caroline's mom is a psychiatrist. They knew that hearing my boyfriend died in the same tragic way as my parents would send me over the edge.

"That makes me really happy. Thank you! I'll have Claire tell Mrs. Jackson that we're going to tell Caroline. I know she'll be so happy!"

"So you're ok with not telling the others?"

"Yes and no. I have you here and that really is the best thing of all. But it's hard letting go of so much of what finally brought me joy. I mean, how do I talk to them and not talk about you? How do I talk about *John* and not feel afraid they're going to hate me for moving on so quickly? I know you know about cutting things off, so please don't think that I don't appreciate the enormity of what you did for us, for me. I just miss them, that's all."

"I understand. It's one thing to want to cut things off. It's another to be forced into it. Let's just start with telling Caroline, ok? And, *maybe*, when all this crap with Marcus is really, truly over, we can talk about telling the others. *Talk*, baby. I can't make any promises. We have to consider Luke and Claire and my mom in this, too." He strokes my face with his thumb and I'm immediately put at ease. Something as simple as his touch can do so much to alleviate my worst feelings.

"That sounds great. Thank you, Will." I wrap my arms around his waist and let his arms cover me like a blanket.

"C'mon. Let's walk," Will says, releasing me and putting my hand in its rightful place within his. "So how have you been doing with expanding your musical tastes?" Will is so good at making any situation feel normal. I've missed that.

"You've been back for this long and this is the first time you're asking me this?" I ask teasingly.

"I've got a list of things to tend to with you, Miss Weston. It's a long list, so it's going to take me some time to get to each item." He smiles crookedly at me and I melt. I love how totally normal this moment is, even though I know Furtick is somewhere close behind.

"I can't wait to see what's on this list! Maybe I should give you some suggestions." I giggle and Will draws me close to him, putting his arm around my waist as we continue to walk. "Well, I have Miles Davis' Love Songs engrained in my head. It was all I listened to for a long time after." We both look sad for a moment, but don't dwell on it.

"Anything else? There are some great new bands out there that you should have picked up." Will doesn't let go of me for a second as we continue to stroll the path through the gardens. You're not allowed to pick the flowers, but occasionally Will *accidentally* does as he touches a blossom, or says *look what I found on the ground* as he hands me a bud. I've got a small bunch gathered but try not to look at them too much so as not to draw attention to our flagrant disobedience of the rules.

"I started listening to Pandora, so I've heard some groups I really like. I don't know all their names, but I've got the Avett Brothers, Parachute, and Cab in my iTunes now. I've also heard a lot more Maroon5, and I love them even more now. Thank you for broadening my horizons." I reach up on my toes and give Will a quick kiss on the cheek.

"That's it? I broaden your horizons and all I get is a peck on the cheek? Horizon broadening should be worth more than that, don't you think?" he teases, wrapping me in his arms.

"Oh, I'd like to thank you further, but you continue to refuse my advances," I smirk.

"Didn't anyone ever tell you that a person's willingness to wait reveals the value they place on what they're waiting for?" Will gives my chin a tug and sends sparks flying through me. "Layla, you have no idea how much I want you, but I want to wake up with you and know that I didn't have to make a deal with your uncle to keep my hands to myself. That we could lie there in each other's arms all day if we wanted, and no one would come looking for us because we would be exactly where we're supposed to be.

"It'd be so easy for us to take off our clothes and have sex. So. Easy. People do it all the time. But opening up your soul to someone, letting them into your spirit, thoughts, fears, hopes, dreams, future – all the things that *we* share – *that* is being naked." Will gazes at me and our eyes seem to meld together in a brilliant blending of blue and hazel.

"You say things like that and I fall *more* in love with you."

"And I am *so* in love with you." Will kisses me deeply, holding on to me tightly in just a fractional preview of what waits for me.

It's been so long since he's kissed me like this. There was a time I thought I'd never be kissed like this again. Even if Will had been dead and I somehow found a way to move on with someone else, I would never be kissed like this. This kiss, this most flawless, fairytale inspired kiss, can only come from your one true love. For me, that will forever and always be Will.

The rest of our night out is more than wonderful and every normal thing a girl could ask for. Will is a dutiful boyfriend and takes me to see the new Justin Timberlake movie. Afterward we get a late dinner and end up running into some of Will's friends from school. As they approach Will leans in and reminds me, "Remember, I'm John."

"Hey, John! What's up, man?" a tall guy who clearly shaves his head rather than deny he's losing his hair says.

"Hey Jason. Just on a date with my girl." Will stands for a moment, doing that handshake, chest bump, hug thing that guys do.

"So this is Layla, huh? You really do exist! I told John here he was going to have to bring you around soon or I was going to chalk you up to his imaginary girlfriend. He hasn't shut up about you for months!" Jason has a sweet and boisterous personality that I immediately like.

"You're not dreaming. I'm really here!" I say with a chuckle as I shake Jason's hand.

"I'm Lisa, Jason's girlfriend. Sorry he's so rude! It's nice to meet you." She extends her hand and we shake politely. Lisa seems quieter than Jason, although that doesn't seem like a real feat.

"It's nice to meet you, too."

"We should go, Jason. They're on a date," she says, tugging at his arm.

"We're on a date, too, and I don't mind having a chat with them!"

"Yeah, well, not everyone is as intrusive as you are. Now let's go!" Lisa pulls on his arm with more force this time causing his feet to move with his body. "It was really nice to meet you. We should double sometime!"

"Definitely!" I say. *Double dating*…what a normal thing to do!

"Later, Jace. Keep him out of trouble, Lisa!" Will calls to them as they make their way to the other side of the restaurant.

Although a bit nervous, it was easy for my end of the short conversation to not mess up and call him Will. This isn't the first time I've been with John and not Will. It still felt strange to hear Jason call him that, but Will didn't flinch. Of course not, he's been John Holland for months now. He's used to it. I need to get used to it, too. I think that maybe I should start calling him John when we're together at home, but that idea makes me sad. I cried big heavy tears at the thought of never saying his name again, but perhaps I could do it because it is my father's name.

I smile remembering the moment Will told me why he chose that name for his new life. Yes, this is a skill I will have to master. For now, I've done well and hope that I'll do just as well in the future.

Will's friends are really nice. They're nothing like the debutants and CEO's in training we knew at Heyward. They're Old Navy, not Prada, so I'm instantly comfortable around them.

"They seem great," I say.

"Yeah, I like them, but we're not exactly close," he says. "It's kind of hard when there's so much they can't know."

"I know what you mean. I always feel like I'm lying by omission about something. It's a natural thing to talk about where you're from, your family, but I'm always changing the subject or being elusive. It's really unfair to them, don't you think?"

"Yes, but as time goes by, *these* people – people like Jason, Lisa, Dana, and Finn – they'll become part of our story. Our life in Davidson won't be primary any more. And one day, when we're at Jason and Lisa's wedding, someone will ask us how we know the bride and groom, and we'll look at them and tell them went to college together." Will clears his throat and I ready myself for a heavy question as that is just about the only time he clears his throat like that. "Do you ever wish I hadn't come back?

"WHAT? NO!" I almost jump out of my seat. I can't believe he would even pose such a ludicrous question. "Why would you even ask that? Do *you* wish you hadn't come back?"

"No, no! I'm sorry. I didn't mean to upset you." Will takes my hand and runs his thumb over my promise ring. "I was just thinking about this very conversation, and the one we had about Caroline and the others. Your life would be less complicated, less secretive if I hadn't come back."

"Maybe, but then you wouldn't be here and I would be devastated every moment of every day for the rest of my life. I would rather lie to everyone than to not have you." I close my eyes to calm myself. "Please don't say things like that again. Please," I beg.

"Ok. I'm sorry." Will kisses my hand and smiles. His assurance that I am where I want and need to be is back and I can rest.

When we get home we tell Luke and Claire that we've decided to tell Caroline about the whole thing. They hesitate for only a moment but agree since Caroline's parents already know everything. Claire suggests we invite Caroline and both of her parents to spend Thanksgiving weekend with us and I couldn't be more thrilled. It's just a few weeks away, so I'm hopeful that they'll be able to make it. I can't wait to see Caroline…and the look on her face when she sees Will!

Chapter 12

I'm busy setting up the guest room when the doorbell rings. I know it's Caroline because she's texted me every hour since they left home. Claire and I bum rush the door and practically tackle Caroline and her mother to the ground. We're so happy for a little bit of the goodness of home. Caroline and I hug fiercely, neither of us wanting to let go. It's been months since we've seen each other, but it feels like forever.

"Let me look at you!" she bellows. I've missed her sweet southern voice, but notice it's not as southern as it once was. California is rubbing off on her and I feel a twinge of disappointment.

"Oh, please, I'm still plain old me. What about you, though? Miss California Girl now! Where's your tan?"

"Oh, it's here, girl, but fading! The sun out there is totally different than back home, that's for sure! I used to lay out with nothing but number four tanning oil but not in Cali! I have to wear sunscreen now! Can you believe it? Sunscreen!"

"Poor baby!" We laugh at the silliness of this *problem*.

"So where is your room? I want to toss my stuff in there and change. The weather is so great here! I'm glad you told me it doesn't get as cold here this time of year as it can in Carolina."

"Yeah, ten degrees makes a huge difference!" I take Caroline's bag and start in the direction of my room when I remember that's where Will and Eliana are hiding. "Good grief! What do you have in here?" I say, putting the bag down, pretending it's heavier than it is. Caroline has over-packed for sure, so I know I can divert her attention here.

"Honey, you know I have to have options! Besides, I'm flying back to school from here, so there's some extra stuff in there that I won't really need here. And...your present is in there!" she replies in her sugary sweet Caroline way. My heart swells as I let her words linger in my ear. My friend Dana has been a good substitute for this southern melody, but while Caroline is here I'll soak in the real thing as much as possible.

"You didn't have to bring me a gift! That's so sweet of you. Thank you!" I say with a pre-gift hug. She'll get another, even bigger one, when I see what it is. "Let's get a drink. You must be thirsty from the drive. I'm always parched after a road trip. It's all the a/c air." I don't know if that's why I'm always thirsty after a road trip, but I had to say something to draw her to the kitchen.

We all decided that we would tell Caroline everything the moment they got here. I couldn't spend a second of her here without her knowing. We also agreed that Luke and Claire would explain the Marcus situation to Caroline's parents while Will and I told Caroline and fielded any questions she had. Caroline would kill me if she found out after we got it under control, and her parents can keep an eye and ear out around Davidson.

We're all gathered in the kitchen, minus Will and Eliana, of course, enjoying the spread of snacks Claire and I prepared. I'm alternating between the pretzel chips and carrots with hummus and the plate of assorted cheeses. My tastes have really expanded since I came to live with Luke and Claire. There's a whole wide world of foods and flavors that I had forgotten about while I was with Gram and Gramps. I'm so glad Claire has revived my palate.

"How was the drive, Carol?" Claire asks. You seemed to make good time."

"It was good. I thought we'd hit more traffic the day before Thanksgiving, but I guess everyone got a head start…or maybe we got the head start," Caroline's mother says. "It's even easier with three drivers. We haven't done a road trip in a while, so it was fun. Caroline took advantage of her captive audience and we got quite an education on interior design and the designers we should be holding allegiance to."

"I wish the others were coming this weekend. It'd be like a homecoming of sorts." I say, giving Claire a knowing look.

"That would have been great, but maybe at Christmas break or for New Years?" Caroline says. "We'll fly down then. I don't think anyone will handle eight hours in a car with Gwen! Certainly not with her driving!" We all laugh and I savor the moment before things get heavy.

I have a feeling that Caroline will take the news of Will's heart beating well. She knows what Will's father was like and I can't imagine her feeling betrayed by the lie I've had to protect over the last several weeks. I know she'll be over the moon to see Will.

"So, Caroline, there's something we wanted to talk to you about," I begin.

"Is everything ok? Ya'll are looking at me like I'm in trouble, or like I'm about to be the center of an intervention," she says.

"Everything is great, honey. Layla just has something she wants to tell you," Mrs. Jackson assures her.

"Ok…what is it?"

"Remember when you came over for New Year's Eve? You told me about you being adopted, and how Will's dad was just awful to you," I say, doing my best to set up the story.

"Yes, of course." Caroline is wary now. Her eyes tell me she has no clue where I'm going with this. If we don't spit it out soon, she's going to go southern psycho on me.

"So you know just how terrible he is…and that Will would have done anything to get away from him." She nods slowly, trying to follow. "Well, he did…he did something to get himself and his mom away from his dad…so that they could live a real life…so that Will and I could have a life together."

"Layla, what are you talking about? Mom, what's she talking about?" Caroline is understandably confused.

111

"Will, and his mom…they're…they're not dead, Caroline," I say cautiously.

"What? How is that possible?"

"It's true." Will's voice rings from the doorway to the kitchen, his mother standing beside him. Eliana is quiet, but smiling bigger than I've seen her smile. She's happy that Will has gotten a bit of his past back. Caroline spins in her seat and just about falls out of it.

"Oh my heavens! Will!" Caroline ejects herself and runs to throw herself into Will's arms. She is thrilled, ecstatic, as I knew she would be. "It's really you? Oh, I can't believe it! Oh, your hair! It's longer! And Mrs. Meyer, you're still so beautiful! I love your hair!"

"Believe it, 'cause I'm here," Will says clutching her. She's leaped up into his arms and Will is literally holding her inches off the floor. "But…"

"But what? Why is there a 'but'?" Caroline says as Will puts her down.

"You can't tell anyone," her mother says. "Will and Layla are going to explain. Are you ok, honey? I know this is a lot to take in."

"Yes! I'm great! I'm not sure that I need any explanation. Gregory Meyer is a terrible, terrible man. I don't question for one second why you did what you did." Caroline takes my hand and draws the three of us together. "And I think it's an over the top romantic thing that you did, Will. I told you he loved you," she says to me.

"I know he does. And I love him," I say to Caroline as I stare into Will's eyes.

"Well, you may not need an explanation, but there are some new developments that you need to be aware of. C'mon, let's go sit on the patio." Will says as he takes my hand and leads Caroline and me outside.

We sit and waste no time in telling her about Marcus. I'm careful with what information I share because Will still doesn't know about the text. I'm going to tell him; there just hasn't been a great time. I tell her about Marcus supposedly transferring and she's just as creeped out by the whole thing, but happy when I tell her about Furtick. Will tells her about changing their names and Caroline swoons at the romantics of it. She has responded just as I thought she would. If any one of our friends was going to fully understand, it was going to be Caroline.

"So, this is going to sound weird, but once you leave here, you can't refer to Will as Will. You have to call him John, ok?" I instruct her.

"Got it. I don't care what your name is. *You* are here, and that's more than we could have ever hoped for. You must have totally freaked out, Layla."

"I was totally stunned. I fainted, but it's been so wonderful having him back. When I think about losing him..." I start to tear up a little as I remember the sorrow.

"Hey...baby, it's ok...I'm here," Will puts his arm around me and pulls me close to him.

"So what should we do first?" Caroline sparks.

"We should eat, right?" Will replies, grinning from ear to ear.

"Yes, let's eat! And then we'll eat some more tomorrow! We'll have a five day feast!" Caroline says cheerily.

We all have a good giggle and another big group-hug. I feel a bit of the weight I've been carrying lift a little. It's similar to the relief I felt when I was finally able to talk to Luke about what I experienced with Gram. I held it in for so long, not having anyone I could share it with. I remember how light I physically felt...like I do now.

Sitting in the kitchen with Will and Caroline I'm taken back to a time in my life when things seemed perfect. I was surrounded by friends who loved and accepted me. I was learning to accept myself after Luke's declaration that Gram had no right to punish me for something that wasn't my fault. I'm missing Gwen, Chris, and especially Tyler, but I'm filled with hope that we'll be able to tell them all soon. Perhaps we'll tell them one at a time, with Tyler being next on the list.

We're gathered around the table enjoying a dinner of nothing but snacks. We did this a lot as a group back home. Gwen, Caroline and I would make real appetizers that required actual ingredients, and the boys would bring bags of chips and containers of dip. We'd play Monopoly and I'd watch the boys discuss their plans for a hostile take-over of the Boardwalk and Park Place properties. When Luke enters the room with our favorite game we can hardly contain ourselves.

"I'm the car!" Will declares.

"Yeah, well I'm the shoe because you can never have too many shoes!" Caroline adds.

"I'll be the hat…because I'm classy like that," I say, taking the small silver top hat to my head and tipping it, giving us all a good laugh.

"Ok, I'll be the banker, too," Caroline says.

"No way! You are the worst banker ever!" Will protests.

"I have no idea what you're talking about," Caroline says coyly.

"Shall I remind you?" Will begins. "One: you forget to give people their properties. Two: you also forget to give people their $200 when they pass Go. And, three: you don't know how to make change, which is weird for a girl who sure knows how to spend money!"

"Ok, ok, ok! You've made your point! *You* can be the banker!" she says giving in.

"I'm going first," I say. "And don't argue with me because it's my house!" We spend the next several hours playing, eating, talking, and laughing. I explain Furtick's place in our family with a bit more detail and how much I've come to love him, which leads me to start referring to him as my Bonus Uncle. I also brag on Will and tell Caroline about him heading up the crew that built the dock. He takes almost no credit for it and tells her how Luke stepped up to make it happen. "That's because he believes in you!" I say, cutting his self-deprecation off at the pass.

Luke really has become like a father to Will. It makes me happy that Will has him. Despite whatever differences they may have had, Luke is a lot like my dad. He's strong, filled with deep conviction, and has the ability to love fiercely. He's a man filled with character and integrity, which makes him the kind of man that Will can confidently model himself after.

At two in the morning Luke says it's time for Will to go home and us girls to at least pretend we're going to get some sleep this weekend. We do have a lot to do tomorrow, but I only see it as a day filled with cooking, laughing, playing more games, and eating more food than anyone should eat in a single day.

"I can't believe you won!" Will says to Caroline as we pack the last pieces of the game away.

"I told you. I know what I'm doing!" she says with feigned sweetness. We walk Will to the door and Caroline gives him just as big a hug as she did when she first saw him earlier today. "I'm so happy that you're here. It was just awful when you were gone," she says softly into Will's neck. "My world just got a whole lot better."

"I love you, too Caroline," Will says echoing her tenderness.

Releasing her, Will takes my face in his hands. "But not as much as I love you," he says sweetly, followed by a kiss.

"Aww! I missed your disgustingly sweet displays of affection," Caroline gushes, her sweet sarcasm reminding me of Gwen.

"Ok, you two. Don't stay up too late. I'll be over in about," he checks his watch, "six and a half hours."

"Ooh, 8:30. Sleeping in I see!" I tease him. Will gives me another quick kiss and is gone all too soon. I grab Caroline's bag and finally lead her to my room. We ready ourselves for sleep and collapse on the bed.

"Are you ready for your present?" she asks.

"Oh, right, I forgot." I still have a hard time receiving gifts, but I'm working on it since Claire and Will have been diligent in their efforts there. Caroline pulls out a Kindle cover with her school's logo on it. "Oh that's so cool! Thank you so much!"

"Now, whenever you're reading, which I know is all the time, you'll think of me!" She reaches over and gives me a tight hug. I grab my Kindle from my side table and immediately put the cover on.

"It's perfect. Thank you," I say hugging her again. We settle ourselves into the bed, facing each other. There really is nothing like a good old-fashioned slumber party with your best friend. "I'm so glad you're here. And I'm so glad that we told you about Will. I'm sorry I had to lie to you. I wanted to tell you right away, but…"

"It's ok, Layla. I totally understand. Kudos to you for being able to keep this a secret! I'm still in shock! When did all this go down?"

"I accidentally ran into his mom on campus last month. At first I thought I was imagining things. You know, too stressed from not talking about Will being gone. Then when I saw her again I just couldn't stay away. I followed her and it all got exposed from there. I wanted to tell you, but there's still so much at stake. This whole thing with Marcus has made things very difficult."

"Yeah, what's his deal?" she asks, twisting her face with her question.

"He's got some crazy crush on me, but don't tell Will. He doesn't know the extent of it," I say putting it lightly. I really don't want her to worry. "I think he thought he could pick up where Will left off. Since I can't tell him about Will, I'm not sure how we're going to deal with him. He hasn't been around in a while, and I have Furtick as my permanent shadow, so I'm feeling relatively in the clear…for now."

"Well, let's put all that aside this weekend. We're going to savor every second we all have together. Layla?" she begins. "Thank you for trusting me. I know it was a big deal to let the cat out of the bag, and I want you to know that you can absolutely rest assured that I will carry this secret as long as you need me to. You're the sister I never had and I would never do anything to betray you."

"I know, and thank you. Thank you for being so trustworthy. There isn't anything I can't tell you. I never had a friend like that until I met you.

It means more to me than you'll ever know." We reflect each other's smiles and drift off to sleep. My heart is full of love and peace and, for now, all is right in my world.

Chapter 13

This is by far the best Thanksgiving of my life. I'm spending the day with my love, my future-future mother-in-law, my best friend and her family, my Bonus Uncle, and…my parents.

It took some time, but I remember the moment I knew Luke and Claire had successfully filled that parent-shaped hole in my heart. Claire and me crying on the stairs to my finished basement, Luke and Will standing by watching me love and embrace Claire, telling her that she was the best mother. The finished basement, wall-hung photos of my parents, trunk full of memories…they were the most amazing tangible gift I've ever received. The best gift that day was the heart and soul knowledge that I could let Luke and Claire be my parents and I didn't have to feel guilty about it. They embody what it means to be a parent in every sense of the word and I couldn't be a luckier girl for it.

"So, Caroline," I begin with an already teasing tone. "Are you going to spill the beans about this boy toy of yours?" I ask, pulling ingredients from the fridge.

"Oh, so you're interested in *my* love life, eh?" She cocks her head to one side in the cutest Caroline way. "Well, he's studying film and is an actor, but who *isn't* an actor out there! I can't tell you how many times I've been asked to be someone's model. Then I stand up and they're like '*Oh, you're short, never mind.*' Whatever! One thing I can tell you about Californians is that they tell you like it is. There is no sugar-coating going on there!"

"So does Layla need to send Tyler and Chris out there to check on the worthiness of this guy?" Will teases.

"I don't know, Will, he could give them a run for their money!" she says.

"Does this boy have a name?" I ask.

"His name is Ryan and he really is just about the most adorable thing you've ever seen." She takes out her phone and pulls up what seem to be a dozen pictures of Ryan.

"He's cute. He's no Will Meyer, but he's cute," I comment as she swipes through her phone's camera roll.

"Thanks, baby," Will says, followed by a kiss to the top of my head as he passes me.

We spend the rest of the day making food and grilling Caroline on Ryan and when I might get to meet him. We discuss the possibility of him meeting Will as John Holland and decide to put that on the back burner until there's more to their love story.

Furtick passes through the kitchen and I give him a look that he immediately recognizes as *"Is there any new development on Marcus?"* He shakes his head, grabs a few baby carrots from the relish tray and makes his way out of the kitchen and on to the porch

I watch him for a while through the window and think how happy it makes me that he's taking some time to relax. He and Eliana are engaged in a steady stream of conversation and both look pretty happy. I watch Eliana tuck her hair behind her ear and smile. Is she flirting with him? I don't know, but whatever they're talking about, whatever she just did, elicited the biggest smile from Wesley Furtick I've ever seen.

"I know we don't do this as a habit, but I'd like to say grace before we eat," Luke says surveying the table full of family and friends. I can't help but think that Luke may have thought he'd never see this in his own home, and the fact that we're all here makes me so happy for him. We all bow our heads in approval and anticipation of Luke's prayer. "God, we're so thankful for all that you have given us. Life. Love. Friends. Thank you for this abundance of food, and may we remember that there are so many who will go without today. Amen."

We all give a collective Amen and begin to pass plates and serving bowls. Our plates are full of turkey, green bean casserole, turnips, mashed potatoes and gravy, and sweet potato. The girls discuss the deals we've been scoping out in the Black Friday sales papers, and I'm pleased that I don't have to convince Caroline of how fun it will be. The boys talk about the upcoming game and try not to think about how much money we're going to spend in about eight hours.

*****

Sunday comes all too quickly. Caroline's parents left bright and early for the drive home, so we're taking her to the airport so she can fly back to California. I have treasured every second of having her here. Even though I'll have to refer to him as John when we speak or text, it feels so good to have a friend that I can talk to about Will.

Caroline and I both cry as we say our goodbyes on the curb of the drop-off zone at the airport. I hug her tightly and make her promise to text me when she gets back to her apartment. Will gives her a huge hug, lifting her from the ground, and thanks her for her unwavering friendship.

Will and I climb into the back of Furtick's Jeep and we're off as soon as I know Caroline is safely inside. Because of the insane airport traffic, Furtick insisted on driving us rather than following. It was a valid point so Will and I didn't argue.

"Furtick, would you mind taking us to Stir? We'd like to grab some dinner," Will says. I love the way he can take command of even the most insignificant situations. He's not wishy-washy about it. It's after seven and we haven't eaten, so of course we'd want to have dinner.

"Of course, Mr. Holland," Furtick replies.

"Would you like to join us, Furtick?" I offer. Will gives me a bit of a scowl but lets it go when I give him one of my own. How could we not invite him? After all he does for us, it's the least we could do.

"No, thank you, Miss Weston. I'll wait in the vehicle and keep an eye out after I've done a sweep of the restaurant, but thank you for the invitation," he declines politely.

"Ok, but you can change your mind if you want," I say.

Will and I are escorted to a quiet table in a dimly lit corner. As far as dining locations go, it doesn't get much more romantic than this. Our server appears almost immediately and takes our drink orders. We've eaten so much over the past four days that I seriously contemplate having a side salad and water, but after reviewing the menu I'm reminded of how much I love this restaurant.

When the server returns with our drinks, Will orders their Brie Leek Tartlets appetizer for us to share. He knows they're my favorite so he doesn't even have to ask if I would like them. I could make a meal of them! After another once-over of the menu I decide to indulge and order the chef's signature dish: braised beef. I know I won't be able to finish the whole thing, but it'll make great leftovers. When it arrives I take the first bite and am reassured of my choice. *Oh, so good!*

"So...how was your Thanksgiving?" Will asks, grinning from ear to ear because he already knows the answer.

"It was amazing. Thank you so much!" I answer excitedly.

"What did I do?"

"Letting me tell Caroline opened my world back up. I've been trapped in this alternate universe where I'm in love with *John*, not Will. Sometimes I felt like I was supposed to pretend life before now didn't exist. I don't want you to ever think that I don't love every single minute of my life with you here, but...that was life with my grandmother. I wasn't allowed to talk about my parents, so it was like I had to pretend I never knew them. I like being able to stay connected to parts of my life before Will Meyer died."

"I understand," Will says taking my hand. "It's important that you still have that connection with the things that were wonderful about our life in

Davidson. You are all I need. You are my life, my everything. Not that I don't love Caroline or our friends. It's just not as important to me that I have them in my life now, but I don't fault you for that need. I want to give you everything, Layla, and if telling Caroline is what you needed, I wanted to give that to you. I don't want you to feel trapped."

"I don't feel trapped with you. I feel free with you," I say squeezing his hand. "It's just that I was so cut off from real relationships for so long. I didn't have friends, at all, when I was with my grandparents. I wasn't even sure I knew how to be a friend, but then Caroline and Gwen came along and made it so easy. *You* made it easy. So…thank you. Thank you for understanding me. It's another reason why I love you so much." I lean across the corner of the table and give Will a quick kiss.

We enjoy the rest of our dinner reviewing the highlights of the weekend including the Monopoly rematch where we fashioned a hostile take-over of all of Caroline's properties. Will won that round, and by the time we were done my sides ached from so much laughing. As we finish up our meal we agree that it was an incredible time, and that we'll talk with Luke and Claire about telling Tyler next. We have no idea when that'll happen, but both feel confident that he'll be able to contain our secret.

We exit the restaurant and Furtick is at the door. He's usually so good about being a ghost that I'm shocked that he's put himself out in the open like that.

"Miss Weston, Mr. Holland," he says sternly. "It's time to go. Now."

"What's going on Furtick?" Will matches Furtick's tone.

"Mr. Reynolds is on the move. He left Charlotte around two today, which means, if he made good time, he'll be arriving shortly. I'm sorry, Mr. Holland, but Miss Weston needs to go home immediately."

"Ok, let's get home," Will says in agreement.

"We'll be dropping you at your apartment on the way. I'll make sure you get you have your car in time for class tomorrow morning. Right now, we can't risk anything." Furtick's tone is strong and decisive. He's in "Marine" mode and what he says is law.

"What do you mean? I'm not going to leave her alone!" Will is furious that he can't be there to protect me.

"And what do you think you're going to do if Mr. Reynolds shows up?" Furtick stares at Will but softens for a moment. "Will. She needs you to go home. If you risk being found out, you risk losing her. I need you to trust me. I will take care of her like she's my own. I promise." Will's eyes drop. He knows Furtick is right and he hates it. He's done so much, sacrificed so much, risked so much so that we could be together. I know he hates that he now has to let go and let Furtick and Luke take over.

We scurry to the Jeep and Will and I climb in the back. "Oh, Will," I fall into Will's arms.

"It's ok, baby," he says.

We pull up to Will's apartment and I realize that I've never been here. It's a gated community for which Furtick knows the security code. We drive through the endless maze of buildings and arrive at Will's. I kiss him with a soft, tender kiss, and tell him that I love him more than he'll ever know. No sooner have the words left my mouth than Will is out of the car and Furtick is whisking me away. We're screeching out of the parking lot just in time for me to turn and see Will duck into the safety of his building. I scan the windows and wonder which one is Will's.

"I don't mean to be unappreciative, Furtick, but why are we at DEFCON 1? If he's just getting into town, why the urgency in getting me home and Will anywhere but with me?" I ask, truly trying not to sound thankless. "Aren't Taylor and Cline following him?"

"They lost him when they merged into traffic on I-95 in Jacksonville."

"And you didn't want Will to know that."

"No, ma'am. I...I didn't want him to think my team wasn't capable of protecting you."

"He doesn't think that."

"Just the same, I'd prefer he not know. We'll be able to trace Mr. Reynolds once he starts using his debit card in town. And we're assuming he'll go back to the apartment he set up when he first arrived here. Taylor and Cline are rectifying the situation."

"I know you can protect us, Wes." I use his given name because I want to connect with him personally right now. I know the business and personal are battling it out for his emotions. It's harder for him at certain times, like when there seems to be an imminent threat to me. I can only imagine what it conjures about his daughter, but I want him to know that he's more than a human shield to me.

"Thank you, ma'am." Furtick doesn't say another word to me on the drive home. He does, however, have several conversations with Luke and Taylor. His choice of words, especially when he's talking to Taylor, makes me blush. I can't make out what the situation is exactly except that Marcus is somewhere in town but they don't know precisely where. He hasn't made it back to his apartment yet and he hasn't shown up at my house either.

When we arrive at the house, Claire flies out the front door to meet me, followed by Luke who heads straight for Furtick. They're arguing as we all enter the house and find ourselves in the Great Room.

"How the hell did they lose him, *again*? Are you telling me that two professionally trained men can't follow *one* person? I'm having a hard time trusting your team here, Furtick!" Luke roars.

"Stop, Uncle Luke! Stop! It's not his fault! Furtick is doing an amazing job and he *is* keeping me safe! It's no one's fault that Taylor and Cline lost him in traffic. You want them to break the law just to follow him?" I say, just a decibel below Luke's.

"I want them to do whatever is necessary to keep you safe," he says, calming only slightly.

"Well…if they're going to do whatever is necessary, they'd better save their law-breaking tasks for when it's really going to count, shouldn't they?" I rebut.

"Ok, everyone just calm down," Claire adds. "Everyone in the kitchen…now." We all obey without hesitancy because that's what you do when Claire gives an order. "If Marcus is bold enough to come straight here, I don't want Layla out in the open like that where she can be seen from the window. Layla, you don't leave this house without Furtick. Not Furtick as your shadow; Furtick as your third arm. He will drive you to school. He will walk you to class. He will wait outside your classroom. He will not leave your side. Do you understand?"

"Yes," I say with a heavy sigh.

"And no Will. Not even on campus," she adds. "Luke will call him tonight and tell him."

"Why can't I tell him?" I protest.

"Because we need to be selective in the information we give Will," Luke answers.

"How long is this going to go on? How are we supposed to live like this? It's like we traded one hell for another!" I run up to my room like a little girl, but I don't care. I can't believe what's happening. I had Will and then lost him and then just got him back, and now Marcus is having some psychotic break and ruining everything! What happened to having paid my penance? What happened to getting my life, my love, back?

I can't think. My head is swimming in an overflowing goop of unfairness so I go into the bathroom and turn the shower on. Steam begins to fill the room and fog up the window and mirror. I get in the shower and let the hot water wash over me. It's calming and peaceful. All the tense muscles in my body begin to relax and the goop in my brain is melting. I lean my head from side to side, stretching my neck. *Ahhh.*

As I wash my hair my mind seems clearer and I start thinking of things I could say or do to reason with Marcus; give him all the reasons he doesn't really want me. I'm damaged, and everyone I've ever loved has been killed. *Do you really like those odds, Marcus?* How about I just reiterate the truth that I don't feel the same way about him? *You don't want to be with someone who doesn't love you.*

By the time I'm finished my fingers are sufficiently pruney and my mind is full of ideas that I'm more confident will be shot down than considered. I grab a towel and dry my hair briefly before I wrap it around my body. I tuck the corner into the top of the towel and reach up to wipe the steamy mirror, but stop in my tracks. Written in the steam are the words, DON'T KEEP ME WAITING.

I scream.

Chapter 14

Luke has put us on silent lock down. It took him twenty minutes to convince me that the creepy note had been written on the mirror before I took my shower, and when the mirror steamed up the words appeared. The idea that Marcus had been in my room, my bathroom, makes me want to throw up.

Once I was calm enough to understand and believe him, Luke issued the decree that we were all to be silent. If Marcus could get into the house unnoticed, there's no telling what he did while he was there. Luke and Furtick are scouring the house for audio or video devices, waving little black electronics around like old men looking for treasure on the beach. They turned my room upside down, as well as the kitchen and the Great Room. Luke even has Furtick check the porch, patio, and the dock, although the dock is so heavily shrouded with limbs and Spanish moss that I don't know what he could possibly do there.

My naivety of thinking I could reason with Marcus has become obvious. This is so much bigger than I thought. All I can think is that in order to keep my family safe, I need to talk to him. I'm the only one who's going to be able to reach him. I need to know what he meant when he said he knew what I wanted. Luke comes through the kitchen and indicates that the house is clean. I formulate a shaky plan and decide to present it to Luke, Claire, and Furtick.

"I think I should talk to him," I say bluntly.

"There's no way in hell you're going to talk to him, Layla," Luke says immediately, matching my directness.

"Uncle Luke, just hear me out. I'm the one he wants, so I'm the one he's going to talk to. He's not going to listen to anything you or Furtick have to say. If we're going to have any idea what he wants, I'm going to have to talk to him." I watch all three of them for their response. They're all deadpanned and I don't know what to think.

"It's actually not a bad idea, Mr. Weston," Furtick finally says. "We're following him and watching him, but that's not deterring him. If Miss Weston set up a time and public meeting place, I could watch her. We could find out what's really going on and may be able to negotiate with him."

"Luke," Claire begins. "It scares me, too, but I think they're right. We're working on some theories right now but we don't have anything solid yet. He could say or do something that becomes the missing piece we've been looking for."

Luke stares at all of us like we have three heads. Clearly he thinks this is a terrible idea. I know he just wants to protect me and is doing everything he can to do that. It must be killing him that Marcus was able to get into the house, but after a few extremely long moments, he concedes.

"Fine, but I determine the place and time. Furtick will be there in plain sight so you know where he is at all times. Furtick, he makes one move that puts Layla in danger and you shoot him. You don't shoot to injure. You kill the bastard." We all nod, knowing that it took a great deal for Luke to agree to this and any argument of the rules will take the whole thing off the table.

I pull my phone out. My heart is pounding, about to beat out of my chest. I scroll through my still-measly contact list and touch Marcus' name and the text icon. I sit there for a minute trying to think of what to type. Am I playful to ease the tension or get him in a good mood? Do I simply tell him I need to talk to him? I decide my best option is to be as blunt with him as he has been with me.

Layla Weston: I got your message. Very creative…and creepy.

It takes exactly eleven seconds for Marcus to reply.

Marcus Reynolds: I wanted to make sure you knew it was from me.

Layla Weston: Of course I knew it was you. No one else I know would so heinously invade my personal space like that.

Marcus Reynolds: I'm assuming that you've come to your senses.

Layla Weston: I've done no such thing, but I think we should talk.

Marcus Reynolds: That's too bad, but perhaps I'll persuade you when we meet.

Layla Weston: Unlikely.

Marcus Reynolds: When would you like to meet, my love.

My skin crawls at his term of endearment. Luke dictates his parameters for my meeting with Marcus, and I transcribe them into text.

Layla Weston: Don't call me that. Tomorrow. North end of the quad. 1 pm.

Marcus Reynolds: I'll be there with bells on. Until then.

Ugh! I feel like I need to take another shower. I can't believe I ever let him near me. More than that, I can't believe I trusted him. He had really been there for Will and me. I thought his advances were harmless flirting that I was able to handle at the time. I had no idea or clue that inside Marcus Reynolds was a psycho stalker, festering, waiting for the perfect time to show up. Will's death was just what he needed to send him over the edge. I don't know exactly what will happen tomorrow, but if Marcus doesn't watch his step, *he's* going to end up the dead one.

*****

I'm fidgeting. It's 12:55 pm and I can't help but think that Marcus is here, slinking in a corner watching me from a distance. My next thought is about Will. I've answered his texts vaguely, trying to put him at ease. I've reassured him that Furtick is now a fixture at my side, which is the only reason he let me come to campus today. I begin to wonder what Luke told him to keep him from discovering me in conversation with Marcus, but I remember that Will's classes are on the other side of campus and that is why Luke chose this spot at this time.

I take a deep breath and watch as Marcus emerges from the shadows of the corridor to the north parking lot. He looks....good. He's wearing dark jeans, a white t-shirt, and a black leather jacket. He looks like he's been working out by the way the t-shirt is hugging his body. I'm startled by my own reaction to him, but it's fleeting as I remember that he's here to destroy everything I have paid and sacrificed to have.

He approaches and I can immediately see that he's a different person. Standing before me is the not the Marcus I met at the little bookstore on Main Street. It's not even the Marcus that sat on the patio and told me he *begged to differ* about us being together. Believe it, or not, this Marcus is even more arrogant and I'm suddenly filled with fear.

"Hello, Layla. Aren't you going to ask me to sit?" he says.

"Hello, Marcus. Would you like to sit?" I reply coldly.

"Why, I'd love to. Thank you for asking." He sits next to me, a little too close and I scoot myself away from him. "Are you trying to hurt my feelings?"

I don't even want to gratify that statement with a response, so I ignore him. "Marcus, this...what you're doing, it's not you. I don't understand. All I keep thinking is that something awful must have happened to make you change into something so...so *not* you."

"Layla, there comes a time in our lives when we have to make a choice. Do we stay on the same, going-nowhere path, or do we forge a new path for ourselves? A new path that leads to getting anything and everything you've ever wanted out of life. I tried living a boring life – a dorky bookstore employee, math major, tutor – but I was tired of not getting what I wanted, what I deserved."

"And you think you deserve me." It's not a question.

"Yes. I watched you with rich boy. I know what you want, Layla," he says.

"What does that even mean? Marcus, I don't know what you're talking about," I say. I'm literally confused. He has this way of talking and I'm not even sure what he's saying.

"You want it all. You want the life that Will Meyer could have given you. The problem is he didn't embrace what he had when he had enough to give to you. He scoffed at the wealth, the legacy."

"That's not what I wanted at all. I loved Will Meyer and it had nothing to do with his money. You don't know me at all, Marcus." I'm keeping my calm better than I thought I would if he brought up Will, which I was sure he would. I'm incredibly proud of myself for referring to my love for Will in the past tense. Technically it's true. Will Meyer doesn't exist anymore.

"Come, now, Layla. Let's be honest."

"Ok, you go first. What do you want from me? Why are you here?"

"That's simple, my love. I want you. And I'm going to have you." His reply is dirty and I feel violated by it.

"Marcus, you can't just come here and proclaim that we're going to be together," I protest.

"Wrong. I can do anything I want. Do you know why I can do anything I want, Layla?"

I shake my head. His tone has become aggressive and commanding and he's frightening me.

"Because it's in my blood."

"What does that mean?" There he goes again, talking in some kind of code.

"We take what we want and make it ours. It's a talent I learned from watching my father."

"I don't understand. I don't know anything about your father, Marcus."

"Sure you do. Oh, but that's right. You don't know him as *my* father, you only know him as Will's father." Marcus' delivery is cold and angry.

"What? That's not true! How is that even possible?" He's lying. He's got to be lying. He really thinks I want the wealth, prestige, and legacy of the Meyers so much that he's making up some connecting that I could never prove otherwise.

"My mother got cast away like some old piece of garbage. He didn't even care that she was pregnant."

The rumors Claire told me about…

"The first three Mrs. Meyers lasted four, three, and then two years when they were swiftly divorced with a small settlement as agreed to in their pre-nup. And then they vanished… The sad part is the rumor at one point was that wife number three was pregnant but Gregory didn't know."

Could it be that Marcus' mother was wife number three?

"He had his driver take her to a Planned Parenthood office to have an abortion. She went inside but couldn't go through with it. Dear old Dad wasn't too happy about that, but there was nothing he could do by the time he found out. Oh, he took care of us financially – God knows he can afford it – but that was just to keep it all out of the press. By the time I arrived he was already priming Will's mother to be the next in a long line of Meyer wives.

"I begged him for a chance to be his son so many times, but he turned me away every single time. My little brother didn't even want what our father had to offer him. Will had no idea what he had." Marcus' tone is agitated, but his demeanor is calm. It's creepy and very much like Gregory Meyer. But now he's said it. He called Will his brother. My head is full and feels as if it could explode any minute. "When Will died, I went to my real father to receive the legacy he had built for his heir, which, as the oldest, rightfully should have been me. Do you know what he said to me?" I shake my head again, too afraid to speak. "He said he may have fathered me, but I would never be his son."

I'm frozen. I can't think of what to say or do. Part of me wishes Marcus would make a move so Furtick could take the shot and this would all go away, but then I scold myself for wishing him dead. Another part of me feels terribly for him. If he had any idea the pain that Will suffered all those years, too, maybe he wouldn't be so angry. He'd see that Gregory Meyer's dismissal had nothing to do with him; that he's not capable of loving *anyone*.

"Will had everything that was supposed to be mine. The education, the wealth…anything he wanted, he got. And if I can't have the wealth, I'll have you. You see, Layla, getting what I want is in my blood. I'm finally embracing that now, and I have to tell you, it feels pretty damn good."

I sit there, stunned. Never in my wildest of dreams would I have ever imagined this scenario. Marcus and Will are brothers. I feel light-headed from the effort it's taking to wrap my brain around this concept. I feel like I should keep him talking, maybe at least *try* to reason with him.

"Can I speak now? I've got a few questions." I say timidly. I don't want to upset him, but I'm confused by this whole thing.

"Of course, Layla."

"I don't understand how he could deny you. Can't you demand some kind of blood test to prove to the world that you're Gregory Meyer's son? He'd have to claim you as an heir then, wouldn't he?" This is me trying to reason with someone who I'm pretty sure has lost his mind.

"You don't think I thought of that?" he says, annoyed at my assumption that he left any stone unturned. "It wouldn't matter. I'm a legal adult so he's not required to provide or share any of his wealth with me. And he's made sure his Will specifically names those to whom his estate goes. If your name isn't in it, you don't get a dime."

"Oh. Well, that doesn't seem fair," I say attempting sympathy as a new line of defense.

"Quite. Anything else you'd like to know?" Marcus is still so calm. His tone is irritated at times, but he never loses his cool. It's creepy.

"Did Will know that you two are…were…brothers? If he did, he never said anything to me about it," I say, prying for more information.

"No, not that he would have cared." Marcus' answers are short and curt. I don't argue this point with him. I honestly believe Will would have been thrilled to not be so alone. Had he known early in life that Marcus was his brother, I think he would have been happy.

"Was that the real reason Mr. Meyer didn't want Will to date Holly?" I don't know why I'm asking this. I suppose I still think about what could have been between them had Will followed after her.

"Nothing my mother did was ever good enough, including the children she gave birth to. It was all about making sure Will wasn't distracted from his legacy…the legacy that should have been mine." He pauses for a moment, seeming to collect his thoughts. "You know, I thought Will had everything and I had nothing, but then you came to town, and you walked yourself into the bookstore and into my life. I knew the minute I saw you that there was something different about you. I should have been more aggressive then, gone after what I wanted. But I waited too long and Will took yet another thing that should have been mine."

"I'm not a *thing* to be possessed, Marcus. I never *belonged* to anyone." This isn't entirely true, as I have entrusted everything I am to Will's heart. But, the sentiment is true. "And I don't belong to you now."

"Layla," he says, his tone strong and reprimanding. "That's just semantics. I really don't want to argue with you…"

"Then don't Marcus. Please. I considered you my friend, someone I could trust, but now you've turned into this guy modeled after the one person you said you despised and I can't even be friends with someone like him."

"Pretending that I'm not a Meyer never got me anywhere," he says coldly. "Remember Halloween?"

"Yes...you pointed the figure at Will's rage and declared *that* to be what the Meyer men were really like, but it's *you* that's just like him, not Will. Will was kind and gentle, like his mother. I've had more than one run-in with Gregory Meyer, and now...seeing you like this...you've really embraced his ways, haven't you? You stay calm in a chaotic situation so that everyone around you looks crazy. You're cold and calculated. And you're relentless." As I speak I realize that in order to make this situation go away, something drastic is going to have to happen.

"My father didn't get anywhere by giving up...a trait I now willingly embrace. I was too patient with you in Davidson. I won't be making that mistake again." He stands up, finding a position of dominance over me. "The next time I see you, I expect that pathetic excuse for a ring to be gone. You have three days." Marcus takes my right hand and kisses it. My skin crawls and my stomach ties itself in knots. "Until then." With that, Marcus gets up and walks away, back into the shadowy corridor from which he appeared while I sit there frozen.

Three days and then what? I hunch my body over, releasing all the muscles from their tensioned state. I want to cry from sheer exhaustion after holding myself together for what seemed like an eternity. My head is in my hands but I feel Luke and Furtick rush to my side.

"Layla, honey, are you ok?" Luke asks. He can see how physically upset I am. "What did he say?"

"Taylor's got his car tagged and bugged, so we'll know where he is at all times. I was also able to get close enough to ghost-sync his phone. It's not the full sync I have with yours, but it'll be enough. We got him, Layla." Furtick touches my shoulder tenderly. It's the first time he's touched me and it makes me feel better.

"I...I can't...I need to go home. Can we please go home?" I can't think straight. I've got so much information streaming through my mind.

What do I tell them first? Marcus is Will's brother? How do I tell Will? *Oh, no!* "Is Will going to be at the house?" I ask. I know I won't be able to keep all of this from him, and I don't have the words to tell him in a calm way right now. I need time to tell Luke and Claire; time to try, in some feeble way, to sort it all out.

Chapter 15

It's all hitting me now. I run through the conversation with Marcus in my head like a checklist. *Marcus is Will's brother. Marcus has decided to adopt the Gregory Meyer approach to life. Gregory Meyer has rejected Marcus as his son. Jealous of the life he thinks Will had, Marcus is determined to step into that life and take over where Will's death left off.*

"Will's not at the house, which would mean he's following orders. But I'll take care of him if he shows up." Furtick says hanging up his phone.

When we arrive home Will is still not there. Strangely, this makes me happy. I don't want him to see me like this, and I don't want to have to explain anything to him yet. I need to get it all out to Luke, Claire and Furtick first. They'll know just what to tell Will and *how* to tell him.

After a cup of tea, made lovingly by my sweet Claire, I'm soothed into a better place where I feel confident in communicating coherent statements.

"Thank you, Aunt Claire," I say, putting the cup and saucer on the counter.

"Layla? Can you tell us what happened? What does Marcus want?" Claire asks in the soft voice I've come to hold so dear.

"Well...he wants me." I say after a beat. "But it's not that simple. Marcus is Gregory Meyer's son."

"Wife number three," Claire says in a whisper.

"Yes. Mr. Meyer had been taking care of Marcus and his mother for years, but when Will...died...Marcus went to him thinking that he could take Will's place; you know, receive the Meyer legacy, but Mr. Meyer rejected him. So, he determined if he couldn't have Will's wealth, he'd have Will's girl," I explain shakily.

"How serious do you think he is?" Luke asks.

"Very. He's intent on embracing his Meyer genes." I say. "Hold on. Why are none of you surprised by this? I was totally freaked out!" Everyone is way too calm for this news.

"Do you remember when you said that Marcus told you he *begged to differ*?" Luke asks. I nod. "That's a Gregory Meyerism. It's a trademark phrase he uses in the boardroom when opposing counsel indicates they think they're going to win. He doesn't use that phrase out in the open. Greg would have had to say it directly to him, and probably on more than one occasion."

"So you knew?"

"We were confused as to why Marcus would say it because there was no obvious link to the Meyers, but it makes sense now," Luke says. "We'd been digging to find any kind of a connection, but Marcus and his mother's medical records are sealed. No doubt a move on Greg's part. We didn't have any way to view his birth certificate to track the theory, but Marcus just put it all out there for us. This may seem scary, but with the information he's given us, we're not walking blind anymore. You did well, Layla."

"Why doesn't Marcus just go public with it? Wouldn't Mr. Meyer take some philanthropic action just to save face?" I wonder aloud.

"It sounds like a good move, but it's not. While he'll pose for the cameras in front of the courthouse, he'll have a destructive plan in his back pocket. You have no idea how many young, unaware attorneys have had *accidents*. They challenged him, made him look foolish, and they paid for it. Marcus knows that if he goes public with this, Greg will be humiliated as a man who didn't really care for a child he had full knowledge of. All that will do is pour gasoline on an already blazing fire," Furtick says directly.

"So what do we do?" I ask feeling hopeless.

"Well, he doesn't have the resources Greg has, so I'm not so worried about what he'll do necessarily. Although, he was bold in breaking into

the house, so there's a concern over how erratic his behavior may be."
Luke is in thought. He's weighing everything and working to come up
with a reasonable solution.

"He said I have three days," I warn.

"Who said you have three days?" Will's voice echoes through the
kitchen. *I thought Furtick was going to head you off at the pass?* Furtick
reads my mind and looks at me apologetically. "I got a little tired of
waiting for a phone call, text, anything...so I decided to come over for an
update. Is anyone going to tell me what's going on?"

"Oh, Will, I'm so happy to see you!" I throw myself into his arms.
This move is both needed and strategic. I need to feel Will's arms around
me, loving and protecting me, and I need to divert his attention, even if for
just a minute from the craziness of what has transpired today.

"I'm happy to see you, too, baby. I've barely heard from you since
Furtick tore you away from me last night. What's been going on? And
don't tell me *nothing* because I stood in meetings like this with Luke six
months ago."

What do I say? I've just gotten all the information out to Luke. Telling
Will that Marcus is his brother is going to be a shock that I have no idea
how he'll take. Even if Will Meyer were legally alive, I can't see him
being happy about this brotherhood. Perhaps when he was younger, but
certainly not now. The harder part to explain without Will going over the
edge will be Marcus' creepy insistence that he and I *will* be together. I'm
afraid that if I tell Will of Marcus' obsession with me that he'll do
something desperate that will blow everything out of the water. If Marcus
discovers everything will he tell Meyer? If he does, our only option will
be to run...forever. My head is spinning and now I'm overwhelmed with
thoughts of all the "*what ifs?*" of what Mr. Meyer will do if he ever
catches us.

"Marcus has indicated he'll be back to see Layla in three days, and it appears that he expects her to respond to his romantic interests," Claire has a remarkable way with words.

"His *romantic interests*?" Will asks, his anger immediately present in his tone.

"Yes. It seems he's had a thing for Layla for some time now. And, with your passing he's under the impression that he can somehow pick up in Layla's life where you left off," Luke answers.

"I thought he was just doing that back home to get at me. So why don't you just tell him that you're not interested?" Will's tone is irritated, not understanding the dilemma.

"Well, I did, but…" I begin. I'm feeling brave since both Claire and Luke got the explaining started. "He's being pretty aggressive in his pursuit. You already know he drop out of college and moved down here. And that he told me he transferred to FSU, but Furtick found out that's he's not even an official student there." I understand Will's questioning. If only I could tell him it's much more complicated than it appears. I can't just turn him down because he's not going to go away. And if he doesn't go away, we can't live our lives here, together, in peace.

"What do you mean *aggressive*? Has he hurt you? If he's laid a finger on you, I swear I'm going to kill him." I can see the rage building in his eyes. This is what I was afraid of, and we haven't even told him everything!

"No. You're not," Furtick says, his firm tone settling Will. "Luke…just tell him. We can't move forward if we're trying to resolve the situation and keep certain facts from him. He's going to have to know."

"Know what? Will someone please tell me what the hell is going on?" Will looks to me for an answer that I'm not sure how to give, so I give Luke a just noticeable nod of approval. I'm glad Furtick has directed Luke to tell Will. I'm not always so great about explaining things. And because it's about Will, I know my emotions will get the best of me.

"I think you should sit down, Will," Luke suggests.

"I think I'll stand." It's clear Will is frustrated by the situation. He's out of the loop and that must feel strange to him. He and Luke and Claire have been a team since the inception of the plan to fake his and Eliana's disappearance, but now he's walking blind.

"Will, please," I say taking his hand. "I need to you to calm down so you can really hear what Luke is going to tell you. Please." Will takes a deep breath and nods his head. Luke cleanses his breath after Will is seated at the kitchen table.

"Marcus has made a claim that, at this point, we don't have reason to believe is untrue." As Luke begins I'm so grateful that Eliana isn't here. I'm just now considering how the news that Will has a brother may affect her, assuming she doesn't already know. "You're aware that your father was married before your mother."

"Yeah, three times," Will says. The look on his face tells me that he has no idea what his father's ex-wives have to do with what's going on with Marcus right now.

"Yes, that's right. Well, Marcus is claiming that his mother was your father's third wife, and that Gregory is his father." Luke's delivery is steady and his words are deliberate and to the point.

"What?" Will stands and we all take a collective step backward, not sure of what his next move will be. "And you believe him?" he asks no one in particular.

"As I said, there's no reason not to believe him. We were already looking into it after he first came to see Layla. We were stopped cold, though, when we discovered that both his and his mother's medical records had been sealed," Luke explains.

"Why would you even be looking into that in the first place?"

"When Layla told him that she was not interested in getting romantically involved with him, he told her that he *begged to differ*," Luke answers, watching Will closely.

"Oh." Will is stunned. He recognizes his father's trademark statement and knows that what we're telling him is true. And after a moment of this sinking in, the dominoes begin to fall. "He's...my brother. I had a brother and my father kept that from me. Does my mother know about this?"

"I don't know," Claire says in her own trademark calming tone.

"How long have *you* known about this?" he asks me directly.

"I just found out today. I met Marcus in the quad this afternoon and...."

"You did what? He could have...where were *you*?" His fury is pointed at Furtick now, proving that Will is out of his mind with anger. No one in their right mind would intentionally take on Furtick.

"I was less than twenty yards away...*fully* prepared to kill him if he did anything to hurt Layla." Furtick's answer soothes Will, but only because they share the same sentiment about the longevity of Marcus' existence on the Earth should he put one hair on my head out of place. "Luke was there as well – unseen, but there."

"So what does this have to do with Layla? Why drag her into it?"

"Layla, I think you're best to explain that," Luke instructs. I don't want Will to hear these words come from my mouth. I want someone else to tell him, but Luke has left me no choice.

"Well...your dad has been supporting Marcus financially all this time. But after you...you know...he went to your dad thinking he could pick up where you left off. Your dad refused, told Marcus that he could never be his son, and sent him packing." I take a moment to collect my thoughts because what I have to tell Will next is not going to be easy. "When I met with him this afternoon he told me that he was embracing your father's approach to life. You know, take what you want at any cost. He said that if he couldn't have the wealth you had as a Meyer son, that he'd have me, because I was yours. And then he told me I had three days."

"Three days to what?" Will reiterates the question on everyone's mind.

"I don't know. I only know that he expects me to take my ring off," I answer quietly. I'm trying not to cry as I recall the creepy intensity of my conversation with Marcus.

We all stand in silence as we watch Will process the last thing he expected to be told. He's already angry with Marcus for his overly convincing portrayal of my boyfriend in front of their father last fall. *Their father*. And now to hear that he's come claiming some right to me because Mr. Meyer rejected him…like I'm the only piece of the Meyer fortune that he can lay stake to…it's a lot for Will to take in. It seems like an eternity before Will speaks again, but I'm put at ease when I hear his smooth and confident tone.

"Ok. So what's the plan? Layla's not taking that ring off until I replace it, so we have three days to figure out how to get rid of him." Will's voice is strong and he's moving into a decisive frame of mind, which brings me peace of mind in this chaotic time.

"I was too freaked out earlier, but…why don't I just ask him what happens in three days? We can't play games with him. He's dangerous and we need to know exactly what we're dealing with," I suggest.

"What do you mean he's dangerous?" Will says, his coolness being replaced by rising heat. It was a poor choice of words on my part.

"Mr. Reynolds gained entry into the house last night while everyone was out. He left Layla a disturbing message on her bathroom mirror," Furtick answers matter-of-factly.

"On her…ok…I'm trying really hard right now not find Marcus and kill him. If there's any other information like that, it's probably best that you keep it from me until this whole thing is over." Will closes his eyes, seeming to count to ten to extinguish the fuse that keeps getting lit.

143

"I agree with Layla," Claire says getting back to a plan of action. "I think it's best that she's direct with him. He's already shown us how bold he can be. If we play games with him that's just going make him angry, and who knows what he'll do then."

"Yes. We can't underestimate him," Luke says.

"Don't do anything quite yet," Furtick instructs. "He's given us three days. Give me twenty-four hours to see what I can find out and we'll map out a plan from there."

I turn to Will when I feel his disappointed stare. I take his hand and lead him out to the dock. He's silent as we walk, brushing away the branches and Spanish moss. He wouldn't express his displeasure in me in front of everyone, but I have a feeling a reprimand for not telling him what was going on ahead of time is on its way.

We sit, silently, for several minutes while we both collect our thoughts. I'm not sure if I should say something first. I'm not sure what to say, really. It's chilly by the water on this December afternoon and all I want is to sit close to Will, being warmed by his arms blanketed around me, but he's in no mood to warm or soothe me right now.

"Why would you do that? Why wouldn't you tell me? Don't you think I can protect you?" Now that he's speaking, I see what's really going on. Will isn't mad. He's hurt. Now I'm sad because I am the one who hurt him.

"Of course I think you can protect me, but aren't I allowed to protect you? This isn't any kind of typical anything. There's no manual for how to deal with someone like Marcus when we're in the situation we're in. You can't speed in and beat the crap out of him like you did before. You can't do anything at all because Will Meyer doesn't exist anymore. If he finds out about you…" I take his left hand and run my thumb across his ring. "I didn't tell you because I knew what you'd want to do. I didn't tell you so I could protect all that you have done to make a life for us here."

"I just feel like I'm failing you." Will's tone is sad. He looks lost, which is disheartening since Will is usually my compass.

"Will, you could never fail me. All you've done from the first second I met you is exceed every expectation I could have ever had about what being loved truly means. You're my hero, but sometimes even the hero needs to be looked after."

"I have so many plans for us, Layla. I want to give you everything. I feel like I'm in this holding pattern of being so ready to offer you the world, but there's always something that makes it impossible to take the final step. Now I'm so pissed at Marcus for ruining everything, and there's nothing I can do about it." Will puts his head in his free hand. I want to comfort him. I want to bring some light to this dark time.

"What kind of plans?" I ask, hoping a new focus will be that light in the darkness. There are no answers right now, so the best I can do is create a bubble around us; a bubble where the only thing that exists is our life together.

Will looks up at me his eyes softening, and the crease in his brow smoothing.

"What kind of plans do you have for us?" I smile as I think of my own thoughts and ideas for my future with Will.

Will smiles and I see a wave of peace wash over him. It's working. He's joined me in this glorious bubble. "Well, I'm going to exchange this for something more official," he says, lifting my left hand to show my promise ring.

"But I love this ring," I smile.

"You can keep it, silly. You'll just have to move it to the other hand." He smiles his brilliant smile and all the craziness just melts away.

"Ok. What else?" My heart swells listening to Will talk about our future together.

"Huge and ridiculously amazing church wedding," he continues.

The smile on my face is so big my cheeks are beginning to hurt. I don't care because I want to smile like this forever; smile at all the wonderful things that are ahead for Will and me.

"Followed by an even more amazing honeymoon with my bride. Someplace…tropical?"

"You know me so well! And what happens after the honeymoon?"

"After the honeymoon? Hmm…whenever I think about this I get caught thinking about how wonderful it's going to be to have you all to myself on a tropical island. I don't get much farther than that." I blush because I get stuck thinking the same thing. "But…after the honeymoon…I spend the rest of my life making sure you know the honeymoon will never really end. We'll build a life together, have a beautiful family courtesy of your stunning beauty, and through the best and worst of life, we'll be there for each other, knowing that no matter what happens, we'll make it. We'll never be apart. I'll be yours, and you'll be mine – forever and always."

"Oh, Will." I throw my arms around his neck and my body into his arms. "I love you so much. We're going to have the best life together."

"Yes, we are."

Chapter 16

It's been a rough day. Furtick banned Will from the house last night, so we're stuck texting and calling. He says Will and I can't risk being seen together. I understand. Until everything with Marcus is over I'm back to my life before I knew Will was alive.

I can hardly concentrate on my classes and finals are next week. Now that Marcus is back Furtick can't be seen, so he's resumed his place as my shadow. So I'm not completely alone, I'm hanging out with Dana more. As we get coffee and move to my favorite study table in the coffee shop, Finn asks where John is.

"Oh, we're on a break. You know, just trying to concentrate on finals," I say satisfying his curiosity.

"Ahem...*who* is John?" Dana asks.

"John is...he's my boyfriend," I tell her. It sounds so strange to say all of those words together in the same sentence.

"When were you going to tell me?" she asks in her sweet southern voice.

"Well, it's still pretty new, so..."

"What does the other guy think?"

"What other guy?" I ask. Is she referring to Furtick? He did walk me to class and wait for me a few days last week.

"You know, kinda tall, dark brown hair...he was following you around like a puppy dog a couple of months ago." *Marcus*. She bats her eyes and tilts her head in a way that makes me think it's a romantic gesture.

"Oh, no, there's *nothing* with that guy. Have you seen him around lately?" I ask slowly.

"No, but if you don't want him, I'll take him! He's cute!"

"No!" Finn and I shout in unison. He knows the creep factor with Marcus, and even though he doesn't know Dana, he'd never let Marcus anywhere near her.

"I mean, he's…he's the stalking type. If it didn't work out with you two, you'd never be rid of him. Trust me." Dana gives me a sideways look, but then seems to decide to take my word for it and drops the subject.

We haven't been studying for long when I get a text from Furtick letting me know that we have to leave campus immediately, and that he's on his way into the coffee shop to get me. I gather my books and apologize to Dana for the short study period. I tell her a quasi-lie that I got a text from my uncle and there's a family emergency. I'm standing just as Furtick enters. He gives a nod of acknowledgement to Dana and I promise to connect with her before our final next week.

"What's going on?" I ask as Furtick ushers me by the elbow to the car. He's looking around feverishly for something, or someone. He opens the back door and practically shoves me in. We're driving down the road before he answers me.

"Marcus' father, uh, stepfather, reported a break-in last week. The only items missing from the home were his two .38 Specials." Furtick finally says.

"Those are guns, right? Big ones?" I ask nervously.

"Not big, but powerful enough. Most people prefer the .38 Special due to its superior stopping power."

"And you think Marcus has them?"

"I don't know yet, but I'm not taking any chances. The timing is too coincidental." We pull up to the house and it looks like a used car lot. Everyone is here – Luke and Claire, Will and his mother, Taylor, and now Furtick and me. I can only assume Cline is manning his post watching Marcus.

I'm so happy to see Will when we enter the house, but am shocked since he was told in no uncertain terms that he wasn't to come to the house until we knew what we were going to do. "What's the word?" Furtick asks Taylor as we enter the Great Room.

"We have every reason to believe he's got the guns, but haven't confirmed. At this point in time, we're assuming he has them. We followed him to a different apartment about fifteen minutes from here. It's gated, a nice place, and no roommates, but there's more," Taylor reports, handing Furtick a file. He reviews it and hands it to Luke who does the same.

"It looks like Greg supported Marcus' family until he turned eighteen…an unofficial child support payment of sorts in the amount of $25,000 a month. He even paid for Marcus' college tuition and books in full. When Marcus turned eighteen the payments to his mother stopped and he began receiving a single $10,000 deposit every month until he turned twenty-one, which was in May. But…huh! He didn't spend a dime of it. He's got almost $400,000 in his bank account." Luke shakes his head. "It's not Meyer wealth, but he's got more money than he could ever need right now. He could go anywhere…do anything. What sent him over the edge? It couldn't be as simple as Gregory's refusal to take him in."

We all stand there for what seems like forever. This doesn't make sense. I'm still having a really hard time wrapping my head around Marcus' mental break. Part of me wants to reach out to him – to the Marcus who was my friend and not my stalker. I have fond memories of my time with him and had truly hoped that we could be friends again one day. I remember how my heart leaped at the site of him when he came to say goodbye. It meant so much to me, but now I have to wonder about his motives. Was he there to see just how distraught I was and how long he might have to wait before he pounced on my heart? If only we could know what happened after we left.

"Wait…" I begin. I'm nervous to make this suggestion but it may be our only hope. "Holly. We should ask Holly what happened."

"Layla, I don't know…" Will says. "She may not know about any of this with my father. I don't want to open anything there. I…I don't want her to get hurt by my family, again."

"That's very noble of you, Will, but she's the only one who's going to have a clue. He stayed with her when he went back to North Carolina. She's not stupid – she's got to know something is wrong. We have to at least try. Maybe she would even be willing to come here, to come get him and take him home. He would listen to her." I try my best to be as convincing as possible, although I think it's me I'm trying to convince the most. I don't want to see Holly. Did Marcus tell her about the lengths Will and I went to so we could be together? Am I on her black list because Will did that for me and not her? I have no idea how this will go. All I know is that she is our lifeline to Marcus. If we don't at least try we'll continue to walk blindly.

"I'll call her, Will," Claire says. "I'll be gentle. I won't tell her anything unless I absolutely have to. We don't want to hurt her any more than you do." This puts me at ease. Claire is marvelous with words and delivery. If any of us can get information from Holly, it's going to be her.

Will takes a deep breath before he agrees. "Ok. Just be careful with her." This is how I know Will is nothing like his father: he cares about Holly's wellbeing. Claire wastes no time and goes to the office to call Holly, her phone number, I'm sure, filed away in the myriad of intel Furtick has gathered.

"Finn misses seeing you," I tell Will, making light conversation in the interim.

"Does he?" Will raises an eyebrow.

"Yeah. I told him we were on a break. He didn't seem to like that. He likes us together." I wrap my arms around Will's waist and feel the embrace of his around me.

"I like us together, too," Will says giving me a sweet squeeze.

Claire is back in the Great Room faster than I expected. "Was she there? Did you talk to her?" I ask not seeing how that's even possible.

"She wasn't there, but I spoke to her roommate," Claire says. "Holly's on a plane to Tallahassee right now."

I haven't had time to even begin processing this before Furtick has left the room. Knowing him, he's finding out which flight Holly is on and what time she lands. But if she's coming here to see Marcus, how do we intercept that? Marcus will either be at the airport or expecting her to arrive at his place not long after he knows she's landed…unless he doesn't know she's coming.

"She was originally on the 12:55 flight, but it looks like she got bumped to the 3:55," Furtick reports the moment his foot approaches the threshold of the room. "I checked his email and phone log. There's been no communication between Mr. Reynolds and Holly, and since she got moved to the later flight and hasn't contacted him, her trip most likely wasn't prearranged." It's amazing how he can track Marcus' phone and activity like that.

"That's good. That means we should be able to catch her at the airport and bring her here," Luke says. This news has filled him with confidence that he can *do* something. I've discovered that a Luke who feels helpless is a very sad thing.

"I'll get Cline on it. Taylor can keep eyes on Mr. Reynolds," Furtick says.

"You can't just have Cline show up at the airport with her name on a sign and a chauffer's hat on his head!" I protest. "If no one knows she coming, how are you going to explain that?" I swear, sometimes these men are too single minded. She's going to think she's being kidnapped!

"She's right, Luke. I'll go with Cline to get her," Claire adds giving me a knowing look. She hears how crazy their thinking is, too. "I can debrief her on the way here."

"Ok, but only if Taylor can confirm that Marcus is nowhere near the airport." Luke puts his arm around Claire and gives her a look. *That* look. It's the kind of look you give someone that tells exactly what you're thinking. It tells them everything is going to be ok, that you appreciate them, are proud of them, that you love them, and that you would be lost without them. I see Luke and Claire give each other this look a lot.

"It's almost five now. She'll be landing in about an hour. Get with Taylor and have Cline pick Claire up and confirm that they still have eyes on Marcus. If this is going to work, we've got to get to her fast." Luke says to Furtick. In less than a minute Taylor is gone and Furtick is back with confirmation that Marcus is still at his apartment. Less than fifteen minutes later, Cline is at our door.

"Make sure Will is gone before we're back." Claire kisses Luke goodbye and is gone within moments of Cline's arrival. Luke and Furtick disappear to the office leaving Will and me alone in the Great Room. We stand there together in the calm after the storm of whirlwind activity.

"Are you ok?" Will asks.

"Am *I* ok? I was just going to ask you the same thing?" I reply. I'm shocked. Holly is going to be here in a matter of a few hours and he's not fazed a bit?

"Besides the obvious in that you have a psycho stalker…why wouldn't I be ok?" He furrows his brow making that little V above his nose.

"Well, Holly is going to be here. I wasn't sure how you felt about that. I mean, I know how you feel about that, but…" I say, flustered.

"Hey, hey, hey…I'm ok, but it's clear you're not." Will pulls me into his arms and holds me. "It's going to be ok, Layla. You know, you could just let Claire talk to her. You don't have to even meet Holly if you don't want to."

"I want to. Well, I do and I don't. What if she hates me? What if she thinks you didn't try hard enough to make things work with her like you did with me? She could be coming here as an ally to Marcus and then all of this…this intercepting her…could backfire." I can feel my heart begin to race with nervousness of the impending unknown.

"Just wait for Claire to get back. She'll tell you where Holly stands with Marcus, and then you can decide from there. You don't have to do anything you don't want to do." Will holds me tighter and I feel so safe, like nothing can hurt me. This is where I want to be forever and always. "And it doesn't matter how she may or may not feel about you. You had nothing to do with how things played out between Holly and me. If she's going to hate anyone, it should be me. Besides, that's in the past. You are my future."

Will leaves and I spend the next hour pacing my room thinking of what to say to Holly. I wonder if I should apologize, but then wonder what I'm apologizing for. It was Will's choice to pursue our relationship the way he did. And if I remember both Will and Marcus' recounting correctly, Will tried to get in touch with her but Marcus wouldn't give him Holly's number. If she's going to be upset with anyone it should be her brother, not me or Will.

If I tell her that I'm not interested in Marcus romantically, will she think it's because of anything other than still being in love with Will? Will she believe that I'm just like all the other Heyward Prep socialites? I remember how Marcus expressed his disdain for them. That's the farthest thing from who I am. The fact that Will wanted both of us should be evidence of that. He once told me that Holly and I were a lot alike.

My hope is that she's knows Marcus has gone over the edge and she's come to take him home. If she knows he's had a mental break, surely she knows that Gregory Meyer is his father and I can only further my hope to her being willing to help us.

I hear the front door close and muffled voices. After a minute Claire calls to me. "Layla, can you come down please?"

She's here.

Chapter 17

I walk slowly down the stairs and take in Holly as she is revealed inch by inch, from feet to head. She is beautiful. She's got shoulder length dirty blonde hair and blue eyes. Her height falls somewhere between me and Claire, and her face is soft, warm and inviting. When she smiles at me, I see the light that drew Will to her.

"Hello, Layla. It's very nice to finally meet you," she says. She speaks first, which puts me at ease. She stretches out her hand and I hesitate for only a minute before I reciprocate.

"Hello, Holly. It's nice to meet you, too." Whether this is really true or not remains to be seen, but I'm going to play nice.

"Why don't we sit?" Claire suggests, opening her arm to direct us to the Great Room. Luke leads the way and the rest of us follow. I'm cautiously optimistic about how this is going to go. Surely Claire would not have brought me down so quickly were she not confident in Holly's ability to help rather than sabotage the situation. "Thank you for coming, Holly," Claire says as we all get situated.

"Layla...I'm not sure where to begin. But I just want to tell you how sorry I am. Will's death was a terrible tragedy." She stares at me with eyes that continue her sympathy. "And I'm so sorry about what's happening with Marcus. He...he's not well," she continues, head hanging in slight shame by association.

"Thank you, Holly. I appreciate the sentiment." I don't mean to sound cold, but I'd like to hear how she's going to be of help to us.

"Holly, would you mind telling Layla what you told me in the car?" Claire asks.

"Of course. It's, well, it's hard to explain...please just stick with me as I try to convey everything." Holly pauses and collects her thoughts, finding the best starting point after having relayed the whole story to

Claire already. "Marcus has been through a lot in his life. My mom…she's not the best person. My dad knew her before she was married to Gregory Meyer and he says that what Mr. Meyer did to her put her in a pretty dark place. That place got darker and darker as the years went by. I grew up hearing about what an evil man Gregory Meyer is, and that one day he'd pay for what he did to her.

"Marcus was twelve the first time she sent him to Mr. Meyer's office to ask him to take him in. He dismissed him and Marcus came home with nothing but tears. And my father…he wasn't very accepting of Marcus either. I guess he had a hard time since Marcus wasn't biologically his. They just never really bonded. My mother didn't help the situation." Holly's tone is a mixture of sadness and anger, but I can't tell who she's angrier with, Mr. Meyer or her mother.

"Why didn't she just expose Meyer as Marcus' father?" I ask the elephant in the room question. I know everyone else has given me an answer to this, but I have to hear it from someone who was enmeshed in the insanity.

"When Marcus was born Mr. Meyer agreed to take financial responsibility for him and Mom until he graduated from college. When my mom married my dad shortly before Marcus turned one, Mr. Meyer changed the terms to support them until Marcus turned eighteen, then just Marcus until he turned twenty-one. The terms and conditions of the contract included a non-disclosure agreement that both she and my dad had to sign. They were legally bound to keep the truth to themselves or they'd be in breach of their contract and lose all the money," she answers.

"So what's going on with Marcus now?" I ask.

"My mom never hid the fact that Gregory Meyer was his biological father. She never sugar coated her feelings about him either. So, Marcus spent his whole life wanting to be everything Gregory Meyer *isn't*. He didn't want to go to some Ivy League school, even though between his grades and Mr. Meyer paying, he could have gotten into any school he wanted. He tried so hard, but when your whole life is spent being a pawn in your mother's game to destroy your father, well, you crack a little bit with every move until you eventually break."

"You said he was twelve the *first* time she sent him. How often did she make him do this?" I'm horrified at the idea of sending a child to face Gregory Meyer alone.

"I'm not sure exactly, but the way Marcus described it, it sounded like it was about every six months." *Oh, my gosh!* I can't imagine the fear and anxiety he must have felt. After the first few times he had to know that Mr. Meyer was going to reject him each and every time, and then he watched Will live the life he would have had if his parents hadn't divorced.

"Marcus hadn't been to see him since he turned eighteen," she continues. "But when Will died he gave it another shot, on his own. My mom didn't have anything to do with it. Only this time, somehow it was worse for Marcus. I guess he reasoned that Mr. Meyer had been denying him all those years because of Will. So after Will was gone and he was still rejected…it was the final crack. He just broke." Holly's eyes well up with tears. She tries to hold them back but one escapes and makes its trail down her cheek and rolls under her chin.

"When Marcus told me about you and Will, he was angry but still had nice things to say about Will. But when Will wanted to come after you, Marcus wouldn't tell him anything," I say trying to fit some of the pieces of the puzzle together, also trying to let her know that Will didn't abandon her.

"Marcus never held anything against Will. He knew it wasn't his fault. Will was just as innocent in the whole thing as Marcus was. But, well…" Holly catches her breath, her face creasing together in concern. "I'm not proud of this, but…my relationship with Will was based on another one of my mother's plans to get back at the Meyers."

"What?" My brows furrow together as I question her statement. A soft look from Claire lets me know that I should prepare myself for what Holly's about to tell me.

"After a while Marcus refused to play my mother's games, so she enlisted me. Layla, I was sixteen and didn't know how to refuse my mother," she begins. "I spent that summer at the Green, every Saturday night, working to get Will's attention. Eventually I did. At first it was just part of the plan. We hung out, I flirted, Will responded. But…we started dating and I started to *really* like him. He wasn't anything like his father. He was kind and genuine."

"What was the plan exactly?" I'm doing everything I can right now not to leap across the coffee table and have an all-out catfight with this girl. She toyed with Will's feelings and for that I want to slap her right across the face.

"I was supposed to get Will to fall for me while my dad found a way into the law firm. It was all about inserting ourselves into the Meyer's lives so that Mr. Meyer would have to be reminded of what he did every day."

"How *did* your dad get hired into the firm? Gregory Meyer is obsessive about an in depth background check on anyone he shares more than two words with." I say condescendingly. It seems obvious to me that no one works for that man without a thorough background check, so how could her father even get past the application process? Mr. Meyer would know who he was and there's no way he would bring him on.

"Not everyone at Meyer, Fincher and Marks is as loyal to him as he'd like to think," she replies. "My dad passed the North Carolina Bar but was coming in as a paralegal. He's had some trouble moving up in his career. He's got a bit of a…gambling problem. He knew Meyer wouldn't handle the application or interview process for that, so my dad got through the interview and then paid an old college buddy at the firm $500 to clear the background check. No red flags meant that Mr. Meyer wouldn't even know he was there until long after Dad had his desk all set up." Wow. Looks like Mr. Meyer and Mr. Reynolds are cut from the same cloth. *Get whatever you want at whatever the cost.*

"Ok. Let's get back to how you stabbed Will in the back," I say. Claire gives me a disapproving look for my lack of grace but since I'm not in a forgiving mood right now I don't back down.

"I deserve that. I know I hurt Will. I didn't want to hurt him. I really did care about him, Layla. Under any other circumstances I think we could have been good together. But…Will and I weren't meant to be. He would never have found you if I had stuck around. You were so good for him," Holly says smiling genuinely. "Marcus told me how you and Will defied his father so you could be together. I'm glad you had the time with him that you did."

"So the plan was to get Will's father to pay your family off to leave town and to leave Will alone?" I can't reply to her statements about Will and me. She knows she hurt him and let him effectively die without knowing the truth. I momentarily ponder the idea of telling him what a conniving witch Holly really is, but quickly come to the determination that it would change nothing. He's never going to see her again, and I'd rather him live the rest of his life under the assumption that Holly's intentions were always pure.

"It wasn't necessarily to pay us to *leave*, but for my mother to squeeze more money out of him. Considering how much Mr. Meyer paid them, my parents were fine with the stipulation that we move. I think Mr. Meyer would be surprised to know that my mother was better suited for him than he realized. She would have spent the rest of her life as the woman he wanted her to be. I love my mother, but she's not a good person. As soon as I graduated I was out the door. I had a job and an apartment close to campus and have been moving on with my life. My parents are still in Charlotte, but I haven't spoken to them since I left home."

"So Marcus is broken and you think I can fix him?" I'm full of questions but can only manage to digest one answer at a time.

"No. Marcus had always been satisfied with his life. He never wanted anything that the Meyers had. But when you came along and chose Will, well…"

"So this is my fault?" I bellow in interruption. "You have got to be kidding me right now." I can feel my face getting hot. I can't believe she's actually insinuating that I sent Marcus over the edge by choosing Will over him. He wasn't even a choice!

"That's not what I'm saying. I'm sorry. I'm not being clear." I give Holly a moment to think and choose her words a little more carefully as she presses on. I'm also giving myself time to calm down. "Marcus could handle you choosing Will. What I'm saying is that each of these things separately – my mother's conniving, Mr. Meyer's repeated rejection, Will's acceptance by his father, you choosing Will – they're all manageable to different extents. But if you roll them all into one, it was just too much for Marcus to take." I take a deep breath and digest her words. I can understand what she's saying. Each of the things I've experienced in my life – Mom and Dad's death, life with Gram and Gramps, losing Will – had they not all piled one on top of the other, my life may have been very different.

"Will didn't have anything more than Marcus. His father didn't love him. He was a game piece in building the Meyer empire. Marcus and Will wanted the same thing: a father who loved and accepted them. If Marcus could understand that, he'd know that Will's life wasn't perfect," I say softening my tone. I feel bad that I laid into her like that. I won't apologize, but I'll move forward in the conversation a bit more gently.

"He knows Will's life wasn't perfect. But a father, one who acknowledged him as his son, hugs and kisses aside, would have been better than what my father offered him." Holly sighs matter-of-factly. "Listen Layla, I've been through enough therapy over the last year to

159

understand just how jacked up my family is. Marcus has been starving for love his whole life. My mother has spent her life so focused on this vendetta that she missed out on what an amazing person Marcus became, despite her. And my father was so blinded by his own selfishness that he lost out on the gift of having a son.

"Then you came along and the real light inside Marcus came on. He called me the day you met and told me he had just met the girl who was going to change his life. I could always tell when Marcus had seen or talked to you; he was happier, lighter. And from what I understand from your aunt, you did that for Will, for everyone. Don't you see, Layla. You're the redeeming factor. You brought love and hope to Will's life. Marcus wants that, too."

"Let me get this straight. I fell in love with Will and *changed his life*, and now, because I did that for Will, I'm responsible for changing Marcus' life, too? I told him that I'm trying to move on and that I don't care for him like he cares for me. I would have been happy to be a part of Marcus' life if he hadn't gone all Fatal Attraction on me." *So much for proceeding gently.*

"No, Layla. No one expects you to be responsible for Marcus. When Holly told me everything, it helped put things in perspective. Marcus really has lost his connection with reality. He's been rejected his whole life, and the one thing he's fixated on as the solution to his heartache isn't coming to him," Claire offers in her usual calming manner. She's leaning forward, trying to add emphasis to her words.

"I want to help Marcus. Despite everything, I still care about him as my friend." I say in a softer tone than my last comment. "Does he know you're here?" I ask Holly.

"No. He didn't know I was coming. I knew I needed to get here as fast as I could when my father discovered two of his guns were missing. The last time I saw Marcus he said that sometimes in order to get what we want, we have to resort to drastic measures. I didn't really have a plan. I

160

just thought I would find you when I got here and figure it out from there. I was afraid if I tried to contact you ahead of time that you wouldn't want to see me. I really just want to help, Layla," Holly pleads.

"We appreciate that, Holly. Thank you for everything," Claire says before I can ask any more questions.

The room is silent for a few long moments while I think about everything Holly's just told me. I know there's an answer here somewhere. And while I run through the beginning of just a few plans, I keep going back to what I said earlier. "Let me talk to him," I say.

"No. That's not happening," Luke replies instantaneously, his eyes fixed on mine, driving his directive home. He and Furtick have been silent this whole time. I can't imagine what they're thinking.

"How else are we supposed to get to him? No offense, Holly, but you really think you're going to get him to back off? Let's be real here. If you could have kept him in Charlotte, you would have, right?" Holly nods, seemingly put off by my approach. "If anyone is going to have any impact on the situation with Marcus, it's going to be me. Look at what I was able to get from him today. Let me meet with him again."

"I said no, Layla. Today was it. Now that we know more from Holly there's no way I'm letting you near him. He's having a mental breakdown and there's no telling what he'll do. We'll figure out how to get him out of town and have him followed for the rest of his life if we have to. Having you sit face to face with Marcus is more than a last resort. Do you understand me?" Luke's tone is strong and a little frightening. I'm trying to put myself in his shoes. Knowing how freaked out I was earlier today I can't blame him for being as protective as he is, but it just doesn't seem fair. Everyone else was allowed to risk so much for Will and me to be together. Why won't they let me do the same?

"So we're just supposed to spend the rest of our lives navigating through the fields of *how do we protect Layla this time?*"

"I said no, and that's final. Do you understand?" Luke's eyes are burning with rage and I can see that now, more than ever, he is not going to back down.

"I understand what you're saying," I say. The wheels in my head are still turning though. I've got to figure this out.

"Well, now that we're all on the same page, let's take a breather. There's a lot here to digest. I'll make us something to eat and we can take some time to think about how we can best help Marcus." Claire stands in a soft command for us all to follow.

As we shuffle into the kitchen, I watch Holly. I haven't decided if I like her, or if I even need to have any feeling toward her other than gratitude for the insight she's given us into Marcus' life.

Claire fixes a few plates of fruit, vegetables, cheeses, crackers, and nuts. Everyone else munches but I just can't eat. I feel like I should have an answer; there's something I should be able to do or say that will bring Marcus back to reality. Surely the Marcus who knows in his heart of hearts that Gregory Meyer is the Devil himself, a man to be despised and not followed, is in there somewhere.

I step quietly out of the room, take my phone out, and pull up my contacts. There he is: Marcus Reynolds. I stare at his name for a moment before I touch Send Message. I quietly ask Luke for forgiveness as I begin typing in silence thanks to having put the phone on vibrate.

Layla Weston: Can we talk?

Marcus Reynolds: Of course. I'm pleasantly surprised to hear from you.

His response comes almost immediately.

Layla Weston: I need to know what happens in three days?

Marcus Reynolds: Technically it's now two and a half days.

Layla Weston: Cut the crap.

Marcus Reynolds: Touchy. Where's your sense of humor?

Layla Weston: What happens in two and a half days?

I don't have time to entertain his wit so I don't respond to his comment.

Marcus Reynolds: I take possession of what is mine.

Layla Weston: Meaning me.

Marcus Reynolds: Meaning you.

Layla Weston: How exactly do you plan on doing that?

Marcus Reynolds: I'd prefer to talk about this in person.

I take a moment before I reply. I don't want to disrespect Luke, Claire, or Furtick and all they're doing to protect me, but I just can't feel so useless and helpless anymore. I have to do something. I take a deep breath and begin to type.

Layla Weston: Meet me tomorrow at the campus coffee shop at 1:00.

Marcus Reynolds: With pleasure.

What's done is done. Furtick is monitoring my phone, so I know I have to get to him before he tells Luke or Claire what I've done. I walk back to the kitchen doorway and wait. Furtick is in his usual unengaged, observing state. He's scrolling the screen of his phone impassively. When he stops, he immediately looks up at me and nods his head once.

He's on board.

Chapter 18

I spend the first half of the ride to campus wondering if I should ask Furtick why he didn't flip out at my texting Marcus and the other half figuring out how to beg Luke's forgiveness. Furtick didn't even flinch as he read the texts. He knew I would follow through with or without him. There's no way I couldn't. Reneging on an arranged meeting with Marcus has the potential to escalate the situation into whatever is worse than DEFCON 1.

"Are you mad at me?" I ask Furtick softly.

"Not entirely," he answers curtly.

"Why not?" I thought for sure he would be.

"Because despite how asinine this idea is, I agree with you. Marcus isn't a computer I can hack into, and he's too unstable to respond to my other tactics. The only way we're going to really know what's going on is to get it directly from him," he says, concentrating his eyes on the road. I smile just a little knowing that Furtick and I think the same way.

"But you are a little bit angry with me," I say. I want to give him the opportunity to be honest with me. I'm hoping our past conversation gives him the confidence to be honest with me now.

"Yes," he replies with the same curtness.

"Why?" I sound like a four-year-old.

Furtick is silent and unresponsive for a moment before his face softens and he answers. "Because I care about what happens to you, Layla. Marcus is unpredictable and I couldn't bear it if something happened to you, especially on my watch."

"Thank you, Wes." I say nothing else knowing Furtick doesn't like to get emotional. He's let out enough already and I don't want to make him uncomfortable by eliciting anything more. I know that he associates his protection of me to his own daughter. That's not easy for him and I'm having pangs of regret that I've just done that to him, as well as Luke and Claire when they find out about this.

I have a pretty breezy morning in class as this is my light day, which is great since I haven't been able to concentrate on anything but my meeting with Marcus. I've got English 201 and Sociology of the Family. My final for both classes is already done since all I had to do was write a topical paper for each. Finals are technically next week but my instructors allowed us to turn in our finals today if they were done. This is going to give me two days off next week and an early start to Christmas break. And while I'm flying high on that knowledge, I'm brought back to my own reality as I begin the walk across the quad to the coffee shop. I wonder how long Marcus has been there. I wonder if Finn has tried to kick him out. *I should have warned Finn.*

Before I reach the coffee shop I get a call from Furtick. He's never called before so I answer it immediately. "Hi," I say tentatively. I'm a bit nervous as to what he's going to say. Will he tell me to abort the mission, or give me some quick self-defense tips?

"I just wanted to check in with you before you walked into God knows what," he says. It's Wes, not Furtick. I appreciate the strong Furtick we have most of the time, but I am always pleased when I get even the smallest glimpse of Wes, my compassionate, loving bonus uncle.

"Oh…well…I'm good. I'm nervous, but I'm good. Where will you be?" I'm most nervous about not knowing where my protector will be hiding. He's such a good shadow, but today I need to know where to look to find him.

"I'm already in the coffee shop, watching Marcus." Furtick speaks softly. I don't know why since the coffee shop usually is usually buzzing with noise.

"So he's there," I say. "How does he seem?"

"Like an over-confident sociopath." Furtick's delivery is quick and I'm not sure if it's meant to be sardonic or if he's serious.

"Ok, well…um…I'm approaching now. Wish me luck," I stutter.

"You don't need luck. You've got me." Furtick's confidence in his ability to protect me makes me well up with emotion. I remember days with Gram where I wished someone would come swooping in and shield me from her sharp words and cold passiveness.

"I know." I smile and hope that Furtick can see me through a window, seeing how his presence makes me feel. I hope that he can experience some redemption knowing that I appreciate all that he's doing for me.

With that we both hang up and I walk, slowing up the last few steps, and into the shop. Finn immediately calls out to me and I step up to the counter. Finn darts his eyes to his left to alert me to Marcus' presence. I nod, but just slightly so as not to irritate anything in Marcus. I don't want him to know or even think that I've discussed him with anyone. There are a dozen different scenarios that could play out if he did. Finn makes my chai tea latte, which is especially great since it's pretty chilly outside, and I'll have something to do with my hands while I sit with Marcus.

As I turn around from the counter I spot Furtick, and I'm at ease. I have to scold myself when I smile internally at his admittance of being ready to kill Marcus if he tries to hurt me. I take a deep breath as I look to my left and locate Marcus.

He smiles at me and I feel sad. There's so much light in him that I can't believe he's letting this darkness consume him. I remember how he could make studying trigonometry kind of fun just by using a silly voice when he read the problems. I can still see that guy and I want so desperately to pull him out.

"Layla, it's good to see you. You look lovely today," Marcus says, standing as I reach the table. He seems so *him* in this moment. His eyes are kind and his expression is soft.

"Thank you, Marcus." I sit down across from him. I put my backpack next to me on the chair and my drink on the table.

"As I said last night, I was pleasantly surprised to hear from you. I had assumed that you were not going to make me wait the whole three days, but I see you're still wearing that," he says pointing to my ring. And just like that, his kind eyes are replaced with disgust.

I ignore his comment and get right to my objective. "How *are* you, Marcus?" I ask.

"What do you mean?" he says, tilting his head, genuinely perplexed at my question.

"Well, I thought about some of the things you said to me the other day and I thought that maybe we could talk about them," I say, not exactly sure where I'll start, but hoping to open up our dialogue with him knowing that I care about his well-being.

"Walk with me." This isn't a question. Marcus stands, takes my books, and waits for me to join him.

"It's cold outside. I really want to stay here," I rebut.

"Walk with me," he says throwing my backpack over his shoulder. His tone is stronger now and I can see I will not be given another opportunity to refuse him.

This is not part of the plan. I suppose we'll be ok as long as we stay in the quad. It's teaming with people and Furtick will be able to follow us without being obvious. *But what if we leave the quad?* No, no...that's not going to happen. I'll just keep us strolling in the quad. After thinking this through I stand and take my drink. As I follow Marcus to the door I give Furtick a quick look and he nods in recognition.

As we begin to walk, Marcus takes my free hand in his. It's not an unfamiliar feeling as he did this any time we were in public together during our façade of a relationship. It reminds me of a time when Marcus' heart hadn't been infiltrated by the demon known as Gregory Meyer. I didn't mind it then, but now my skin crawls at even the idea of being close to him. I'm not worried as we walk, though. I'm sure that's because I know Wesley Furtick isn't too far behind.

"What did you want to talk about, Layla?" he asks, finally breaking the silence.

"Well, you gave me a lot of information when we talked. I guess the first thing I wanted to know is how you *really* feel about me. You told me that we were going to be together, but I never heard you tell me how you felt." I'm hoping I can appeal to his heart. If I can reach in there, perhaps I can bring out the old Marcus.

"Isn't it obvious?" He stops and turns our bodies to face each other, not letting go of my hand. He's standing close and I'm barely able to squeak out a syllable.

"No." I feel a surge of nervousness run through my body so much that the electric pulses even make my teeth hurt.

"I'm in love with you, Layla. I started falling for you that first day when we sat in the coffee shop. A bit poetic that we would meet in a coffee shop today, don't you think?" His eyes are soft again and his words sincere. *He's in there. The real Marcus is in there.*

We begin to walk after a beat and I collect my thoughts and try to plan what to say next.

"Marcus, I'm concerned about you," I say.

"What is there to be concerned about? I'm better now than I ever have been." He is matter-of-fact in his delivery. Confident.

"Well, you say that you love me, but you're trying to coerce me into a relationship with you. I don't think that's very loving." I'm choosing my words as carefully as I can.

"I'm not coercing you, Layla. I'm reminding you of what you were afraid to admit because you felt you were tied to Will. I know you felt the same way about me – I could feel it when we were together. I can feel it now. I'm sure it was a confusing time: wanting to be with Will because he could give you any *thing*, but wanting me because of how you know I made you feel."

"And what is it exactly that I was afraid to admit, Marcus?" My stomach is doing flips and I think I might throw up.

"You're in love with me, Layla. I know you feel like you're betraying some promise by saying it, so I won't make you...not yet. I'm sure somewhere in your mind you think it's too soon, but it's not. It's not because I know you didn't *really* love Will." *He's delusional. He really believes that I'm in love with him.*

"And so because I'm in love with you, and you're in love with me, that makes me your possession?" I'm going back to his text, trying to understand someone who is losing his mind.

"Yes. Wouldn't your aunt and uncle say the same about each other?" Marcus' delivery is unnerving. He's looking at me like I'm crazy for not understanding what he sees as basic truth.

"I suppose," I say nervously. I don't want to encourage him, but his statement isn't completely off base. I would say wholeheartedly that I belong to Will, but that's because I truly am in love with Will. "You haven't told me what happens in three, well, two days now."

"Well...I wanted it to be a surprise, but since you asked...we're going away together," he says smiling bigger than I've ever seen him smile. He's almost giddy.

"What? Where?" I'm officially freaking out on the inside now.

"It's a bed and breakfast in the mountains, not far from Davidson actually. It's beautiful and you're going to love it." He's so pleased with himself, like he's just hit a homerun in the game of romance. That couldn't be farther from the truth. I barely want to be here with him right now, let alone go anywhere with him!

"Shouldn't you have asked me about that first, Marcus?" My nervousness is coming through in my voice now. Marcus can tell I'm uneasy and he's become offended.

"I was being romantic." His demeanor has turned agitated. I've definitely not said the right thing and he's starting to squeeze my hand.

"You know, you could show a little appreciation. Will never did anything like that for you. He couldn't because you two couldn't even be in public together. But I can. I can because I can give you everything that Will did and more." He's snowballing and I'm getting scared. I don't know where Furtick is and I don't know how to signal him.

"It's a very romantic gesture, Marcus. I just don't think my uncle and aunt are going to be ok with letting me go," I say, trying to provide a reasonable excuse while brightening my tone. I'm certainly not going to get into the lack of physical relationship Will and I had. I'm confident he'd read it as I was saving myself for him.

"You're a grown woman, Layla. You don't need their permission." Marcus' pace begins to quicken and I'm doing my best to keep up. Clearly Furtick can see that I'm trailing behind a bit and in need of his intervention. *Will he take the shot?*

"Where are we going, Marcus?" We're heading toward the corridor that leads to the north parking lot. *Where is Furtick?* The quad is teaming with people – too many for him to take the shot.

"Perhaps a preview of what's to come will help," he answers curtly with a smile.

"That sounds lovely, but doesn't tell me where we're going right now," I say in between catching my breath. He's walking fast now, but my legs are moving closer to a run.

"Well, when I got your text I knew you weren't going to make me wait, so I've got something special planned for us today." We stop when we reach his car. Not the crappy hatch back he had in Davidson. A black Prius, just like Will's. He presses my back against the passenger side back door and leans in closely. I can feel his breath on my face and my lip quivers as nerves take over completely. "You're going to love my new place."

Chapter 19

Before I know it Marcus is putting me into the passenger seat of his car. "Seat belt," he says in a soft directive. When I don't respond quickly enough he pulls the seat belt out and I take it from him. He's still agitated by my comments. Only when I'm fully buckled does he close the door. *Get out, Layla! Now, while he's circling the car!* I scream to myself. But I don't move. Even if I did scamper from the car, he's just going to chase me. I can make this harder or easier. The easier, compliant way will hopefully yield me some answers and in turn help Marcus.

Sorry, Furtick, I think. I'm sure he's cursing me to high heaven right now. I wonder where he is but remember that Cline put a tracker on Marcus' car so I feel a bit of comfort in knowing that I won't be completely MIA. And as I recall, Cline also bugged the car so I know I should get Marcus talking.

"So we're going to your place. What about your roommates?" I ask knowing full well that he's moved to a new apartment.

"I'm not living with those immature frat boys anymore, Layla. I've moved on to a place more suitable for us." *Us?* His irritation with me is softening. He smiles and I can't help but feel good about it. As long as he's happy, things are going to go just fine. I need to keep him calm, which means I have to keep calm. "We'll have all the privacy we need." He gives me a wink and puts his hand on my leg. He's inching it up too high on my thigh and a shiver runs through me. I take his hand in both of mine so he's not even touching me. "That's more like it," he says giving my hand a little squeeze.

"So I guess you'll be getting a job soon. With your experience at the bookstore, I'm sure you'll find something on campus, or nearby." I do my best to make normal conversation. I really don't want him to get upset like he did while we were walking. The last thing I need is for him to do is floor the gas and slam us into a tree in some crazy murder-suicide attempt.

"Nope. I won't be doing anything that will take my attention from you," he says. His delivery is eerie. It reminds me of the tone Mr. Meyer used when he found me on the trail during his early morning walk while we were in the mountains. My stomach turns at the memory.

"But how are you paying for your apartment and school?" I know the answer to this, too, but I need to appear as if I don't.

"Let's just say I've saved enough money to last us for a while." His vague response leaves a harder look on his face. He's not going to tell me any more about Gregory Meyer, at least not right now. And he's using that word again, *us*.

I'm silent for the rest of the drive to Marcus' apartment. Every few minutes of the fifteen minute drive Marcus volunteers a giddy comment. "This is going to be so great," or "I can't wait for you to see," he says. I give the best smile I can pull together and nod in feigned excitement. We approach the gate to the complex and Marcus enters his code. I try to see what numbers he punches, but my view is obstructed by Marcus' hand and the shape of the metal box.

The gate opens a moment after he enters his code and soon we're winding through the maze of buildings. I'm doing my best to pay attention to where we're going but it's too much. *Left, right, right, left, left, left...* I know Furtick, Taylor, and Cline know where Marcus' apartment is, but I'm trying to remember in case I end up having to make a run for it.

Marcus parks the car in a space close to the building. "Wait right here," he says with a bright smile. When his door closes I take a deep breath and let out a heavy sigh.

"If you're listening Furtick, I'm sorry," I whisper before the door opens. Marcus takes my hand as he helps me out of the car.

"So, Marcus...uh...when did you decide you would move to Tallahassee?" I ask timidly as we walk toward the building. Knowing what the catalyst was I'm not sure how he's going to respond, but perhaps it will be a good lead-in to talk him out of what he's doing. I'm trying to nonchalantly look for Taylor and Cline, hoping that they were monitoring our conversation in the car, although I'm not sure how the whole bugging thing works. I don't see them, but then again, they're not supposed to be seen.

"Well, that's hard to say. After that night at Halloween, when Will exploded as he did, I knew it would only be a matter of time before you'd come to your senses. And then when Will went missing, I knew you would want an appropriate amount of time to mourn so as not to appear to be heartless. But I suppose when you moved here, which I knew was out of complete obligation, I knew you'd miss me so I started tying up loose ends and working on the logistics." Marcus' confidence seems to rise with each step we take toward his apartment. And as we begin to take the stairs up to the second level my fear level also rises. Marcus really believes that my relationship with Will became a lie; that I really wanted, and now want, to be with him.

"Then why all the comforting talk about how they'd find Will and everything would be ok?"

"I couldn't present myself as a completely insensitive jerk, Layla."

We reach his apartment and my dread has reached an all new high. I have to believe that I can reach him. That has to be my sustained objective. If I lose focus for even a minute I don't know what will happen. Marcus smiles at me as he unlocks the door. "Ready?" he asks with a new tone of joy. I nod with a faint smile.

The door opens and Marcus puts his hand on the small of my back to usher me in ahead of him. As I cross the threshold I am overwhelmed with the loveliest aroma. It's beautiful and immediately calms me, even if just for a moment.

I walk past the kitchen on my right and enter the living room. It's large, bigger than I would have thought for an apartment, but then this is a gated development and these are high- end units. There's hardwood flooring in the entryway and kitchen, which I noticed has brown, black and silver granite counters and dark wood cabinets.

He's already furnished the apartment and everything is nicer than what I'd expect a bachelor to have. But beyond the furnishings, flooring, and granite is a site that overcomes me with mixed emotions. The apartment is filled with flowers – vases and vases of flowers. Roses of all shades, long stemmed and spray. Violets both opened and closed, and my favorite, Gerber daisies, in an assortment of colors. There are so many, hundreds, that I don't even recognize.

"I didn't know what your favorite flower was, so I had them bring something of everything. Do you like it?" Marcus says in a voice that reminds me of the man he used to be. He's not cocky or arrogant. Right now, he's a guy who's crazy about a girl and going to extremes to impress her. Were he not on the other side of a mental break down, I'd think this was sweet.

"They're lovely," I say still taking it all in. Marcus takes my hand and leads me into the living room.

"Here, let me show you around," he says happily as he puts my backpack on an accent chair. I'm glad he's back in a good mood. It eases my nerves and makes me feel like he's reachable. "You saw the kitchen when we walked in. Obviously this is the living room, and the dining area is over there. And over here..." he begins as he takes me toward a hallway. "...is your room." I still myself in the moment, not knowing how to respond. The wrong words on my end could be disastrous, but to tell him what he wants to hear will only encourage his delusion.

"Wow," I say ambiguously. It's a simple room with a wrought iron, queen-size bed, matching side tables, and a beautifully ornate dresser.

"Do you like it? I wanted you to have your own room at first." He smiles at me as if I should be grateful for his act of valor, but he has no idea how inappropriate and assumptive he has been. Even if I were interested in him, does he really think I would move in with him? Just more evidence that he really does not know me at all.

"Well, I'm not really sure what to think about it, Marcus. You're moving a bit fast." I try to say it shyly so as not to offend him but that doesn't seem to work. I've tried hard to not upset him but I see the heat begin to rise on his face and I brace myself for what may be coming next.

"This isn't fast, Layla. We've had these feelings for each other for a year now. And when two people love each other, they take steps to move their relationship forward." He takes my hand again and pulls me behind him to the other end of the hall. "And this is our next step." He's brought me to his bedroom. The room, just like the living and dining area, is filled with flowers. It's beautifully romantic and terribly frightening at the same time.

"Marcus, I..." I start to object but Marcus cuts me off.

"I know you're nervous. And I know you don't want your aunt and uncle to think that you're disrespecting Will's memory. After all, they think you were really in love with him. But I think if we can just explain to them how we feel about each other, they'll understand. They want you to be happy, Layla." He runs his thumb along my jawline and it takes everything in me not to jerk away. He really is his father's son.

"I think we should talk about this," I say moving out of the room and into the living room. I take a seat on the couch, crossing my legs and arms in my own defense.

"Alright," Marcus says sitting next to me too close. He pries my arms from their pretzel state to hold my hand. I don't put up too much resistance as he's already upset. I sit, collecting my thoughts. I compose myself and quickly formulate an idea that I think will buy me some time, as in days, if Marcus will agree.

"Well, I think you're right about my aunt and uncle. I don't think they'd understand me wanting to be with you right now. But, you know, what Will and I had being together secretly worked really well. I think we could make that work, too. I mean, just while we're working this out." I look at him with hopeful eyes, thinking that I've offered a viable option. If he can let his guard down, maybe I can reach him. However, I'm dismissed quickly as his face hardens.

"No! That's not how this is going to be. You and Will *had* to hide. We don't." Marcus is angry. "You love me, Layla, and I won't let you think that we have to live in the same secretive state that you and Will did." He takes my face in his hands and pulls me to him. My body is shifted in such a way that my defensive leg crossing comes undone. Marcus' lips are on mine before I know it. I try not to resist too forcefully but I'm too obvious in my struggle and I have set Marcus off. "Layla, don't make this difficult."

"I just…Marcus, I can't do this." *I really can't do this*. I thought I could but I can't play into his delusion any longer. All it's doing is fueling him. "I know about everything," I blurt out but Marcus isn't thrown. He lets me talk, all the while kissing my neck. I continue to try to push him off of me, but he's too strong. "I know about how your mother forced you to play her games in her retaliation toward your father. I know that Meyer rejected you time and time again. I know you hated Will for having a father who acknowledged as him as his son." Marcus stops mid-kiss, his lips feeling glued to my skin. "But forcing yourself on me isn't going to change any of that. I don't love you." I verbally vomit all over him and he doesn't flinch. He just stares at me with dark eyes.

"So you've decided to make this difficult," he says, not acknowledging what I've said at all. "That's ok, Layla. You'll give in to your true feelings soon. In the mean time I'll help you along the way." He stands, holding tight to my hand, and pulls me to stand with him. He releases my hand and slides his arms around my waist. "Put your hands on my shoulders," he directs. I do as I'm told after a moment of hesitancy. I mustn't forget that there are two powerful guns located somewhere in this apartment.

Marcus leans in and kisses me again. It's sweet and, in another universe, nice, but his passion builds quickly and it takes only moments before he's pressing into me forcefully. He's holding my body with more strength than I realized he had. I'm absolutely not kissing him back but that isn't stopping him. He holds me tighter and moves one hand to my behind. I pull my face from his and try to push him off of me.

"Marcus, stop!" I yell, pushing his body away from me with as much force as I can gather. He releases my body and I think I've gained a small victory, but it's nothing but a brief break as he looks at me, fire in his green eyes, taking my hand and pulling me to the hallway that leads to the bedrooms.

Oh, no!

Marcus pulls me into his bedroom and throws my hand from his. We stand there looking at each other for a few long moments. I don't know what to say so I go for pleading. "Please, don't do this, Marcus."

Suddenly Marcus' phone rings, giving me a reprieve, however short it may be. It's obviously a personalized ring because I don't think he would have answered it otherwise, and he doesn't even look at the screen to see who it is. "Hey, I can't talk…" he answers but is quickly cut off. "Why? Ok, ok!" Marcus moves the phone from his ear and presses a command on the screen. The next thing I hear is Holly's voice.

"Layla, can you hear me?" she asks through the speaker.

"Yes, I can hear you," I reply. I can't believe she called. I can just imagine the fury Luke has disposed upon Furtick for this predicament. I hope Luke hasn't fired him. I don't care what Luke says, I'll do everything I can to keep Furtick around. Whoever came up with it, right now I can only assume the thought would be that Holly is the only one who will be able to get through to Marcus.

"Are you ok?" she asks with softness. I can almost see her face, tilting down in a nonthreatening, concerned way.

"Why wouldn't she be ok, Holly?" Marcus interrupts. He's staring at the phone and furrowing his brow. He's so consumed with his belief that I'm in love with him that her suggestion that I might not be ok is beyond him.

"Marcus, you have to let Layla leave now. Ok?" Holly's speech is slow, but not so slow that it's demeaning. I can tell she's trying to reach Marcus and make sure he's really listening to her.

"Layla is fine, aren't you?" Marcus looks to me with bright eyes, still completely confused as to what the issue is.

"Actually, Marcus, I would really like to go home. I appreciate the flowers and all the attention, but…as I told you when you first came here, I think we make better friends." I make my tone and delivery soft like Holly's, like Claire's.

"Layla, love, it's Holly. You don't have to pretend around her. She knows how you feel about me." His anger has subsided but I know that's going to change if the conversation continues as it is.

"Marcus. Layla isn't in love with you. She told me so herself. You need to let her leave." Holly's tone is stronger now. I'm glad she's using that tone and not me. As his sister she can get away with it in a way I'm afraid I couldn't. This is the second time she's told him to let me leave. Furtick, Taylor or Cline must be outside. They wouldn't let her suggest I leave if someone weren't there to protect me.

"That's not true, Holly." Marcus' face is panged again and my anxiety level just increased. "Tell her it isn't true, Layla," he directs. He stares at me for a long moment before I can answer.

"Marcus…I don't love you," I say slowly as I reiterate what I've already told him more than once. As Marcus continues to fix his eyes on me he touches the screen of his phone and hangs up on Holly. I have no one to defend or support me and I'm standing here with a man whose next move I can in no way predict. "I'm so sorry, Marcus. I thought if I could spend some time with you, talk with you, you'd remember the friendship we had. And you wouldn't want to be like *him*. That's not who you are."

Marcus walks to a bedside table and opens the drawer. At first I can't see what he's doing, but as he turns around I see him holding a gun. *So that's what a .38 Special looks like.* As he steps back to his place a few paces from me he's shaking his head.

"Why, Layla? This could have been so beautiful, you and me. I was prepared to do for you what Will never could. Look around you," he says waving his hands, gun included, at the flowers surrounding us. "This is just one *small* gesture of my love. You have no idea what I had planned for you, for us. But now you've gone and dirtied it up with lies. I don't know why you're so afraid to be honest about how you feel about me." He holds the gun casually at his side and takes three steps toward me. I instinctually take corresponding steps backward until I bump into the corner of the bed. I stumble, but just for a second before I regain my footing.

"I tried to tell you, Marcus. I told you when we were in Davidson, when you first came to see me here, and I've told you twice today. We are not going to be together. I don't love you like that. You were always a great friend to me and I wanted us to be like that again. But now *you've* dirtied things up with this delusion that I'm in love with you." I'm scared as hell right now but I can't back down. "I know that the person I knew back home is in you, Marcus. Just stop and think about what you're doing right now. Is this who you want to be? After everything he did to you and your mom…do you really want to be like *him*?" Marcus' eyes begin to lose their fire and I feel a slight ease in the tension between us.

"Being that guy never got me anywhere. All I ever wanted was someone to share my life with. My real father didn't want me. My stepfather couldn't have cared less, and my mother's life work was a vendetta against my real father. All I had was Holly…until I met you. We had something special, something you and Will didn't have. But now you're clinging to a lie, and you've turned my sister against me. So what does that leave me with?" As Marcus holds my eyes I examine his for some trace of the Marcus I'm searching for. Adrenaline has kicked into high gear and I'm breathing harder. We both are. I try to calm my heart rate but it's difficult with Marcus now standing a nose-length away.

"Being that guy is what made you great," I say softly. Marcus steps away giving me room to breathe a bit more freely. "Marcus, let's just go sit down in the living room and talk, ok?" He doesn't seem as agitated as before, so maybe I'm reaching him? He's standing near the door and as I step toward him he looks up at me.

"No," he says firmly. "I have waited for you. I waited for you to be done with Will, I waited for you to get over his death, and I have waited for you to stop lying to yourself about your feelings for me. I'm done waiting, Layla. I don't care how long it takes you to get yourself on board, but you and I are together. For your sake I hope you catch up soon, because until then, this is going to be a very rough road for you." Marcus takes me by the waist with his gun-free hand and pulls me to him. He forces another kiss on me and I struggle and move my face from his. This makes him angry and he pushes me toward the bed. I stumble backwards and land on the bed.

Marcus begins to move toward me but a loud bang and crash distract both of us. We both look to the door and hear a rush of commotion and men's voices calling out both of our names. The voices get closer and I finally recognize one of them as Furtick. In seconds, my personal guardian angel is positioned in the bedroom door, gun drawn.

"Marcus Reynolds! Put your hands where I can see them!" Furtick instructs. His arms are extended in front of him pointing his gun at Marcus. "Put the gun down, Marcus. Put it down real slow." My heart is racing as I huddle on the bed watching Furtick ride in on his white horse and save the day.

180

"Layla! Where is she?" I hear Luke call out. I see him come into view behind Furtick, but I don't move. I don't know what to do. I suppose I'm waiting for a directive from Furtick. "Oh, Layla! Thank God you're ok!"

"Layla is going to get off the bed now, Marcus. And then she's going to walk slowly over to me and then to her uncle," Furtick says in a slow instruction.

"Layla is staying right here with me where she belongs," Marcus counters. They're not taking their eye off each other.

"Marcus, please," I beg. I move slowly off the bed and am now standing a few feet behind Marcus in his periphery.

"I said NO!" Marcus yells and directs his attention to me, breaking his eye contact with Furtick. In a split second Furtick lunges for him, slamming him to the floor. I'm knocked down in the scuffle as I hear a gun fire. It's loud and hurts my ears. I scream and scurry myself to the wall. When I open my eyes Furtick is sitting on top of Marcus' chest. There's blood on both of them but I can't tell whose it is.

"Layla! Layla!" Furtick is shouting my name but it takes me a minute to regain my senses and really hear him. "Get out of here! NOW!" Furtick shouts at me. He's full on Furtick – no Wes here at all, but this is the time when Furtick is needed most. I can't help but hope as Luke takes me from the room that Furtick feels a sense of accomplishment in protecting me in a way that he couldn't with his own daughter. I also hope that catching Marcus doesn't mean Furtick will be going away. I don't know what I'd do without him.

We exit the building with Luke holding me steady with every step. As we near the bottom of the stairs four Tallahassee police officers pass us on their way up to Marcus' apartment. I never dreamed that it would get this far. I really thought I'd be able to reach inside this new, distorted version of Marcus and pull out my old, caring friend. But he's not there. Years of rejection and cruelty at the hands of Gregory Meyer, along with the mind games his own mother played, have erased the guy I used to know and it breaks my heart to think of the man Marcus could have been. He and Will share a brilliance for all things mathematical. The sky was the limit on what Marcus could have accomplished. Now…now I don't know what will happen to him.

The parking lot is scattered with onlookers pressing against the police tape barricading the area. There are two police cars and an ambulance stuffed into the small apartment complex lot. I'm taking in the chaos and realizing all eyes are on me, which makes me unbelievably uncomfortable.

I see Claire coming toward me in a fast-paced walk. I break free from Luke and rush to her, falling into her. Her arms wrap around me and she holds me so tight. "Oh, Layla! I was so worried! I was so scared we were going to lose you!" she says squeezing me tighter. She's crying, which sparks the tears I've been holding back.

"I'm sorry! I'm so sorry! I thought I could…but he just…I'm sorry, I'm sorry!" I squeeze Claire back and nestle my face into her shoulder. I feel terrible that I made them worry and filled them with fear. They've already lost one daughter. It would have killed them to lose me, too. I know I would be devastated if anything ever happened to Luke and Claire.

"We'll talk about all this later. Let's just go home. We're just so glad you're safe. We love you so much!" Luke joins our embrace, hugging and squeezing Claire and me, his girls, and I know that I am an incredibly lucky girl.

Chapter 20

It turns out the blood on Furtick was Marcus'. The bullet hit something major and there was a lot of bleeding. They tried to get it under control, but it was just too much. He died on the way to the hospital. No charges are being placed against Furtick since he caught Marcus in the act and was therefore defending me. He's being heralded as a hero. He's definitely my hero. I don't know what I would have done had he not come to my rescue.

The scene from the coffee shop to the gunfire replays in my mind on a loop. I think about the things I said, the things Marcus said, and I wonder what I could have done differently. What could I have said? What shouldn't I have said? Marcus is dead and all I can do is assign blame to its rightful place: Gregory Meyer. Were he not the devious and malicious excuse for a human being that he is, none of this would have happened.

I shower and sanitize the filth of Marcus off of me. I hate that I feel that way about the person I once thought was my friend and ally, but that guy died long before today. I'm sad that he's gone. The Marcus that died today was an artificial representation of someone who had incredible potential. I wish it had ended differently, but I'm glad it's over.

"Where is she? Layla!" I hear Will's frantic voice echo through the house.

"I'm here, Will!" I respond and I run down the stairs, skipping the last four and leaping into his arms. We hold each other tighter than ever before. Feeling each other breathe and listening to our heartbeats, we clutch each other in frenzied appreciation.

"Why would you do that? That was so stupid! I almost lost you. I couldn't bear it if I lost you!" Will is kissing me and clutching me so tight. After a few moments he releases me only slightly and looks into my eyes. "Is this how it felt when you thought I was dead?"

"Does it feel like your heart is being squeezed in a clamp? Is your stomach cramping because it's taking on the excruciating pain ravaging your body? Do you feel like you're about to lose your mind? If so…then yes. That's exactly how it felt." I hold Will's face and stare into his ocean eyes, making sure he knows that I understand his pain. "I'm so sorry I caused you that pain."

"*I'm* sorry, Layla. I'm so sorry I made you feel this way." Tears begin to stream down Will's face as he buries his face into my neck. "I love you so much."

"I love you, too," I say softly.

"We have to talk about this," Luke says, breaking our intense moment. Will manages to release me after a few gentle pushes on my part. I have a feeling we would have stood like that all night if Will had his way. "What you did…"

"I'm sorry, Uncle Luke!"

"You brought a damn stick to a gun fight, Layla! You had no idea what he was capable of doing!" Luke raises his voice out of fear, not anger.

"I know. I'm sorry. I really thought I could reach him," I explain. "We weren't supposed to leave campus. I thought I would just talk with him like before. But then he insisted that we take a walk. With Furtick following me I didn't think it could go wrong."

"And you…" Luke directs his anger at Furtick. "What the hell happened? What were you thinking? You were supposed to protect her!"

"I did protect her. Layla was going out there with or without me. Had I not been on campus with her, we wouldn't have gotten to his apartment in time." Furtick's response is calm, yet firm. He stands by his decision, and so do I.

"He's right. I was going to go whether he was there or not."

"Why didn't you tell me?" Luke asks Furtick.

"Because I knew you would stop us. Layla was right to contact Marcus. If she hadn't we'd still be walking blind on what he was really capable of, and who knows what he would have done. Today's outcome is unfortunate, but it is what it is. It's over, and I wouldn't have done it any other way." Furtick looks at me with eyes I haven't seen in him. He's happy, proud, relieved. He has redeemed himself and done for me what he has spent years wishing he could have done for his own daughter. "I'll get my bags."

"You're not leaving, are you?" I ask sadly.

"I did what I came to do, Layla." Furtick looks at me for a long moment before he takes me by surprise and into his arms.

"Don't go. Please," I beg.

Furtick releases me and smiles, studying my face. "You're really something, you know that? Thank you for letting me be part of your life."

"Stay. Please, Wes. I need you to stay." I don't know what I'll do if he leaves. "You're family and I just can't lose any more family."

"Sir?" Furtick looks to Luke after a beat.

"What you did today..." Luke begins. He shakes his head and pinches the bridge of his nose. "Thank you. You saved her life." Luke extends his hand to Furtick. "That's what family is about." Their handshake turns into a warm embrace as Luke thanks Furtick properly. They have more in common than they may know. Both could not protect their daughters as they hoped, and both have lived with that regret. But because Luke brought Furtick into our family, all that changed today.

"It's settled then, Uncle Wes," I say happily.

"Uncle Wes, huh? I like it," Furtick smiles.

"You're the closest thing I have to a brother, so I think it's fitting." Luke's endorsement is all that's needed to change the mood and begin moving us to some level of normalcy. Marcus is dead, so things will never really be the same, but we can at least move on knowing that the threat of being found out is over.

The doorbell rings and Wes excuses himself to identify our unexpected guest. I suppose he'll always be on duty. "It's Holly," he says when he returns.

"I'll wait for you on the dock." Will kisses me quickly before he exits through the back door and swiftly disappears through the Spanish moss.

"Hi," she says quietly as she enters with Wes at her side.

"We're so sorry for your loss, Holly," Claire offers. "Would you like something to drink or eat?"

"Thank you, but, no. I'm leaving tomorrow. I've identified the body and he's going to be cremated, so I'll be taking his ashes home." Holly's voice is small and sad.

"I'm really sorry it ended this way," I tell her. "I never wanted Marcus to get hurt."

"I don't blame you, Layla. Your intentions were pure. Next to me, you were the only person in Marcus' life who took him for who he was. Everyone else has used him as a pawn in some twisted game. And, unfortunately, the people really responsible for Marcus' demise will never be made to pay for what they've done." She pauses, sighs, collecting her thoughts. "If it's any consolation, he really did care about you."

"I know he did."

"I'll let myself out. Thank you for all you did…tried to do…for Marcus. And, Layla…maybe one day we can be friends. We must have something in common if Will cared for both of us."

"Thank you, Holly." I nod knowing that I can never be her friend. Will is very much alive so there's no way I can let her into my life in any capacity. I feel badly about that. As hostile as I was with her at our first meeting, she proved to be helpful. She filled in the missing pieces, and her phone call to Marcus bought Wes and his team some time in getting to me.

Holly leaves and I immediately make my way to the dock after closing the door behind her. I push the last vine out of my way and find Will seated quietly, his feet dangling over the edge.

"Hey," I say, getting his attention.

"Hey," Will responds but doesn't turn around.

"Are you mad at me?" I ask him as I take my shoes off and sit next to him.

"I'm not mad, Layla. I was scared. When Furtick called and told Luke what happened, I thought I was going to lose you forever. Marcus was so unpredictable. I don't know what you were thinking." Will's eyes lock on mine and I can see the pain and fear he's pouring out.

"Please don't take this the wrong way, but…now you have an idea of how I was feeling. Only…for all I knew, you were really gone." I take his hand in mine, caressing along the top by his knuckles. Will's eyes fill with sadness for the pain he caused me and I squeeze his hand to let him know that I'm really ok. "I had to try and reach him, Will. After our conversation in the garden, I understood the pain he was experiencing. You experienced it, too, but…you at least had your mom. Marcus didn't have anybody. Holly was there for him, but she couldn't be responsible for his emotional wellbeing. Everyone gave up on him, Will, and I just couldn't do that."

"I understand. It doesn't change the fact that I was scared out of my mind. But, I understand. You're just so incredible. You were so brave today." Will pulls me close and I rest my head on his shoulders.

*****

Waking up this Christmas morning was absolutely the best. Luke and Claire invited Will and Eliana to spend the night after a light Christmas Eve meal. Eliana slept in my room while Will and I slept in the Great

Room in front of the Christmas tree. We stayed up until after midnight just so we could be the first to officially tell the other Merry Christmas.

As I lay on the couch, stretching and rubbing the sleep from my eyes, I see Will, laying there on the floor next to me and know that I have already received the best Christmas gift ever.

We ravage through our gifts in a much less orderly fashion than Luke, Claire, and I did last year. Last Christmas Claire made me wait to open all of my gifts, giving me my cherished Kindle as a grand finale.

There are no big gifts this year as I think we were all a bit preoccupied with the whole situation with Marcus, but the clothes, jewelry, and small electronics being unwrapped are a huge hit with everyone. The fact that we're all together truly is gift enough.

While I'm relishing in the glad tidings we're all enjoying, I can't help but think of Holly. I know her parents aren't mourning the loss of Marcus as they should, but I'm sure Holly is huddled under a dark cloud on what is supposed to be day full of joy. I think for a few minutes about calling her, but decide against it. As much as I owe Holly for the distraction she caused, enabling Wes and Luke to come to my rescue, inviting Holly to be a part of my life is out of the question.

Luke sent Taylor and Cline home to be with their families, discharging them from their service to us with a nice retirement package. With Wes a permanent fixture in our family, we've got all the extra muscle we need. Even though there isn't an imminent threat to me or to our secret anymore, Luke still has Wes in his employment as our private security. It feels a bit silly to have him employed by us…it's not like we're the Kennedys or anything…but it's nice to know that he's staying.

I think Eliana is glad he's staying as well. I've watched her get a little more comfortable, and a little more flirtatious, with him over the last few weeks. Wes seems lighter now, too. It's great to see Eliana embracing who she is and feeling safe enough with Wes to show that.

We fill the day with cooking and music and games. Wes has a booming laugh that no one saw coming, but we're so happy to receive it. I crush Will and Wes in Monopoly and take a victory lap around the kitchen, landing in Will's arms just as Claire announces that it's time to eat.

As we gather around the table it's hard to not take note of how cozy Eliana and Wes are.

"So what's up with your mom and Wes," I whisper to Will.

"I don't know, but they're going on a date on New Year's Eve. It's so weird to see her with someone like that. I've never seen her so happy!" Will whispers back. His lips brush against my ear and I feel a tingle of joy come over me.

"It appears that all is right in the world again, huh?" I say to Will, smiling uncontrollably.

Claire puts the last dish on the table and she and Luke take their places at the heads of the table. I look at all of us seated around the feast and feel the sting of tears welling up in my eyes. This is my family. We have all travelled such rocky paths to land where we are. It feels as though we all give a collective sigh of relief knowing that peace is finally upon us.

"Claire, the roast is to die for! What did you do to it?" Eliana asks as she puts another fork-full in her mouth. Claire says Turkey is for Thanksgiving, Ham is for Easter, and Roast is for Christmas.

"You're going to laugh, but it really is the easiest thing in the world! I put a packet of dried French Onion Soup mix on it, then about a cup of water. I cover it in the pan and cook it on 250 for eight hours. About halfway through I throw the carrots, potatoes, and onions in. I'm so glad you like it!" Claire has done her fair share of internet searches for easy and impressive dishes in her quest to become a better cook. We experiment with different food quite a bit, but she took it on as a challenge to herself. I must say that she's really outdone herself!

"I'd like to make a toast," Will says, pushing his chair out and standing. "This is a very special holiday for me. For the first time in, well, ever, I am seated at a Christmas feast with the knowledge that *each* person around this table loves me. Each of you has sacrificed more than one could ever expect from another person.

"Luke, Claire…you made Layla and me being together possible. Without your support, I'm not sure where we would be. You have given me so much encouragement and guidance. I just don't know how to thank you.

"Furtick…Wes…you saved my life when you saved Layla's. I will forever be indebted to you. No words or deeds will ever be enough to thank you.

"Mom…" Will starts but begins to get choked up. "Mom…you gave up everything for me. You never left me and you did everything you could to protect me. You are so much stronger than you ever gave yourself credit for. Watching you over the last six months…I'm just so glad that you're finally seeing that.

"And Layla…the love of my life. We've been through *so much* over the last 18 months that I can't believe you're still here with me. I will do my best to make the next 18 months as completely uneventful as possible. I couldn't be a happier man. I love you so much."

"I love you, too, baby." I stand up and kiss Will sweetly, joining in his toast. "I couldn't agree more with every word. To family!"

"To family!" everyone echoes.

Eliana and I pack up all the left overs, setting some aside for her and Will to take home, although I'm not sure why since they're both at the house all the time. It used to be just Will, but now that Eliana and Wes are getting close, she's here just as much as Will.

The girls wash the dishes while the guys get the Great Room cleaned up. We tidied up some, but it still looks like Christmas threw up in there.

Once everything is done we reward ourselves with coffee and dessert around the fire pit on the patio.

"Isn't this lovely?" Eliana remarks.

"Yes, it's just perfect!" I say. "Best Christmas ever!"

"Not yet, it's not," Will says.

Will stands, followed by Luke who goes over to the end of the patio near the door to the porch and flips a switch I didn't know was there. All of the sudden the trees surrounding us light up with white twinkling lights. Not just on one tree or even in one section, but every single tree in the back of the house is lit. I look at Will who is standing at the step of the dock holding out his hand and a surge of nervous excitement shoots through every fiber of my being.

"C'mere. I want to show you something," he says.

All eyes are on me and I'm speechless. I follow him, taking his hand. As we move along the dock I'm overwhelmed. The lights carry through the thick trees and are strung and wound around the Spanish moss like icicles. Between the chillier air and the sparkling lights, Will has turned this place into a kind of winter wonderland.

When we reach the end of the dock I'm just as mesmerized. There are white lights wound around the railing with white tulle. Everything is softly glowing and reflecting off the water. It's the most magical scene I've ever witnessed.

"Oh, Will!"

"Don't say anything...not yet," Will instructs before taking a deep breath. "Layla, when I met you I was in a lonely place, but you brought me out of it. You gave me so much to look forward to. You gave me hope. But these last six months...they were some of the worst of my life. I had to let you go, and just when I got you back, I almost lost you." Will takes another deep breath and looks at me with his intense blue eyes. "But I don't want to talk about the past anymore. We're on the threshold of a new year, and I can't think of any better way to end this one."

Will drops to his knee and takes my hand in his. I gasp and cover my mouth with my free hand. Tears well up and overflow from my eyes, running in a steady stream down my face.

"Layla, when you came into my life I expected nothing but maybe a good friendship to come of it. But, somewhere along the way I realized everything I ever needed was standing right in front of me in you. I want you. I want your beauty and poise. I want your flaws and mistakes. I want your strength and resiliency. I want your incredible smile and that infectious giggle of yours. I even want your sarcasm. I want everything that is you because…I want you. There are eight billion people in the world and *you* are the *only* one I want.

"Layla Michele Weston…I was born to tell you I love you…will you marry me?"

Chapter 21

I open my eyes and find my hand resting on the pillow right in front of my face. I smile as I'm greeted by the sparkle of the engagement ring Will gave me just a week ago. It really is the most beautiful ring I've ever seen. It was Claire's grandmother's wedding ring. When Will told me that, I think I cried harder than when he proposed. The white gold setting has five diamonds set across it, with a woven pattern along the front and back. It is exquisite and unlike anything I've ever seen. I couldn't love it more.

I was shocked at Will's proposal. I mean, I've known for a long time that Will and I are going to get married one day, I just thought he'd wait a bit longer before making it official. But, proposal now, or proposal later, there was only one answer I could give him. And even though I starting crying uncontrollably, I was able to squeak out a resounding *yes*.

So much for making the next 18 months as uneventful as possible!

Will is asleep again on the floor next to the couch where I am stretching myself awake. We stayed up to watch the ball drop in Time Square and all the festivities unfold. A few of our favorite bands were playing, and there were awkward on-air proposals, along with the continued training of Ryan Seacrest who will one day take over the whole event from Dick Clark. We ate junk food and toasted with Luke and Claire to a promising New Year.

I lay there watching Will sleep, recalling how I spent my last New Year's Eve. Caroline ambushed my solo plans and made the night so much better than it would have been. That was the night she told me about being adopted and how she, more than anyone else, knew what it was like to have to win Gregory Meyer's favor. It was her reassurance of Will's love for me in the midst of my confusion that was the first major step in bringing Will and me back together.

I take a final stretch and move strategically off the couch, careful not to wake Will. I make a quiet, but quick, trip upstairs to brush my teeth and pull my hair up into a ponytail and then make my way back to the kitchen to put on a full pot of coffee. When I close the fridge I'm startled to see Eliana standing there. And while she looks relaxed, young, and happy, she also seems a bit nervous.

She and Wes had what I'm assuming is their first date last night and it appears she never went home. She's wearing one of Wes' trademark plaid button-up shirts and an uncontrollable smile.

"Good morning!" I say cheerily.

"Good morning, Layla. I…uh…" she stammers.

"It's ok, Eliana. I'm guessing you had fun last night?"

"It's not what it looks like. We didn't…I didn't…I would never…we just slept."

"Oh…well that's fine, too. Believe me, I understand the value of just simply being close to someone like that." I smile and she seems at ease. "Wes is a pretty great guy. I'm glad you two are hitting it off. "

"Yes, he's really wonderful. Very…different, than Will's father." Eliana shifts her weight from one foot to the other before deciding to take a seat at the table. "Layla, can we speak candidly?"

"Of course," I say. I've always wanted to have a better relationship with my mother-in-law than my mom had with Gram, and even though our marriage is an undetermined time away, I want to start early on this mission.

"I didn't fully understand what I was getting into with Gregory," she begins.

"Oh, Eliana, you don't owe me any kind of explanation," I tell her.

"I know, I know. But since you're going to be Will's wife, I really need you to understand a few things." She plays with a napkin ring on the table, not making eye contact with me. She's nervous and fidgety. I finish setting up the coffee and pour us each a glass of orange juice while we wait for the brew.

"If you really feel it's necessary," I say, setting the orange juice in front of her.

"Thank you." She takes a long sip of juice and puts the glass down. "I met Gregory when I was 22-years-old. He and his wife came into my family's store in Hickory. My father and brother are master carpenters and they make the most beautiful furniture. My mother and I ran the showroom and worked with customers on design. Will's inclination toward creating with his hands comes naturally." She smiles thinking about how connected to her side of the family Will really is. It makes me smile, too.

"Gregory bought every piece I showed him, and took every design suggestion I made. There were so many pieces that it was going to take a year to fulfill the entire order. He didn't care...he wasn't in any rush.

"After the order was complete and everything was delivered I received a call from this enigmatic man who seemed to hang on every word I said. He wanted to thank me for all my help and asked me to dinner. I was flattered that this older, distinguished man would show any interest in me. I was just a girl from an industrial town, working my family's business. I wasn't anyone special, but he sent a car for me in Hickory and took me to the most extravagant restaurant in Charlotte.

"As we spent more time together, he continued to be charming and charismatic. He complimented me and said all the right things. He gave me anything my heart desired, and then some.

"When I asked about his wife, he told me they were the latest casualty of irreconcilable differences. It happens all the time, so I didn't question it. I had no idea that she was his third wife until much later." She takes another sip of juice and I use that as my opportunity to speak.

"Will said that, since you've been here, you've missed his father sometimes."

"Yes. As terrible as things were, he was my husband, and there was a time I was most definitely in love with him. I know it's difficult to understand," she says softly.

"Eliana, I'm sorry, really, you don't have to tell me this. I understand how manipulative Gregory Meyer is. You don't have to convince me of that."

"But I want you to know that *I* didn't understand that…not at first. I was young and tired of the life I was living. I loved my family but wanted so much more. I wanted to go to college, study design and bring back fresh ideas to my parents' business. But I had obligations. Gregory promised me a world where all my dreams would come true…then snatched it right out from under me.

"After we married I wanted to go to school but Gregory kept telling me that he wanted and needed me at home. If I was studying all the time, who would take care of him? So I waited, feeling like I was being a good wife. At some point Gregory started growing tired of me. I don't know what I said or did, but it started becoming clear that I was not enough. He worked later and later, took overnight trips to see clients, and when he was home, he barely spoke to me. I lived for the moments when he showed me any attention. When I got pregnant, I thought things would change. They changed, just not in the way I hoped they would.

"Gregory became obsessive about William from the moment we found out we were having a boy. He chose to name him after his father and himself: William Gregory Meyer. It's a strong name, though, don't you think?" I nod in agreement. Everything about Will is strong to me. I can't believe she's telling me all of this. I wonder if she's ever told anyone the whole story.

"I endured all I could for several years, but when William was little I wanted to leave Gregory, go back to Hickory where he could grow up around family. But Gregory wouldn't allow it. If I left I would never have seen William again." Eliana lets out a heavy sigh and looks at me with pain in her eyes. "William knows everything, which is why he has worked so hard to be nothing like his father. I tried to convince him ages ago to leave, but he wouldn't go without me. I thank God every day that he inherited the Hufford genes for kindness, compassion, and love. He's a protector, Layla, and if there's anything you need to fully understand about my son it's that he will love and protect you until the day he dies."

"Thank you for being so transparent. You didn't have to tell me anything, and I want you to know how much I appreciate it. I know how incredible Will is and how lucky I am to have found him, and I will love and protect him, too. There isn't anything I wouldn't do for him. And you need to know, *really know*, that Will is the great man he is today because of you. Left in the hands of his father, Will would have turned out very differently. You should be very proud. You've endured a lot in your life, Eliana, which is why I'm so glad that you've found Wes. I don't know where you think it might go, but I know that right now, you couldn't be in better hands."

Eliana stands and I join her in a warm embrace. She's opened herself up and let me in in a way I never expected. She has had years of closing herself off, not being allowed to tell anyone about the real nature of her husband, so I appreciate her sharing. I know it took a tremendous amount of bravery to share with me as she has and I'm honored that she found me worthy of carrying her story.

"What the hell? Why are you barely dressed...in one of Wes' shirts?" Will's shocked and disapproving face at his mother's appearance makes me laugh.

"Oh, uh..." Eliana isn't sure how to respond.

"They had their own prom night," I tell him. It takes a moment for him to understand what I'm saying and recall our beautiful, non-sex filled night, but when it sinks in he seems a bit skeptical. They are, after all, two grown adults.

"Ok...I guess," he finally says.

"I'm going to put some clothes on." Eliana scurries from the kitchen and disappears around the corner back to Wes' room.

"Good morning, fiancée," Will says, wrapping his arms around me.

"Good morning to you, fiancé," I say, followed by a sweet kiss on his sweet lips.

Will is about to go in for a deeper kiss when it seems the masses have awakened and enter the kitchen. Happy New Year greetings are exchanged all around as Will and I break and gather coffee cups for everyone.

"So, Wes...how was your night?" I ask teasingly.

"It was..." he begins, but looks to Will before continuing. I have to give Will a nudge so he stops with the obligatory stink eye. "It was great," Wes smiles.

"What did you do?" I ask.

"Yeah, Wes, what did you do?" Will asks with only half-teasing chastisement.

"Ok, ok...I'm only going to subject myself to your Spanish Inquisition once. So let's get it over with." Wes takes a sip of his black coffee and leans back in his chair. "The answer to your first question: I took Eliana to dinner at Stir, and then we went downtown to walk around and watch fireworks. Next."

"Are you going to go out again?" Claire asks, joining in. She is a hopeless romantic so I know she's totally into this.

"Yes. Next," he smirks.

"Did you kiss her?" I ask, making my voice sound sugary sweet.

"A lady never tells," Eliana says as she enters the kitchen with a full set of clothing on.

"Yes," Wes says smiling.

"Wesley!" Eliana protests.

"What? You said a lady never tells. No one said I couldn't!" Wes' smile spreads across his face as he stands and gives Eliana a sweet embrace and an honorable kiss on the cheek.

"But, in all seriousness," Wes begins. "We want to know that you're ok with this, Will. It's important to us." Wes puts his arm around Eliana's waist as they both look hopefully at Will.

"Are you happy, Mom?"

"Yes. I am very happy," she says looking into Wes' eyes.

"Well...it might take me a little while to get really used to it, but...if you're happy, then I'm happy." Will smiles genuinely, giving his blessing to wherever Wes and Eliana's relationship takes them.

Chapter 22

The months come and go and for the first time since before my parents died, I feel normal. I'm a normal college student with two parents, a fiancé, an uncle, and a whenever-to-be mother-in-law. Life is utterly ordinary…just the way I like it.

My and Will's class schedule didn't sync up the way we had hoped it would this semester. I've got a full day on Tuesdays and Thursdays and Will's working with a packed schedule on Monday and Wednesday. While we're both on campus every day, we literally have 30 minutes in the middle of the day to see each other. It's not ideal, but Will makes up for the time by practically living at my house.

It's been so busy that we haven't even had a real date since…well…we've actually never had a real date. When we were in Davidson, all the time we spent together was in secret so while I was always excited to spend time with Will, it just always felt off. On our first *date*, Will brought me back to Luke and Claire's for a picnic on the dock. It was beautiful and I wouldn't change a second of it, but we were always hiding in the shadows. And up until Christmas, Wes followed us everywhere. It would just be nice to have Will ask me out on a date, come pick me up at my house, and have me home at a reasonable hour.

We haven't set a date for the wedding either. Will wants to get our wedding date on the calendar but I've just wanted to enjoy being engaged. Now that all the drama in our lives is over, it's nice just existing. But, I know Will is getting impatient, so I'll have to woman-up and set a date for the happiest day of my life.

I've wanted to plan something special for Will since his birthday, too. He turned 19 in December and the occasion got totally overshadowed by the situation with Marcus. In fact, it was days after that Eliana insisted on a special birthday dinner. I suppose 19 isn't a big deal but I think his next birthday is monumental, so I've got to catch him by surprise. I've got about 20 minutes to kill before I get my 30 minutes with Will so I'm making lists and jotting down party ideas in the campus coffee house. A hoard of people rush through the door and startle everyone already seated and casually enjoying a cup of joe. When I look outside I see that the sky has opened up causing the stampede. I notice one of the last empty seats is next to me when a guy I don't know starts making a beeline in my direction. He looks at the seat and then looks at me as if to say "Please, for the love of God, save me that seat!" I smile at him and put my hand on the seat of the chair so I can ward off any other takers.

"*You* are a life saver!" he says as he sits. "This is nuts!"

"No problem," I say. "Yeah...the coffee house suddenly becomes cool to everyone when getting soaked is on the line."

"Tell me about it! I'm Eli, by the way." He offers his hand after wiping on the dry part of his cargo shorts. "Eli Briggs: journalism major." Eli isn't tall like Will, but still taller than me, like everyone else. He's got shaggy brown hair and brown eyes. He's cute and I immediately think that Dana would like him.

"Layla Weston: undeclared but leaning heavily toward psychology. It's nice to meet you, Eli."

"So, Layla Weston, probable psych major...where are you from?" Eli asks. It's such a simple question. Six months ago I would have been so closed off that the idea of having this conversation with Eli would have been non-existent. Truth be told, I wouldn't have made eye contact with him long enough to secure this seat for him, but now...now that I'm living my utterly normal dream life? I've got this.

"I'm from a little town in North Carolina," I say. I decided long ago that this would be my solid answer to this question. "What about you?"

"New York, but we moved around a lot," he replies.

"Military brat?"

"Brat, yes…military, no," he laughs. "My dad's job took him all over the place. I was happy to finally get into college so I could stay put for a while, but I'm on my way out. Just one semester left, so the light at the end of the tunnel is getting brighter." Four people are trying to squeeze around a two-person table next to Eli and he gets shoved right into me. To make the room we have more comfortable, Eli puts his arm around my chair. "Do you mind?" he asks.

"No worries," I say. "That's awesome about being so close. This is my first year, but with all the AP classes I took my senior year of high school, and the credits I earned last semester, I'm technically a sophomore now." I tuck a loose lock of hair behind my left ear and Eli gets a look at my engagement ring.

"Whoa! Well done to the guy who put that on your finger!"

"Oh, yeah. I just got engaged at Christmas." I'm a little embarrassed. I don't know why. I couldn't be prouder to marry Will. I'm just not a fan of all the attention. This has sparked quite a few conversations about the kind of wedding Will and I will have. I'm all for small and simple, but Will wants to make a huge spectacle of his love for me. While that's sweet, it's totally unnecessary.

"Boyfriend from back home or college romance?" Eli asks.

"Aren't you inquisitive! Guess you're well suited for that journalism major, huh?"

"It's in my blood! I can't help it," he smiles.

I see Will enter the coffee shop so I make a buzzing sound. "Oh, I'm sorry, your time is up! My fiancé just walked in the door and he's going to need that seat. I guess you'll have to quiz me some other time," I chuckle.

"That is actually a great idea. I'm on the student newspaper and would love to interview you for a student spotlight. What d'ya say?" Eli looks at me eagerly. "You should say *yes* because I'm not going to take *no* for an answer. You'd be great! Ok…I had someone set for the next student spotlight but they got busted for having pot in their dorm so they got expelled. Not exactly the kind of student we're wanting to highlight."

"Well...I guess," I say reluctantly. "Here, give me your phone. I'll put my number in it and then text myself. Ok...now I've got your number, too. Just let me know when you want to get together. You know you're going to owe me, right?"

Will gets his drink from Finn and makes his way over to where I'm sitting with Eli. His face is hard and I can almost see the daggers shooting out at Eli. Will is so protective of me. I'm going to have to diffuse this immediately.

"Hey babe. This is my new friend Eli. Eli, this is my fiancé, John," I say giving Will the look that says "Behave!" I've become quite adept at referring to Will as John around other people. It took some practice, and sometimes I have to think for a second, but, for the most part, I've got it down now.

"Hey John. It's nice to meet you," Eli says, extending his hand to shake.

"Eli," Will reciprocates. "Thanks for keeping my girl company and my seat warm," he says. Eli takes Will's cue and gets up, making the way for Will to take his rightful seat next to me.

"Absolutely. I'll call you in the next few days, Layla. Thanks for helping me out. I appreciate it!"

"Definitely! It was great to meet you, Eli! We'll see you soon!" I say as Eli walks away. I pour on the sugar wanting to make up for Will's icy stare.

"You have something you want to tell me?" he asks seriously.

"No." I take a sip of my coffee, ignoring his macho jealousy.

"Layla. I walk in here and you're sitting here with another guy and his arm is around you. Do you even know who he is? Where he's from? What if he..."

"First of all, his arm was around the chair, not me. He was only sitting like that because those idiots over there were pushing him into me. And just so you know, he *asked* if I minded. Secondly, how can you think for even a nanosecond that I would be unfaithful to you?" I put my hand on Will's cheek.

"It's not you I'm worried about," he says. "I don't like that our schedules are so off. I can't protect you like this." Will is frustrated. He wasn't able to protect me like he wanted when Marcus was a threat to us, so he's working at making up for lost time.

"W-…John," I say correcting myself. I'm speaking in a hushed tone, and the coffee shop is so loud and busy, but I still need to watch myself. "Let's go outside. I've got an umbrella, and you need to start making your way to class."

We step outside into the rain and I pop the huge golf umbrella open. Will takes my free hand and we begin walking the path across the quad to his building. I love walking in the rain with Will. It's like a scene from a movie – the kind where couples stay together forever. Maybe that's why it feels so good.

"I've really been enjoying these last few months. They've been…normal. I need normal, Will," I tell him.

"I know…" he begins.

"No. Don't say anything. Just listen. Ok?" Will nods and I continue. "I know that you love me and are just looking out for me like you always have. And I love that about you…about us. But we've spent our entire relationship playing both offense and defense. Can't we just move forward in our life together like…like two people who haven't gone through hell and high water to be together?"

"Layla, that's part of our story," he says in defense.

"That's part of Layla and *Will's* story. What's my and John's story?"

"Layla…"

"Will…I need life to be normal. Think about it. My parents died and I spent the next five years being punished for their death. Then I moved in with Luke and Claire and spent the next year on a roller coaster of loving you and dodging the consequences of that. I lost you, and just when I got you back I faced everything with Marcus. Good grief! I'm a Lifetime movie, Will! I just need to live a normal life as a college student, daughter, fiancée, and friend, and that includes you maintaining a *normal* level of jealousy because you can't stand for me to be around another guy and not because you think I need protecting."

"You're right," he says with a sigh. "I'm sorry."

"Thank you." I give his hand a squeeze and his cheek a kiss.

"Ok…so this is me being a *normal*, jealous fiancé. Who is this Eli guy?" Will smirks.

"He's on the student paper. He came in with the swarm of people when the downpour started. He needed a seat and I had one open next to me. That's all," I tell him.

"So why is he going to call you?"

"Oh, he needs a fill-in for the student spotlight. He had someone but apparently they got busted for having pot in their room, so they're not exactly eligible for the feature. I told him he could interview me."

"Well, I guess that's ok. Just still be careful what you tell him. Remember not to use John or Elisabeth's last names. We may be out of the woods, but we still want to be cautious."

"Got it. I know the drill. Wes throws different scenarios at me once a month to make sure I'm on guard," I reassure him.

"This is me," Will says as we reach the building for his economics class. "I'll be over after class. I've got a ridiculous amount of homework, though. It's not due until Monday, but I'd like to get it done between tonight and tomorrow. That'll give us Friday and Saturday night to do something fun."

"Really?" I say excitedly.

"Yeah…I know it's been crazy busy. I really want to start making us a priority now that things are…*normal*. John Holland would really like to date his fiancée. So, Miss Weston, if you're not busy this weekend, would you do me the honor of letting me take you out on an official date?" Will smiles that brilliant smile of his and I melt just like I did the first time I saw it on the Green in Davidson when we met.

"Why, Mr. Holland, I would be delighted," I smile sweetly and bat my lashes a few times. He's read my mind and feels the same way I do about the lack of quality time we've had. I'm giddy with excitement and can't wait until our date, or dates.

We kiss each other goodbye and I leave Will on campus to head home and tackle my own mound of homework. I've waited too long to have a normal life to let anything stand in the way of my weekend with Will.

Chapter 23

I've just gotten out of the shower when I realize that I've only got 20 minutes before Will is supposed to pick me up for our date. I begin to rush but then decide to take my time. There's a normalcy to the boy having to wait on the girl, so I casually get dressed in the light cotton red skirt and soft white shirt I picked out last night. I dry most of my hair and pull it back into a high ponytail, letting my new bangs swoop across my forehead and some locks hang loose to frame my face.

I stare at myself in the mirror for a long time. The last time I considered my appearance this much was the day of Gramps' funeral. I was embarking on a new chapter in my life – one of freedom and found redemption. I remember wondering if I looked as different as I was beginning to feel. There was no sign of change then, but that's not the case now. I stand taller, my face is happier, and my eyes are brighter. All I can think is that I may not have gone where I intended to go, but I know I've ended up exactly where I need to be.

I check the clock and realize that even with all my casualness about getting ready, I still have five minutes to spare. I hear the doorbell chime and think it's odd at first. No one ever rings our doorbell, but for the past couple of months Claire and Eliana have been chummy with our neighbors. Claire said it was time to stop acting like recluses and make friends.

When I open the door I don't find a middle-aged northern transplant standing on our front step, but instead, the love of my life, bouquet of flowers in hand, smiling like a fool in love. He looks more handsome than I've seen him since prom. He's got on dark jeans, a white dress shirt with the sleeves rolled up just past his elbows, and the hottest black vest I've ever seen. I take a deep breath and relish in the fact that the man standing in front of me is all mine.

"Hello, sweetheart," he says smiling.

"Hello," I say mirroring him.

"These," he holds out the bouquet for me to take, "are for you. I saw them and they made me think of you."

"They're lovely. Thank you, Will." I step aside, inviting him in. Will gives me a sweet kiss on the cheek as he crosses the threshold.

"Layla, who's at the door?" Claire asks entering the room from the kitchen.

"It's Will," I tell her.

"You rang the doorbell?" Claire looks quizzically at Will. "You never ring the doorbell!"

"I'm here to pick up Layla for a proper date. A proper date does not just walk into his girl's house." Will smirks at me. "I'll be taking Layla out to dinner, Mrs. Weston. Is there a particular time you and Mr. Weston would like her home?"

"No particular time, Will. We trust you both will be responsible. Have fun!" Claire stifles a giggle as she retreats into her and Luke's bedroom. I hear the muffled talking and laughing of them both as she relays the little act Will is putting on for my benefit.

"Is this normal enough for you?" he asks wrapping his arms around my waist.

"It's definitely a strong start. Thank you." I push up on my toes and kiss Will square on the lips.

"Whoa, whoa, whoa! This is our first proper date. I'm not the kind of guy who kisses on the first date!" he teases. "Oh…who am I kidding? C'mere!" With that, Will presses his lips to mine and kisses me like he really means it. It amazes me how our kisses get better each time. I suppose that's because our love gets better and better every day, too.

"You don't really think we haven't dated, do you?" Will asks as we pull out of the driveway.

"No, I suppose not. It's just...forget it. It's silly," I say, embarrassed that I'm allowing myself to be so particular about this. I really should just be grateful that I get to spend the rest of my life with Will. How we got to our life together shouldn't matter so much.

"C'mon, Layla...please tell me. It's obviously bothering you," he pleads. "I don't care if you think it's silly. It matters to me."

"Well...it's not that I don' think we've dated. We have...in our own way. And I guess that's what matters most. I love that we have our own special love story...minus the threats, manipulation, and secrecy, of course. I just really want us to have a life where we're not always looking over our shoulders. Does that make sense?" I press my lips into a hard line, not wanting to cry as I think about the life-threatening terrain we've travelled to get to where we are today. I don't ever want to go back to that.

"It does. I understand, and I want you to know that my life's mission is to give you the best, most normal life ever. I guess it's a little harder for me to transition into this normal life. I'm just so used to being in protective mode with you. When we were in Davidson, every move I made was calculated to protect you. Even when Luke, Claire and I decided something drastic had to be done and Mom and I disappeared...Layla...that was the hardest thing I ever did in an effort to protect you. I guess I just don't know how to *not* guard over you. You are the most precious thing in my life and I would sooner die than lose you." Will takes my hand and brings it to his lips, kissing my knuckles. He really does truly love me. It's in moments like this that I know that I would face 100 years of Gram's fury if I knew that Will was waiting for me at the end.

"Well, there's nothing to worry about now. Marcus is...gone...and your father is destroying lives in Davidson, gloriously oblivious to anything but his own selfish gain. Since Wes insists on continuing to monitor the firm's staff for any suspicious changes..." I say grasping his hand in both of mine "...we are free to be John and Layla, happily engaged couple, working our asses off to finish school before the end of time!"

When we pull up to my favorite restaurant, Stir, my stomach is filled with excited butterflies. It reminds me of the flutters I felt the night Will took me on my first date and we picnicked on the dock. I experienced a release of emotions I didn't know I still had. Then, when Will kissed me on the porch... That's the night I felt like I really started living again.

We're halfway through dinner when Will brings up the subject of our wedding. Any normal girl would be chomping at the bit to get wedding plans underway, but I just haven't been able to focus on that. When I looked at the calendar earlier this week, I was hit in the face with a reason other than the commitment to my education.

"We have to at least talk about a time frame, Layla, even if it's when we're finished with school. There has to be a destination here." Will is visibly upset by my lack of initiative in planning our wedding.

"I just can't right now," I say, tearing off a piece of bread. I don't eat the bread. I just examine it.

"Layla, I know you want to marry me. I just don't understand why you don't seem to care about how we go about executing it, beginning by setting a date." Will takes the bread from me and tosses it back into the basket.

"Their anniversary is next week," I say softly.

"I thought Luke and Claire's anniversary was in October?" he asks, his eyebrows furrowing together.

"My parents' anniversary is next week. It would have been their 25th."

"Oh, baby, I'm sorry. Why didn't you say something?" Will takes my hand in his and rubs his thumb across my fingers.

"I just noticed it last week." I can't even look at him. I'm afraid I'm going to cry and I just don't want to do that.

"I can see why that's upsetting to you, and maybe why you don't want to talk wedding stuff now, but…what does that have to do with why you've avoided the subject for the past four months?"

I think about his question and realize that I'm still stuck. I'm stuck with the same baggage I've been carrying since I was 12-years-old.

"It's a chain reaction – a domino effect that I will never escape. I'm marrying you because I met you when I moved to Davidson after my grandparents died. I moved to live with my grandparents because my parents died. If my parents hadn't died, I would never have met you." I swallow hard, rehashing this painful truth again. I've tried but don't know if I'll ever reconcile these feelings. "Babe, my parents had to die in order for us to be together. I have a hard time moving forward with my life sometimes, knowing that theirs was cut so short."

"You want a normal life, right?" Will says and I nod immediately. More than anything I want my life to be ordinary. "A normal life means that you take what happens to you in it and press on, using those experiences to make you a better person. You can't spend your life living with guilt and regret. You can't spend your life so focused on all the death you've faced that you forget to live. And from everything you have ever told me about your parents, they would be so mad at you right now for not embracing the life that you have. You survived that car accident for a reason, Layla. I'd like to think that *we* are that reason."

"How do you do that? How do you know exactly what to say to me at exactly the right time?" I say squeezing Will's hand.

"I have no idea," Will says with a bit of a chuckle. "Tell you what…promise me that we'll sit down next week and set a date, and I won't bring it up again until then. Deal?"

I lean over the corner of the table and place a small, sweet kiss on Will's lips. "Deal."

I'm still gazing into Will's gorgeous blue eyes when I feel like someone is staring at us. I move my eye and then my head and find it was more than a feeling.

"Hey Layla! I thought that was you!" Eli says approaching our table. All I can think is that I hope I put Will's worries to rest the other day, but it does seem strange that Eli would be here of all places.

"Hey Eli. What's up? You remember John," I say casually but so Will knows I haven't dismissed his normal level of jealousy.

"Yes, of course...John," he says as they shake hands.

"What can we do for you, Eli?" Will is curt. He's not messing around in working to convey that, while I may have agree to help him out of his bind with the student paper, he is not really welcome into our world.

"Oh, I just saw you guys over here and thought I'd come say hey. So...hey! But since I'm here, you can save me a phone call, Layla. Is it ok if I come by next weekend to do the interview?" Eli stands there awkwardly as I consider his request.

"Layla and I have plans next weekend. Perhaps she can meet you on campus one day?" Will offers as an alternative. I just gave him my word that we would sit down next weekend and set a wedding date and there is no way he's letting me out of that.

"Well, I'm pretty jam packed all week. It should only take about an hour. I know an interview for the school paper doesn't scream Friday night fun, but I would be more grateful than you could ever know if I could just have a little bit of your time. Please?" Eli looks pathetic. He's in a real bind and I hate to say no to him.

"If you think it should only take about an hour, then I think Friday should be fine." Will squeezes my knee under the table – a definite sign that he is not happy with me. "I'll text you my address. Can you be there at five?"

"That'd be so great! Thank you so much, Layla! I appreciate you, too, John. I don't blame you for being a little hesitant. Layla seems like the kind of girl a guy would do anything for. You'll be there right? I mean, you guys are engaged. I can't exactly interview Layla without her other half being there!"

"Oh, yeah...I'll be there," Will says with a smirk. Like he's going to let me out of his sight with some guy we both just met. I have to admit that I do like being protected by Will. It makes me feel safe.

"Awesome! Ok...let me get out of your hair. You two did not come out tonight to have a third wheel talking your ear off." Eli starts walking backward, making his way to the front of the restaurant. "If I don't see you around campus, I'll see you on Friday! Thanks, again!"

I'm getting a stare-down again, only this time it's from Will.

"What?" I ask.

"You know what," he says.

"I'm not dodging the wedding planning. I swear! He's in a bind! Helping out a new friend at school is a very *normal* thing to do. And it's only going to take, like, an hour. If he's there at five, we'll be done by six or so. Then we have the rest of the evening and weekend to argue over our wedding date and the kind of wedding we're going to have. Ok?" I smile and tilt my head playfully at Will. "You love me, remember!"

"How could I ever forget?" Will laughs quietly and kisses me on the cheek. "Ok...normal it is! Are you ready to go?"

"Done so soon?"

"I have a very *normal* date planned for us tomorrow. Not that it starts early...I just want to take you home and make out with you on your couch. You know...just your *normal* date stuff."

"Ordinary making out sounds like fun! We'll have to be extra quiet because we don't want my parents or my uncle to hear us," I whisper. Will smiles and motions for the check.

"I've noticed you've been doing that more lately: referring to Luke and Claire as your parents," he says.

"Yeah. It started out as just being an easier way to talk casually about my family without going into the whole mess about my parents. But the more I did it, the more it seemed a better fit. I haven't called them Mom or Dad to their faces yet, but I have a feeling it's going to happen sooner or later. The only problem is, that when I think about actually making that switch, I can't help but think about the problems between my dad and Luke and Gram and Gramps. I never did talk to Luke about the whole not-defending-him-in-court thing. It feels like it's looming out there. I don't know if I have questions or not, and if I do, if they're even about the explosion at the cosmetics factory," I tell him.

"Just tell them that. Layla, they're going to understand. They want to fill in any blanks you may have. Honey, you were only twelve when they died. I'm sure there are some things you want to know about your parents that aren't criminally related. Promise me you'll talk to Luke and Claire soon, ok?"

"I'm promising an awful lot tonight," I jest.

"Yes, well, that ring on your finger is the biggest promise of all, and you can't take that back!" Will grabs my hand and leads me out of the restaurant.

I spend the drive home in quiet anticipation of our make out session. It's been a while since we've been close and I'm actually a little nervous. I don't worry about Will stepping over any lines. He's always been so incredibly honorable…no matter how many times I tempt him. He's committed to us waiting, which is why he's probably a little anxious to get a wedding date set.

Well what d'ya know? I just found my motivation for setting my wedding date!

Chapter 24

I've been flipping through the pages of my parents' wedding album for hours. Staring, examining each picture…hoping to extrapolate something more about them, but every picture, every scene, tells me what I already know. In the midst of the big hair of the 80's, when wedding fashion called for puffy sleeves and headpieces with veils that looked like they could snap your head off, my mother walked her own path. On her wedding day she wore a long, flowy, soft white dress that made her look like a Greek goddess, a crown of white daisies in her hair, and, of course, no shoes. Yes, my mother was a card-carrying, tree-hugging, granola-crunching hippy.

Oh, my gosh. I can't believe I haven't noticed this until now. The flowers, the brick path…they were married in the gardens Will took me to in the fall! I immediately want to go back there. I want to walk the brick path again knowing this time that my mother took it as she stepped closer to her life with my father. I want to touch the same flowers and trees she did. And I want to hear the wind whip through the leaves the same way she did 25 years ago.

"Layla?" I hear Luke's soft voice say at my open door. "It's getting late. Are you ready for some dinner? Claire's got a pot of spaghetti sauce simmering. Should be her best one yet," he smiles.

"Tell me about them," I say quietly.

"What would you like to know?" I love that Luke doesn't need to ask me a clarifying question to understand what I need. He just knows, like a father knows his child. He sits beside my limp body on the bed and rubs a few small circles on my back.

"Was it really the legal stuff that tore you all apart?" I breathe a heavy sigh having felt a sense of release by Luke's comforting touch.

"No. Gram did that," he says without hesitation. "She was a hard woman and didn't like inconveniences. Your father was eleven when I was born. No one, let alone John, was expecting a baby to interrupt their lives. But there I was, completely oblivious to the disruption I was causing.

"We both heard the phrase 'Why can't you be like your brother?' more times than either of us could count. It was ridiculous, really. John was so much older than me that there was no reason for either of us to be like the other. But...he was my older brother and I *wanted* to be just like him. He was so incredibly smart, and could make or build anything." There's a look of admiration on Luke's face and I can see that, despite any differences, he really did love and respect his brother.

"By the time I was in kindergarten and he was a senior, my mere existence was a problem. I learned early on that I was going to have to carry my own...make sure I didn't cause any problems for our parents, or John. But there was always this competition. Looking back, it's so dumb. I was just this little kid, trying to keep up with the intelligence and talent of a grown man." He sighs and looks lighter. I don't think he's spoken of this with anyone outside of Claire. It must be a great relief sharing this with the only other person on the planet who knows what Gram was like. I understand what he's saying and can see how she would create dissention between them in some wacked out effort to make them into men.

"You're in their wedding pictures. I guess things were good at some point?" I open up the album to a page with a picture of Luke and my father. He's got his arm around Luke's shoulder, a tall young man now, and they're both smiling.

"Yeah...things got a little better as we got older. There were times we were able to put aside our lack of interest in each other for the greater good."

"But I don't see Gram or Gramps anywhere in here," I say, flipping through the pages in case I missed them somehow.

"Nope. Gram refused to go to their wedding. And Gramps only didn't go because he had to show support to his wife. Gram didn't like your mom, but don't take any offense to that. She didn't like anyone. No one was good enough for her boys."

"She didn't like Claire?" I'm astonished. How does anyone *not* like Claire?

"Well…she lightened up a bit by the time Claire and I got married. Your parents had been married for ten years by the time my wedding rolled around. Gram and Gramps didn't come to ours either, but that was because we did a small destination wedding in the Caribbean. It was literally us and, like ten of our friends who thanked us for giving them an excuse to go on vacation."

"Where were Claire's parents?" I ask, hoping that Claire didn't come from the same stressful family that Luke and I did.

"That's…that's a story for Claire to tell you," he says. I understand and don't ask any more about it. I know better than anyone that there are stories that can only be told by their owners.

"So, since you had never been close, the thing with my dad and the cosmetics lab just exacerbated the situation," I say, doing the math.

"Yeah. Had that not happened, I'd like to think that we would have grown into a more civil relationship. And you would have met Penny," Luke says with a smile. He can't help but beam when he says her name. I can't imagine losing a child at just two in such a tragic way. But I'm so happy that I can be here and be part of the new family they've created. "Layla, I wish I could tell you more about your parents. I wish I *knew* more to tell you, but our life as a family was not what I think any of us wanted it to be. I don't really know what Gram and Gramps were like before I got there. I don't know if she was soft or kind. I don't know if your father ever had a good, loving relationship with either of them.

"But what I *do* know, what I *can* tell you about them, is that they loved you more than words or deeds could have ever expressed. So don't look at

217

them in relationship to me or Gram or Gramps. Look at them as you always did. See them as the parents they were to you. Reflect on the goodness that they cultivated in you. And know that even though they're gone, they would want you to grab the bull by the horns and take on this one and only life you've been given."

I can't speak so I wrap my arms tightly around Luke's neck and squeeze. He crushes me in a hard embrace as we sit there for a long time. There's a knock at my door and I see Claire and Will standing there with anticipation in their eyes.

"Come here," Will says, extending his hand. "We have to do something."

I've learned not to question so much when Will says we're going to do something. Whatever it is I know his heart was full of love as he put it together.

All four of us make our way downstairs and out the back door, not stopping until we reach the end of the dock. There's a large box with white, billowy things overflowing from it and I feel my brow furrow as I try to make out what they are. Before I can come to any conclusions, Will pulls the objects from the box and hands one to each of us.

"It's a floating lantern," Will says answering my unspoken inquiry. "It's time for some closure, Layla."

"I don't understand," I say quietly.

"I'll start." Luke takes a lighter from his pocket and lights the wick on each of our lanterns, instructing me to hold it so the heat from the flame can fill the ballooning top. "This is for John and Elisabeth. They were taken from us far too soon. For my brother…who I hope knew just how much I loved him." With that, Luke lets go of his lantern and lets it float up and over the lake, releasing with it his sadness for having lost his brother so much earlier than my father actually died.

My heart begins to beat quickly, and my breathing becomes slightly labored. I don't know that I can get through another memorial like I did with my friends for Will. It was so painful, but…it really did help me begin to move forward. When Mom and Dad died not a single person asked me how I was doing or what I was feeling – with the exception of the mandated counseling I attended. Talking with Luke and sharing with Will about my parents has been incredibly helpful, but ever since Will and I got engaged I've been feeling stuck. I can't escape the guilt I feel for being so happy in a place I wouldn't be in had my parents not died that horrific night.

"This is for Marcus, who never knew the unconditional love of a family." Claire's soft voice fills the air like sweet perfume. She smiles sadly and releases her lantern. I know Claire felt so deeply for Marcus when she found out how terrible his mother had been to him all those years. His mother had an incredible opportunity to replace the cruelty of Gregory Meyer with love and joy, but she threw that away for her own selfish gain.

"This is for John and Elisabeth…for all they did to make Layla who she is…for giving life to the one person who makes my life complete." Will releases his lantern and gives me a long look, letting me know that it's ok to say whatever I have to say…to feel whatever I need to feel right now.

I open my mouth to speak but only sobs pour out. I don't want to cry over them again. I don't want to feel the pain again. I learned how to shove it down so deep that I don't feel anything. But now…in this moment…being given permission to speak of them like this, to mourn. I don't know how to mourn them. I'm so angry for allowing Gram to shut me up so tightly that I didn't give them what they deserved from me, their daughter, their only child. I listened to that woman when she told me we were not to talk of them again. I erased them from my life because she was so hard and bitter and angry. I didn't do what my parents taught me to do.

"I'm so sorry," I whimper. "Mom, Dad, I'm so sorry I believed I had to pretend you never existed. I'm so sorry that I didn't say good-bye to you the way you deserved."

"Now's the time, baby. They're listening," Will says putting his arm around my shoulder.

I try to stop crying and when I can't, decide to push through the tears and get out as much as I can. It's been bottled up so long that I'm not sure if any of it will be coherent, but it's all I've got and I can't pretend that I don't want to let it out.

"This is for Mom and Dad…for loving me…for always taking care of me," I choke out in between sobs. "This is for my parents who taught me how to fight for what I love and believe in. I'm so sorry I forgot how to do that for so long. I promise not to let you down anymore. You were the best parents a kid could ask for." I take a deep breath before I make my final statements and find real closure to all that has burdened me for the last seven years. "This is for Gramps…for being my ray of sunshine in an otherwise dark place. And for Gram…" I consider finding something kind to say, but I can't. "…the most I can say is…thank you…thank you for my first father, John…and my second father, Luke. I choose to forgive you. I'm not going to let what you did to me keep me from the life I have in front of me now. I'm letting you all go now. I'm moving forward with my life, just like my parents would want me to." I squeeze my eyes shut and whisper *I love you* to my parents and let my lantern go. I watch it float away for a few long minutes before I feel arms, lots of arms, surrounding me.

"Thank you," I say to Will. "Somehow you always know exactly what I need. I love you."

"I love you, too." Will kisses the top of my head and I feel a smile come to my face. It seems like an odd time to be smiling, but I realize that, for the absolute first time in my life, I'm at peace.

"Layla, I know what you said, about the *father* thing, I just want you to know that…" Luke starts but I have to cut him off. This really has been a long time coming.

"I need parents – a mother, and a father. I need to say those words, call someone by those names. Please…Dad?"

"Oh, Layla!" Luke and Claire are on me in the fiercest hug I've ever received.

"We love you so much!" Claire says through tears.

"I love you, too…Mom."

Chapter 25

I haul my heavy bags in from the car and plop them down on the coffee table in the Great Room. There are so many that the stack of slick pages slide out and scatter across the table, with some falling to the floor. I had only planned on buying a few, but after I started looking at all the choices I just couldn't make up my mind. The look on the cashier's face was priceless, especially after she caught a glimpse of the gorgeous ring on my left hand.

"What's all this?" Claire asks helping me pick up my mess. She flips through a magazine and raises her eyebrows in excitement. "Bridal magazines?"

"Yeah. I promised Will we would set a date this weekend. I've been avoiding it like the plague, but now…I'm actually getting really excited," I tell her.

I was on my way to excitement last weekend when Will and I talked about setting a date, but after the lanterns on my parents' anniversary…everything is so different. I had no idea just how much I had been carrying. I guess I had been shoving it down so long, I forgot just how much there was. I thought about being angry at Gram for the rest of my life. And, to be honest, it would be easier to be one of Gram's victims – one of the people whose lives she destroyed with her harsh words and cold heart. The lack of people in attendance at her funeral was evidence that I wasn't the only one she hurt. I'm not that girl anymore, though. I'm Luke and Claire's daughter. I'm Will's fiancée. And that girl? She's strong, tenacious, independent, and full of love and goodness. That is who I am.

I'll never understand how someone as wonderful as Gramps married someone like Gram. I can only think that at one time in her life she was kind and good. I'll never know, but I'd like to think that something happened to her and she wasn't as lucky as me to be surrounded by people who cared more deeply for her than she does herself. That somehow, that was the one time Gramps missed the mark. All of that is in the past now. My future is waiting for me, and I'm not going to delay any longer.

"I'm glad you're finally embracing your engagement!" Claire says hugging me.

"Mom, uh…how are *you* doing with this?" I ask.

"What do you mean?"

"Well…I don't really know how to say this, but…I keep thinking about Penny," I say hesitantly. I can't pretend that my getting married isn't a reminder of what they lost when Penny died. I want them to enjoy all the wedding planning and not be sad because it's not Penny's wedding they're planning.

"Layla, I'd be lying if I said I hadn't thought of her, too. Luke and I have let go of all that we lost that day. We will always be sad that we won't have all the momentous occasions with her that we anticipated having, but we'll also be eternally happy having those moments with you. You filled part of the Penny-shaped hole in our hearts. We couldn't be happier to be a part of all the special things that are to come for you. *You* are our daughter, too, and we will celebrate with you as such."

"I wish I had known her."

"I do, too." Claire kisses my cheek and moves back to the table to shuffle through the magazines. "Are you going to show all of these to Will?"

"I don't know. I want us to make some decisions together. Will wants a big to-do, but honestly, I'd be happy getting married in the gardens like my parents. It's not like we'll have a ton of people to invite. I just can't see myself walking down a long aisle in a mostly empty church."

"Well, you've got time, don't you? When *are* you considering having the wedding?" Claire asks.

"Will would like it to happen tomorrow. I would like to wait until the suffix 'teen' is not part of my age. That would be a little over a year from now. It'll be summer, but the middle of my junior year. I don't know..."

"Layla? You don't seem sure about this. Is everything ok?" Claire's soothing tone always puts me at ease. And, like a mother, she's learned how to read my face and my own delivery and tone.

"Yes, everything is fine. I *want* to marry Will. Sometimes, though, I just feel like...well...we haven't had very long together when we weren't running or being secretive. I feel like things just calmed down. I'm just afraid that we haven't had time to get to know each other without being in survival mode. Does that make sense?"

"That makes perfect sense. You and Will have had quite a journey. I don't think there's any doubt that you and Will were made for each other. You love him, and he loves you. And even though you said 'yes' and you're wearing that gorgeous ring, only you know when you'll be ready to walk down the aisle, brick path, or sandy beach and say *forever* to him. There is no rush, Layla, but because I know you love Will with every fiber of your being, don't let those fears overtake you and convince you that this isn't right. You have fought long and hard for your and Will's love. To let anything come between you now, even your own qualms, would be a travesty. Set a date that gives you time to have all the normalcy of dating and being engaged that you need."

Claire is right. She's usually right. Will and I have a love most people only dream about. The lengths that we have gone to be together are what great love stories are made of. We *do* have time. We have all the time we need. And while I want to be Will's wife more than anything, there really is no rush. I hope I can convince Will of this. I think that once we have a date set, no matter when it is, he'll be happy that there will be a tunnel to go through and a light in the foreseeable future.

"Thanks, Mom," I say smiling. It feels so good to say that. I've missed the talks my mother and I had about all the various and sundry things a pre-teen talks to her mother about. I remember one of the last conversations I had with my mother about a friend at school who wasn't acting very much like a friend. She told me not to be afraid to tell my friend that she had hurt my feelings, and that if she didn't apologize then she wasn't my friend to begin with anyway. Sound advice to an 11-year-old. "Oh, gosh! We need to get dinner in the oven if it's going to be ready when Eli's done interviewing me for the paper."

"Right! I've had the meat marinating overnight, so it should be ready by now. What else did I need to do to it?" Claire asks. Her cooking has improved by leaps and bounds, but she's still a little scared when it comes to using the oven, which is so funny to me since the oven is the easiest thing in the world. Set the temperature, put the food in, and wait for the timer to go off. She's my mom, and I wouldn't have her any other way.

The house is starting to smell insanely good with the aroma of beef stew cooking to perfection, low and slow, in the oven. The men of the house have descended upon the kitchen, begging for a taste. When Will walks through the front door the first thing out of his mouth is the sound of rejoicing.

"Please, God, let that be the smell of Layla's beef stew!"

"Of course! What else would it be?" Will kisses me and whispers *thank you* into my ear. "It's a special night so I thought I'd make your favorite."

"Special night?" he says with a wink.

"Don't tell me that setting our wedding date doesn't constitute a special night!" I slap Will gently on his stomach and he grabs me around the waist pulling me closer to him.

"It will be the second most special night ever," he says sweetly. "I can hardly wait to argue over it with you."

"Silly! We won't have to argue if you just concede that the date that I pick is the best!" Will squeezes me and sneaks a brief tickle to my side, sending me flailing. "Will!"

"Ok, ok, you two," Wes says.

"Oh, like you and Eliana aren't as bad!" I tease.

Wes and Eliana have been going strong since New Year's. It was a little hard for Will to let go at first. He's been so protective of his mom for so long that he just, instinctively, wants to keep her from getting hurt. He spoke with Wes on several occasions, making sure Wes knew how fragile she was. Eliana spent so long with Gregory that she's been learning how to say *no* and assert herself. If Wes didn't encourage that, it could be very easy for her to fall back into the quiet, submissive woman she was before. Fortunately for her, Wes is all too familiar with Gregory Meyer and has known how to challenge Eliana. I once heard him telling her that she needed to tell him no because he was being unreasonable. A little lover's quarrel that seemed to have turned out just fine by the way I saw them kissing and making up.

The doorbell rings, putting a damper on the teasing I was planning on giving Wes. You'd think the President was standing at our doorstep, the way the whole family left the kitchen and made their way to the Great Room. When I open the door Eli is standing there looking thankful.

"Hey Layla! Thanks again for doing this. You have no idea what this means to me!" he says walking into the house.

"It's no problem, Eli. Seriously!"

"Wow! It smells amazing in here!" he says, closing his eyes and savoring the aroma of my to-die-for beef stew.

"Oh, thanks! We've got a family meal planned for tonight when you're done grilling me." I don't want to be rude, but I want to be clear that we have other plans for tonight that do not include Eli. Will smiles at me, recognizing my effort to stay committed to our plans of setting our wedding date tonight.

"That's cool. I'll try not to take up too much of your time then. Oh, awesome! Your whole family is here!" he says, finally noticing my entourage.

"Yeah, I hope that's ok. We're kind of ridiculously happy together," I tell him. I don't care if he thinks it's weird that we're so close. No one will ever understand the life we've lead and how bonded we are. I never want us to be a family that complains about each other. We may do things that get on each other's nerves, but family is family and nothing will ever change that.

"That's perfect, actually," he says with a smile.

"These are my parents, Luke and Claire. This is John's mom, Elisabeth, and my Uncle Wes. And, of course, you know John," I say in a round of introductions. Handshakes go all around accompanied by *hellos* and *nice to meet yous.*

"Wow, I can't believe how great this is. You know, the student spotlight interview usually just has the student. This is totally bonus!" Eli says as he pulls a huge binder from his backpack. "I've got a lot I'd love to know. Actually, if it's ok, can I ask John a question first?"

"Me? Uh…sure, I guess," Will looks puzzled but goes with the flow.

"Great!" Eli flips through a few sections in his binder, finally landing on the section he was looking for. Finding it, he looks straight at Will with the most serious face and says, "Are you sure your name is John, because you look more like a Will to me."

It takes less than three second for Luke, Wes, and Will to have Eli pinned to the floor on his chest. The three of them were a blur of hair, skin, and clothing as Claire, Eliana, and I instinctively jumped back and out of their way.

How can this be happening? How could Eli possibly know about our family's secret? Surely he wasn't clued in by any pre-interview research he may have done on me.

"You have exactly five second to tell us who you are and what you want." Furtick has appeared and is in full-on security mode. I thought it had been silly to keep Wes on the payroll as private security but am thanking my lucky stars that he's here now.

"C'mon, guys, ease up!" Eli chokes out. It's clear he's having trouble breathing. Understandable, considering he's got three grown men all over six feet tall holding him to the ground.

"Three," Wes advises.

"Ok, ok…I can't breathe, man! Get off me and I'll tell you. I promise!"

The guys release their hold on him and Wes flips him over and drags him from the floor. After he's been tossed into a chair, Wes sits on the coffee table in front of him in the most intimidating pose I've ever seen on him. His fingers are laced together and his elbows are on his knees.

"Talk," he says.

"Layla…" Eli starts.

"You don't talk to her," Will says. "Who are you?"

"My name really is Eli Briggs," he says after a beat. "But I'm not with the school paper. My father was an investigative reporter for the Charlotte Observer. He was investigating Gregory Meyer when he died last year. Meyer killed him."

"What?" Eliana's eyes are huge and she's trembling.

"Claire, take her in the kitchen," Luke instructs. "Layla, you go, too."

"No. I'm not going anywhere." I look at Luke and he knows I'm serious. I brought this into our home and I have to know what's going on. I won't wait for some watered down report from them.

"What do you mean Gregory killed your father?" Luke asks.

"My father, Alexander Briggs, spent five years investigating the bastard…all his ethics violations and flagrant abuses of the law. And just when he was so close to blowing Meyer out of the water, he dies." Eli's eyes are fiery. They aren't the same soft and friendly eyes I met in the coffee shop. They're on a mission.

"You still haven't told us how Gregory Meyer killed your father," Wes says. "I'm getting impatient. You don't want to see me lose my patience."

"He had his goons give my father a pretty severe beating. My dad's heart wasn't so great. At least they took him to the hospital after they beat the crap out of him, but even that couldn't save him. His heart just wasn't strong enough to handle the stress. He had a heart attack." Eli's tone is filled with disgust. I understand his hatred for Gregory Meyer. It's a common thread we all share. "Can I show you something?"

Wes nods and shifts his position slightly so Eli can retrieve his binder. He pulls out a photo of him and his father. They're sitting on a picnic table on what looks like a beautiful day with gorgeous Carolina Blue skies behind them. His father, an older, attractive man with salt-and-pepper hair, looks happy. He also looks familiar.

I see Wes' eyes get big and he immediately stands up. We make the same discovery at the same time. I've never seen Wes' eyes so filled with fear. He excuses himself leaving Luke and Will with confused expressions painted on their faces. I follow Wes out, knowing that I am the only who can reach him right now.

"Two, Layla. Two! I'm responsible for the deaths of two men!" he says as I meet him on the patio. Wes paces a few times before landing on a bench and covering his face with his hands.

This has to be devastating for him. The man in that picture is the same man I saw Wes and Cline beating that day outside the law firm. It's difficult to process. Until now he had been no one. I never considered that he could be someone's husband or father. I was sad for him at the time and hoped the wrath of Gregory Meyer would be short, but that wasn't the case.

"You took him to the hospital, Wes," I say reassuringly. "You weren't some monster that beat him up and left him for dead. Your heart has always known the right thing to do. You did your best, Wes."

"I don't know how to fix this."

"You can't." I sigh. "You know, when Meyer came to my family and tried to tear me apart from Luke and Claire with his *House Call*, I was furious. I was furious at Luke and Claire for not telling me about my father. I was furious at my father for doing something so stupid, but Will helped me realize that the person to be furious with was Meyer. All he does is destroy people's lives.

"Wes, he took advantage of you and manipulated you. He didn't care that you would lose everything that was important to you. You have to see it for what it is. Now, I don't know what Eli wants, exactly, but if he was going to expose us, don't you think he would have done it by now? You have to let this go. Take that rage you're feeling and direct it where it needs to go."

"You really are the best," he says squeezing an arm around me.

"I love you, Wes. You're my family and I will always look out for you. Are you ready to go back in and see what Eli wants?"

"Yeah, but I can't make any promises. If he threatens you…"

"Let's just cross that bridge when we get to it, ok?"

We enter the Great Room in time to hear the tail end of what sounds like Luke summing up whatever it is that Eli is after. It sounds like he wants the dirt that Luke has been collecting all these years. I don't know if Luke is actually considering giving it to Eli or not. It's a real risk. Even if Eli doesn't divulge his source, there's no way Meyer won't know that Luke gave it up because there are things that only Luke knows. Perhaps Luke won't give him those pieces of evidence.

"So tell me why I shouldn't throw you in my trunk and leave you stranded in the middle of the Everglades?" Wes says.

"Because I'm on your side." Eli is standing now and has summoned the audacity to take an intimidating stance in front of Wes. He's a lot braver than I realized. "I want to take down Gregory Meyer just as much, if not more, than all of you. I don't care about your little secret here. Kudos to you for pulling it off, though. I don't want to expose you. I want to crush Meyer."

"Does your editor know you're here?" Luke asks.

"Um…" Eli hesitates.

"Does your paper know you're here continuing your father's investigation?" Luke says with more aggression.

"I'm not working for the paper. I'm here on my own." Eli looks away, like he just got caught with his hand in the cookie jar.

"Are you kidding me?" Wes moves forward and Eli takes more than the coordinating steps backward.

"I'm not going to reveal my sources!" Eli says in his defense.

"It doesn't matter! You're not affiliated with a news agency! You don't have the right of protected sources!" Wes is back to pacing again. I imagine it's because he's afraid that if he doesn't move away from him, Eli is going to end up face down on the floor again.

"You have no idea what you've done. You came down here, snooped around, and put our lives at risk so you could somehow avenge your father's death?" Will moves in on Eli, closing the distance between them so they're toe-to-toe. "I love this girl with every breath I breathe. I have and will continue to move mountains so that I can spend the rest of my life with her. If you have jeopardized that in *any* way, be clear on one thing: I. Will. End. You." Will takes my hand and, without saying a word, takes me to our place on the dock.

Chapter 26

I'm quiet while Will moves around the dock, sporadically whispering and sometimes yelling about taking chances and risking lives. In all that we have been through I have never seen him like this. The night he told me he loved me before his father questioned me at dinner, the day he came to me and suggested we run away together, and not even the day after graduation when he knew he was leaving me to begin the charade of his disappearance compare to the torment of feelings Will is experiencing right now.

"Will?" I say softly.

"What?" His reply is sharp and stings a little at first until my mind and heart register that his cutting tone is not directed at me.

"We need to talk about this," I tell him.

"What is there to talk about? Oh, wait, yes, I know…let's talk about where we're going because we can't stay here anymore!"

"Will…please…"

"Please, what? What, Layla?"

"Please can you calm down? You're scaring me."

Will stops pacing and looks at me seriously. Taking me by the shoulders my breath catches and I feel the intensity Will is intending to convey. "I have risked not only my life, but my mother's life, so you and I could be together. And this dick comes in here and starts overturning every rock we've hidden under just so he can avenge the death of his equally nosey father. So, no, Layla, I will not calm down." I wince a little and Will realizes that he's squeezing my arms tighter and tighter with every passing moment. Releasing me he backs up a step and runs his fingers through his hair.

"We can figure this out," I say. "Let's just stop, put everything on hold for a minute, and really think about this."

"Put everything on hold. Right. Well lucky for you Eli showed his hand when he did, otherwise you'd be stuck setting a wedding date with me."

"What's that supposed to mean?" I say, not hiding how offended I am.

"C'mon, Layla…really?"

"We talked about this. I thought you understood where I was coming from. Last week…the lanters…" I'm astonished and so incredibly hurt that Will would think, especially after our talk at the restaurant, that I don't want to marry him. The bubble of excitement that I have been blowing for the past week just burst.

"Yeah, well…" Will turns away from me and faces the water. Putting his hands on two posts I can see his back rise and fall with his heavy breathing.

"You know what?" I say, calming myself. "You're upset right now. There's a lot going on. So…I'm going to go inside and give you some time to think."

Will doesn't say anything in reply. He just stands there, looking out on the water.

I'm proud of myself as I walk calmly, if not just a tad bit quickly, back to the house. What I wanted to tell him was that he was being a total and undeniable jerk. That his implication that I didn't want to marry him was the harshest thing he's ever said to me, and that he's not the only one who has made sacrifices for us to be together.

But what if… What if all of it was for nothing? Not *nothing* but…just not forever. What if Will and I aren't really meant to be together forever? What if we just served a good and solid purpose in each other's lives for a reason? I needed his love so I could be strong enough to move past the torment of my life with Gram, and he needed my love to gain the strength he needed in order to move out from under the tyrannical rule of his father. And now, here we are, two people trying to move forward in the direction we thought we were supposed to go when it seems there is sign after sign that there is no moving forward.

I stop as I approach the back door and take a deep breath. Just like Will, I'm letting all this insanity and stress get to me. There is no doubt in my rational mind that Will and I belong together. I may still have some things to overcome, but I know that once things settle down again, Will and I will be able to handle them together.

Eli is still here, only now he's back in the chair Wes put him in when we started this disastrous discovery. He's yelling at Wes again, which tells me Wes hasn't unleashed his wrath on him...yet. I'm proud of my bonus uncle. I know it's taking an incredible amount of restraint not to *make* Eli shut up.

"Dad, what's he doing?" I ask as I watch Wes rummage through Eli's bag.

"He's looking for all the notes Eli has taken on us since he's been here. Turns out he'd been following you for a week before he met you in the coffee house," Luke says.

"Geez! What is it about me that says 'please stalk me'?" I can't believe I'm finding a place for a bit of humor here, but I suppose it's either laugh or cry.

"Ok, that's all of it here. Are there any more notes about Layla anywhere else? And before you consider lying to me, you should know that I have very effective ways of finding things out." Wes is full on Furtick and I can't help but smile a little. Furtick saved my life and, while I love Wes, I don't want Furtick to ever go away completely.

"Yes...that's all I had on Layla and Will. Do you have to be such a douche?" Eli says. I don't think this has gone exactly as he thought it would. It's his fault. He stalked me, misrepresented himself, and ambushed us in our own home.

"It's part of my charm," Wes smirks. "Where did your father keep the stuff he found on Meyer?"

"I've got it," Eli tells him. "There's a hidden compartment in my bag."

"What? You've got it *on* you? Luke! Get over here!" Wes is frantically searching through Eli's bag again. "This idiot has the Meyer evidence *on* him!"

"These aren't the originals. Is this the only copy?" Luke asks, thumbing through the pages, being the calm to Wes' storm.

"Yes. The originals were in my father's safe deposit box. I made this copy before…" Eli starts as he looks as me.

"Before what, Eli?" I ask.

"Before someone broke into it and stole it."

"You're an idiot," Will says, startling me with his presence. "If you think for a minute that my father isn't going to toss your place and have you followed to make sure there are no copies, you're stupider than you look."

Will is calm now…at peace. He looks at me and takes my hand in his. His eyes are bloodshot and his face is stained with tears. I stare into his eyes that are now so much bluer after crying and see the pain that was misdirected on the dock. He's clearly had time to run the gamut of emotions that were going wild within him and come to some kind of resolution. He's in a much better place to have a rational conversation.

"Wes, can you check on…" Luke begins, but Wes is already down the hall and in the office doing whatever it is that Wes does to make sure we're all protected.

"My guy on the inside says they've already tossed his apartment. He must have left town before they got anyone on his tail. They're exhausting all the search efforts before nosey-boy over here gets a physical shake-down," Wes reports as he re-enters the room.

"Eli, what is it that you want from us?" I ask, adding a little softness to the otherwise overly-testosterone filled room. They've done their due diligence and thoroughly scared the crap out of Eli, even though he's trying not to show it. It's time for a more gentle approach and since Claire is still in the kitchen with Eliana, it looks like I'm up to bat.

"All I want is your help in taking Meyer down. I know, from my father's notes, that you were his closest confidant," he says to Luke.

"I wouldn't use that term. But…when it came to business, I knew more than anyone…more than I should." Luke considers all he knows and it visibly shakes him to his core.

"Why didn't you just report him?" I ask. "Isn't there an ethics committee, or something?"

"It's a very hazy line. Greg got around a lot of things by having me on retainer as his attorney. It's unusual to do that within the same firm, but Greg doesn't typically follow the norm. Under attorney-client privilege, I can't divulge any crime that he told me about."

"But that doesn't mean I can't," Wes says. "The smartest thing Luke ever did was to suggest that Taylor, Cline, and I keep records of all interaction with Meyer…and record our conversations."

"You have recorded proof? Oh, this is awesome!" Eli charges to his backpack and scavenges for a pad of paper to start writing.

"He can't hear those recordings, Luke," Wes whispers.

"I know. He'll leak them and then the case Agent Croft's been building will be destroyed. But…that's not what you mean, is it?" Luke asks quietly.

Wes takes a moment before speaking. "I just don't think he wants to hear his father having the crap beat out of him."

Luke gives Wes a nod and redirects his attention to Eli who is still searching under the mess Wes made for something to write on.

I love that Luke didn't even flinch when Wes told him about Eli's dad. Luke knows that Wes was working under duress and would never, out of his own volition, beat up a total stranger. They have the kind of brotherhood it seems he wasn't able to have with my father. My heart leaps for them both, knowing that their bond grows stronger every day.

"Eli, you can't write any of this down," Luke instructs him.

"Why not? This is the stuff that's going to take him down," Eli retorts.

"Because you're not a member of the press doing investigative research. You're a son on a mission to avenge his father's death. There's a difference. Now…" Luke says before a deep breath, "I'm willing to work with you but every single aspect of this arrangement is on my terms. This is about my wife and my daughter and I do not take their lives lightly."

"I thought she was your niece?" Eli has an understandable look of confusion on his face.

"You really want to argue?" Luke counters. Eli shakes his head as Wes takes a half step toward him. "Good. Now do we have a deal?"

It takes a good minute before Eli replies. I know this isn't how he imagined getting Gregory Meyer to pay for how he destroyed his own family's life, but if he wants to see justice, he's going to have to get on board.

"Deal. What do we do now?"

"*We* do not do anything. Wes and I will take your father's notes and compare them with what each of us has. We'll figure out what he's got that we can corroborate and not draw attention to ourselves. *You* are going home. You're going to go back to school or work or whatever it was you were doing before you started this mission of yours. We'll contact you." Luke's directive is clear and to the point but is not a satisfactory solution to Eli's quest.

"NO! I didn't bust my ass to get this close just to be tossed out!"

"I understand that you want to have a heavy hand in bringing Meyer down, but you're not equipped to do that. You're a little boy who's pissed off. If you go to the paper with your sob story they're going to pat you on the back, tell you how sorry they are, and send you off. Why? Because *none* of them, no matter how much evidence you have, wants to put their lives on the line to take down *the* Gregory Meyer. You're an even bigger

237

idiot if you think he doesn't have every newspaper within a hundred mile radius in his back pocket.

"And if you're actually daring enough to go to Meyer with it in some ridiculous attempt in getting him to admit his wrong-doing, well pick out a matching headstone next to your father's because that's where you're going to end up.

"So pull yourself together and know that you did the best you could. Let us handle things from here, and I swear to God, if you breathe a word of our secret to anyone, you'll wish you had faced Gregory Meyer's wrath and not mine." Wes always has a way of laying everything out on the table and not holding back. You never have to wonder where he stands.

"How do I know that you're not going to just cut me out of this all together? How can I trust that you're going to keep me in the loop?" Eli is pissed off and not ready to back down.

"What difference does it make? The goal is to take Meyer down. The *key* is to be patient. You can't rush this, Eli. You have to know who you're talking to, who you can trust, and you can't go shooting off at the mouth. It's a process that you're not ready for." Furtick sighs and I see him approach Eli in a way I didn't think he used in situations like this. "Listen, Eli," he says sitting on the coffee table opposite of Eli again. "I know how it feels to have someone take something so important from you. You're so filled with rage that you can barely see straight. All you want is for that person to pay for what they've done. Trust me – I know.

"I thought Meyer was helping me, but…it didn't take long to realize that Gregory Meyer doesn't do anything for anyone that isn't going to benefit him more in the end. He took more from me than I would have lost if I had never met him. We are on the same side. You've done your part. Let us take over from here and I *promise* you Meyer will pay."

Eli looks at me as if I'm his gauge. He barely knows me but somehow is looking to me for some verification of what Wes has just told him…as if whatever I say is going to convince him of what he should do now. This is clear evidence that Wes is right about Eli not being ready. He's not patient enough to strategically find out who can and can't be trusted. Were he to carry this investigation any further on his own, I fear he'd most certainly meet the same fate as his father. He just happened to get it right this time with me.

"You can trust us, Eli," I say to him.

"Ok," he says after a deep breath and a long beat.

"We'll be in touch. And I'll have one of my guys in Charlotte keep an eye on you. He'll make contact once so you know he's with us, but after that he'll be a ghost." Wes extends his hand and Eli grips it for a hard shake. "Thank you, Eli."

I help Eli gather what's left of the contents of his backpack and walk him to the front door. Since Luke and Wes have taken everything but the blank pages in his notebook, the bag is considerably lighter than when he arrived.

"I'm sorry I lied to you, Layla. I just…" he begins.

"It's ok, Eli. I understand better than you might think. You really can trust us. If you only knew what we've all gone through together this last year, you'd know that for sure. And…I know that Wes already threatened you within an inch of your life, but it really is so important, a matter of life and death, that you don't tell anyone about Will or his mother. You know what Gregory Meyer did to your father for snooping. Imagine what he would do to Will and his mother if he knew they had pulled the wool over his eyes and gotten away with it."

"You have my word. I want Meyer to pay for what he's done not only to us, but to everyone whose life he's destroyed."

I close the door behind Eli and breathe a sigh of relief. My gut tells me that we don't have to worry about him. His commitment is to the destruction of Gregory Meyer. If he exposed us then Meyer would have the upper hand and that is the last thing Eli or any of us wants.

Chapter 27

I turn from the door and Will's eyes lock onto mine. My heart drops recalling his harsh words on the dock. With the exception of when he yelled at me after the whole thing with Marcus on Halloween , Will has never had even the slightest disagreeable tone with me. But tonight, he looked almost disgusted with me. My heart breaks a little thinking about his implication that I didn't want to marry him and I look down at my hands. I play with my engagement ring, twisting it around my finger. I start to take it off but only as a fidgeting move. I get it just past my knuckle when Will is rushing toward me.

"What are you doing?" he says frantically, shoving my ring back into place.

"What?"

"Why are you taking your ring off?"

"Oh…I wasn't really…I was just fidgeting. I…I'm not taking it off, Will," I say to reassure him. "But we need to talk."

"I'm sorry I was harsh outside. You're right. We did talk about your reasons for not setting a date, and I do understand them," he says. "Can we just move on…please?"

"No, we can't *just move on*. Will, you were really mean out there. You took something that was really difficult for me to talk about and discarded it like some lame excuse to not marry you."

"I…I can't talk about this right now. I need to check on my mom." Will walks away, leaving me standing there, alone in more ways than one.

I follow him into the kitchen after the minute it takes me to pull myself together. Luke and Wes have already explained to Eliana what Eli meant when he said that her husband killed his father. I don't know if Wes has, or ever will, tell her about his part in Alexander Briggs' death, but I hope our talk helped him put that in perspective. Regardless, I know it has made Wes determined to follow through with the promises he made to Eli.

"I'm sorry I got so upset," Eliana says.

"It's ok, Mom. There's a lot you may not know about Dad," Will says, taking his mother in his arms. I know she's going to be even more at peace now as Will's arms have that effect.

"I know more than you think I do, William. It was just difficult to hear a complete stranger say the words out loud. But…" she says releasing herself from Will and tugging the bottom of her blouse. "That man is not my responsibility any longer. It's just unfortunate that I won't be able to testify against him one day." Eliana moves from Will's side into Wes' arms seamlessly. "I have a new life now and I'm not looking back."

My heart is full watching Eliana and Wes together. He looks at her in ways Gregory Meyer isn't even capable of looking at anyone. In his eyes she finds the love and honor she was never granted by her husband. I have such high hopes for these two. I see so clearly the redemption and freedom they find in each other and I know that they're both so happy.

"I'm going to go," Will says, pulling me aside.

"Where are you going?" I say, confused.

"I'm going home, Layla."

"I know we've had quite a hiccup in our night, but…I thought we were going to talk about setting a date," I say, tears filling my eyes. I can't believe Will is walking out when we have an unresolved issue. I walk out of the kitchen, afraid the others will see my tears, pulling Will with me.

"Layla…" Will says following me outside. "You don't really want to set a wedding date tonight."

"Is that a question or a statement? Are you telling me what I don't want to do?"

"Obviously there are some things that you still have unresolved. We can't set a date while you're dealing with those things."

"The only thing that's unresolved is the fact that my *fiancé* is acting like a total jerk," I say half shouting.

"I'm being a jerk? You're the one looking for any reason to avoid setting a date! Do you even want to marry me, Layla?"

"I can't believe you just said that!" My head hurts already from the shock of his words. I leave him standing on the patio while I retrieve the unreasonable amount of bridal magazines I bought earlier today. When I return I throw the stack down in front of Will. His eyes get bigger watching them slide across the table. "Does this answer your question? You know what, I think you were right. You need to go. Now. Neither one of us is in the right frame of mind to talk about this."

I don't even wait to watch him leave. I storm through the door and poke my head into the kitchen.

"Mom..." I can't even get a full sentence out to Claire. She looks at me and nods her head, following me upstairs to my room moments after I land on my bed.

"What happened? I didn't hear what you said, but it was loud, whatever it was," Claire says lying on the bed next to me.

"We had a fight."

"That was obvious. What about?"

"He doesn't think I want to marry him."

"Why would he think that?" she asks, sitting up and moving me so my head is on her lap.

"Because I've been putting off setting a date. We were supposed to do that tonight but then Eli... He thought I was happy for the distraction."

"Were you?" Claire runs her fingers through my hair, soothing me.

"No...well, I had been putting it off, but, not any more...you saw all the bridal magazines. Mom, I want to marry Will. I just..." I move and throw my face into my pillow. "He really hurt my feelings tonight. You should have heard him. It was like he was disgusted with me or something."

"So you two had your first fight. What are you going to do about it?" she says matter-of-factly.

"*I'm* not doing anything. He was the one being a jerk!"

"Hmmm…you know, Luke and I were still in law school when we got engaged. We'd had some disagreements, but no real fights. We were under a lot of stress with finishing school, internships, and planning a wedding, so it was no surprise that one of us finally just broke.

"Luke was at my apartment all the time because it was easier to study there than at the house he shared with an ungodly number of guys. Well, I came home from a particularly hard day of classes and the terrible internship I was in to find dirty dishes and the frying pan in the sink and Luke chilled out on my couch with a beer and the last of the leftover pizza. I flipped out, yelled at him about disrespecting me, and threw the frying pan at him. I *threw* a *frying pan* at him. What kind of a crazy person does that? Do you want to know what he did?" I shake my head, not believing that Claire could ever be capable of something so undignified as throwing a frying pan. "He went back to his house and came back thirty minutes later…wearing his old football helmet. Then he looked at me and told me that if we were going to fight he thought he should be better prepared."

"Oh, my gosh. What did you do?" I say. That's actually the sweetest, funniest thing I've ever heard.

"I laughed and kissed him like I never had before. You see, Layla, I freaked out over something so stupid because I was stressed out over school and life. You and Will have faced more than anyone ever will, and Luke and I are constantly amazed at how well you've handled it. You have to cut *each other* some slack when you're having a hard time dealing with crisis. What happened tonight was a serious threat to everything Will has done to secure your life together. You have to give him space to sort through the fear that ravages him.

"You have no idea how terrified he is. He is literally petrified of losing you. Now, that doesn't excuse his hurtful words or behavior, but it should give you a point of reference when he says or does something that is uncharacteristic of him. He left everything behind for you, because he loves you."

"I didn't ask him to do that," I say in some kind of defense.

"Oh, but you did. Will told Luke about you asking him if there was any way he could stand up to his father so the two of you could be together."

"I...I wasn't seeing it like that. But...you're right. I asked Will to make it so we could be together and he did. And after all he's done...I've been so stuck in the past. What do I do?" I can't believe I've been so selfish. I challenged Will to stand up to his father, told him that was the only way we could be together. He did that and then risked his *and* his mother's life so that we could spend the rest of *our* lives together. And then I'm going to get stuck focusing on the pain of my past, and not allow myself to enjoy and live in the love I begged for? *I'm* the jerk!

"Go talk to him," she says.

"I can't. I told him to go home." I put my face in my hands and rub the tightness from it.

"He's still here. Luke's telling him the helmet story." Claire smirks and I see, once again, just how great a team she and Luke are.

When we walk downstairs I half expect Luke and Claire to high five each other, but Luke just gives her a wink and opens the door to the patio for me. As the door closes behind me I stare at Will, sitting at the table with the bridal magazines now neatly stacked in front of him.

"Seventeen. You bought seventeen bridal magazines?" he says, raising his eyebrows and smiling sweetly.

"I told you I wanted to marry you, and...I couldn't decide which one to get. They all looked overwhelmingly helpful."

"I'm sorry I was so terrible." Will stands up and his arms are around my waist in one smooth move. He pulls me tighter to him and kisses the top of my head. "You know…when I met you, I tried really hard to keep my feelings inside. Letting them out had only gotten me, or someone I cared about, hurt. Every time I was with you, though, you made me feel everything so deeply that there was no way I could keep it all in. I felt *everything* like I never had before – love, hate, lust, joy.

"I've tried really hard over the last year not to let my emotions get the best of me. I've failed too many times to count, but I'm always trying. But tonight, when I thought that it was all over, that everything we had worked so hard for was blowing up in our faces… I knew I was going to have to run. What I didn't know was if you'd come with me." Will shakes his head remembering the whirlwind of a night we've just had. "I was scared and I wasn't thinking straight. I can't lose you, Layla."

"You're not going to lose me, Will…ever. *I'm* sorry. I spent so much time wanting a future that I never dealt with my past. And then when I was finally getting what I wanted I started feeling like I was betraying my parents somehow…like I shouldn't be so happy about having something I wouldn't have if they weren't dead. I know it sounds crazy…"

"It doesn't sound crazy, Layla. It makes perfect sense." Will holds me close to him and strokes my hair. I feel better being there in his arms. These arms…they make everything better.

"Will," I say pulling away so I can look at him. "I want to marry you. I want to be your wife. I want a future with you. I'm done living in the past and being afraid. We have been through and conquered too much to give up now or ever."

"I'm so happy to hear you say that. I want a future with you more than anything." Will leads me to the other side of the table and we sit in front of the ridiculous stack of magazines, his fingers threaded with mine. "Let's just take this one step at a time. There's no rush."

"July sixth – next year."

"What?"

"That's the day I want to marry you. Would you like to marry me on July sixth?" I smile at Will knowing that I've caught him completely off guard.

"Are you sure?" he says, tears filling his eyes.

"I've never been more sure of anything in my entire life."

"Why July sixth?"

"My only requirement in setting a date was that I had to cross the threshold into my twenties. Also, you promised me a tropical honeymoon, I figured a summer wedding would work. What do you think?" I ask as I wipe a tear that escaped Will's eye and is marking a path down his cheek.

"July sixth will forever be my favorite day of the year. I love you, Layla." Will pulls me onto his lap and holds me. "I love you so much."

"I love you, too, Will. I can't wait to be your wife."

We sit there for a long time like that, me on Will's lap, being held and cradled in his arms so lovingly. It feels as if we've climbed and conquered the highest, most treacherous mountain and survived.

I pull myself away from Will and grab the top magazine off the stack.

"Ok...here we go! Wait...did you dog-ear these pages?" There are dozens of pages marked. Some feature wedding gowns, others flowers or tuxes. "You're really going to be into the whole planning, aren't you?"

"I...may have flipped through the pages after Luke told me the football helmet story. Yeah...I'm going to be one of those guys who actually cares about the details of his wedding. Is that ok?"

"Just as long as you don't turn into groomzilla! I'm really glad you want to be so involved, but..." I'm not sure how to approach the subject of how different we envision our wedding day. Will had always said he wanted a big wedding with all the bells and whistles. I just don't see that happening now and I don't think that's what I want.

"No buts, Layla. Spit it out," he says kissing my cheek.

"I just think we have different ideas of what our day is going to look like," I say softly. "You want all the hoopla and, well…what's all the hoopla if you don't have anyone to share it with. It's not like when we were in Davidson and we had friends and family and scads of people that would come to *the* Will Meyer's wedding. I know, like, ten people here, including our family. It'll look so pathetic to have some big church wedding for nobody but us. So…I really want to get married at the gardens. Just us. My parents were married there and it would mean a lot to me to get married there, too."

I watch Will absorb what I've said, hoping he isn't upset at me for not wanting what he wants. I just can't bear the idea of walking down the aisle of an empty church. My wedding day won't be at all like I may have imagined it to be if my parents were still alive. Since my family is now this non-traditional collection of beautiful people, I think a traditional wedding would be weird. And at the end of the day, all I want is to be Will's wife.

"I totally agree," he says, flashing his irresistible smile.

"Really?" I'm excited and surprised at the same time. He really is so amazing.

"I know I said I wanted all those things, and I would still go with all of it if you said you wanted them too. I want our wedding day to be exceptional, and the only way it's going to be exceptional is if the venue and the flowers and the music mean something to you. So while I'll do my best not to be, what did you call me? Groomzilla? I'm going to do everything I can to make sure that on July sixth, a year from now, you are the happiest girl on the planet."

I'm the happiest girl on the planet right now.

Chapter 28

It took me some time, but I finally figured out what I want to do for Will's birthday. With his birthday six months away, and because I want to surprise him, I'm throwing him an un-birthday party. If I wait until December to do something special for him, I'll never be able to pull it off as a surprise.

So, with Claire and Eliana's help I've put together the coolest Mad Hatter themed party – the cool, Johnny Depp, Mad Hatter since Will is a huge Depp fan. I invited Finn and Dana, and the other friends we've been making at school. Caroline got in this morning and was waiting in my room when I got home, but the best part is that Tyler is coming in this afternoon.

After Caroline's visit in the fall we all decided that Tyler would be the next to find out about our secret, and Luke agreed that now would not only be a great time to tell him, but a great birthday present for Will. Tyler thinks he's coming for a late birthday celebration for me, since my birthday was a little over a week ago. I can't wait to see the look on his face when we tell him! And Will is going to be so happy to have Tyler back!

Will says that our friends and the life we left behind in Davidson aren't as important to him as the life we're building together now, but I know he misses Tyler. They were best friends and brothers. Tyler was the only guy that Will trusted to take care of me when he couldn't. Having Tyler back in his life is going to mean more to him than I think he realizes.

Luke and Wes have spent the last several weeks pouring over the notes and evidence they got from Eli. It's a big job, comparing what Eli had to what Luke's been collecting for 15 years. There's a lot that's just speculation, but there's also quite a bit that is frightfully true. There are things that Luke will tell me, and things he won't. Mainly they're the things that Wes was a part of previously. Violent acts that Wes works hard every day to separate himself from forever.

Eliana proves to be the best thing for Wes every day. Some days, after a particularly difficult revisit to his past, Wes is defeated and questions his worthiness of anything good. I understand that feeling. Eliana is faithful to tell him that she loves him despite his past. Yes, they've fallen in love, and it's wonderful. Through everything they have each endured, in the end, they found the one person who could truly understand them.

"Dad, I've been meaning to ask you something. You mentioned Agent Croft the night Eli was here. You said he was building a case?" I ask sitting on the soft leather couch in the office. I've been decorating all day and if I don't *sit* down I'm going to *fall* down.

"Agent Croft works for the FBI. He's been building a case against Meyer for years." Luke answers, not looking up from the stacks of files in front of him. He's comparing one file to another like he has for weeks now.

"Dad," I call from the couch. When he doesn't respond I pull myself up and stand next to him. "Dad," I say again, only this time I put my hand on his back. When he looks up I can see just how tired and sore his eyes are. He needs a break and he's not going to take one without being forced.

"I know. I'll be done with this stack in a few hours," Luke says directing his weary eyes back to the papers.

"Seriously, Dad! Tonight is Will's party and I want you to have a good time, not be dog-tired. Please. It'll all still be here tomorrow," I beg him.

Luke gives a heavy sigh and pinches the bridge of his nose. "I suppose you're right," he says.

"You *suppose* I'm right? Has being married to Claire taught you nothing?" I tease.

"Of course...my mistake." Luke lets out a tired laugh and pushes away from the desk.

I've been in this room, with files and papers spread across two desks, a hundred times since the comparative search began, but for some reason I'm overwhelmed by it in this moment. It's been a long time since I've really considered Will's father. But…I don't know that I'll ever get over or move past the fact that there's a man out there who would end my life in a heartbeat if given the chance. I feel safe within the walls of the love I have here with Luke and Claire, and, of course, Will. But as hard as I try I know that all of it could be taken away from me if Gregory Meyer ever discovered how he was duped.

"Layla, honey, are you ok?" Luke asks noticing my deadpan stare.

I can't tell him how struck with fear I am in this moment. It will only make him turn around and scour the damning files even more. He'll get a second wind powered by his determination to keep me safe at any cost. No…tonight is not about Gregory Meyer in any way, shape, or form. Tonight is about Will. It's about family. It's about love. It's about everything that Gregory Meyer knows nothing about.

"Yeah, I'm fine. I'm tired just looking at this mess. Now…you…go close your eyes and rest for a bit. Tyler will be here in about an hour and I need you here when Will gets back and we spill the beans." I usher Luke out and send him on his way upstairs.

By the time Claire is back from the airport with Tyler, Caroline and I are jumping out of our skin with excitement. It's been almost a year since I've seen Tyler and I can't wait to throw my arms around him. Every memory I have of Tyler concentrates on his commitment to his brotherhood with Will. Everything from the times he covered for us so Will and I could spend time together away from the house to his insistence that Will was madly in love with me even after we stumbled in on him with Carrie at the firm's retreat, and then the awful night we all said our goodbyes to Will after his funeral. Tyler was always there for Will, and vice versa.

I know walking away from Tyler was one of the hardest parts about what Will did for us, but tonight I'm going to remedy that for him. My gift to Will is giving him back a piece of his life that no one, not even I, could ever replace.

Caroline and I don't even bother to wait inside the house. Tyler's sneakers have barely touched the pavement of the driveway when we're both hovering over him.

"Tyler! I'm so happy you're finally here! I've missed you so much!" I scream as I throw my arms around his neck. It feels so good to have him here, and to know that his place in our lives won't be temporary.

"Layla! You look beautiful, as usual! It's so great to see you!" Tyler hugs me with as much force. "You are in big trouble. I can't believe it's been almost a year! Why haven't you come to visit?"

"You know, I actually wanted to talk to you about that. Let's get inside," I tell him.

"Uh, hello! Where are my hugs?" Caroline has her hand on her hip. She's trying to look serious but her face can't help but crack that cute smile of hers.

"I saw you two weeks ago!" Tyler teases as he gives in to her demands.

"Oh, uh, I should have prepared you," I say to Tyler as we walk in the house.

The house is filled with incredible Mad Hatter decorations that Claire and I found online. It was a real "boutiquey" site with specialty decorations unlike I'd ever seen. Considering the theme of the party, there was no other way to go.

There are ginormous mushrooms and massive silk top hats around the room, and we set a huge table down one side of the room with teapots and cups and saucers. All the drinks are labeled *Drink Me*, and all the food, *Eat Me*. That part isn't from the Mad Hatter storyline, but it was too cute not to include.

"Yeah…it pretty much looks like Alice in Wonderland threw up in here," he says.

I lead Tyler down the hall to Wes' room. He's going to stay at Eliana's for the next few nights so Will and Tyler can have some real time together here with Caroline and me.

"Whose room is this?" Tyler asks. It's clear that this isn't an empty, spare bedroom. There are clothes in the dresser and closet, and there are pictures of Wes and Eliana on the nightstand. "Whoa! Have you seen this, Layla? She looks just like Will's mom!"

"That's because it is Will's mother," Luke says from behind us.

"Hey, Mr. Weston! I'm sorry, I don't understand."

Luke and I spend the next 30 minutes explaining Will and his mother's existence, with Caroline backing up the whole story. Tyler asks questions and we answer as many of them as we can. I tell him about Marcus and have to calm him through most of that story. Tyler would fight just as furiously for my safety as the rest of the men in my life. I also tell him about Wes, my bonus uncle, who is now in love with Will's mother. In the end, Tyler has tears streaming down his face for his best friend who isn't gone forever as he once believed, but is alive and about to be clamped in the manliest embrace in about an hour.

"There is one last thing you need to be extremely cautious about, Tyler. You must call him John tonight. He's been here since he left Davidson, building a life as John Holland, and that's how everyone here knows him," I instruct. I know that Tyler will do his best, but we should be certain that one of us is with him until we know he's got it.

"I understand. I…I just can't believe this." Tyler wipes the tears from his face and hugs me. "I don't know if I should be mad that you're just telling me now, or thrilled that you're telling me at all."

"Be thrilled," I tell him, squeezing him closer. "Will is going to be here any minute. Freshen up and wait in the kitchen. Caroline will show you where it is and then she'll come out to the living room with me. He'll think that Caroline is his surprise. Then, I'll bring him in the kitchen and watch him totally freak out! I can't wait!"

All goes as planned when Will walks into the house. He's shocked at the décor and happy to see Caroline. I explain my idea of an un-birthday party to him and, after some coaxing, he concedes.

"That's good, because all our friends are going to be here in a few hours!" I kiss Will sweetly and take his hand to lead him to the kitchen. "I didn't know what to get you..."

"Oh, honey, you didn't have to get me anything. It's not even my real birthday," he says, but I shoot him a look and he knows he should give up now. "But whatever it is, I know I'll love it!"

"That's more like it! As I was saying, I didn't know what to get you, so I decided to go big, or go home! Close your eyes!"

I walk Will into the kitchen and don't have to say a word. Tyler does it all for me.

"Hey man," Tyler says softly, still not believing that Will is really alive.

"Tyler!" Will races across the kitchen and the two men are holding each other like brothers do.

Tears are streaming down all of our faces as we share in this incredible moment. Will has missed Tyler terribly, but hasn't been able to verbalize it. He left everything behind for me, so the last thing he was ever going to tell me is how much he missed something he left.

"I missed you so much, man! I can't believe you're alive!" Tyler squeaks out.

"I can't believe you're here! How? When did they tell you?" Will looks at Tyler, joy pouring from his eyes.

"Layla lured me here under the guise of a birthday celebration for her. I just got here a couple of hours ago, and she didn't waste any time in telling me everything. She's good!"

"Yes, she is. C'mere," Will says pulling me to him. "Thank you for this. It's amazing to have him back."

"I knew you were missing him but would never say it out loud. He's family and we just couldn't keep him out of the loop forever. You need someone, too. Happy un-birthday, babe."

"I'm speechless. I…thank you, all of you." Will wipes the new tears forming from his eyes.

"Ok…" I say, breaking the mushiness of the mood. "Tyler is going to be here for four days. You have all weekend to re-bond with him. Our new friends will be here in a few hours. Go change and get ready for the party. I brought all your stuff from the apartment for the whole weekend. Wes is staying with your mom and the four of us are going to have an old fashioned slumber party!"

Chapter 29

Will's un-birthday party was a huge success. In all, we had about 25 people here. About half of them were actual friends of ours, but they brought significant others, and then some. Word got out about the theme of the party and everyone just had to see it for themselves. No one left disappointed either, as Claire and I made sure everyone went home with a Mad Hatter silk top hat and a few *Drink Me & Eat Me* favors. At the end of the night, Will said it was by far the best party he's ever had. He quickly followed it up by saying that it will be outshined next year in July as our wedding reception will "kick this party's ass," as he put it.

We're putting Caroline on a plane back to California this afternoon. She's got a great internship with some famous interior designer to the stars and has to be in the office bright and early on Monday morning. I loved every second with her and already miss her as her tiny body disappears into the crowd of people entering the check-in area.

"So you two are really getting hitched, huh?" Tyler says as we make our way home from the airport.

"We're really getting hitched!" Will says.

"When's the big day? I'm invited, right?" Tyler asks.

"July sixth, next year, and, duh! Why wouldn't you be invited?" I say punching his arm from the back seat of Will's car.

"Well…I just found out Will is still alive, so… And, I wasn't sure how it was going to work. You know, Layla Weston marrying some guy named John Holland. How *is* that going to work?"

"It's going to be small, at the gardens where Layla's parents were married," Will smiles his brilliant, heart-stopping smile at me in the rear view mirror. I smile back feeling grateful to have a fiancé who truly cares that our wedding day is as special and filled with meaning as possible.

"We won't do any of the things we would have been obligated to do if things were different and we were getting married in Davidson. Like, there won't be any newspaper announcements or a professional photographer. Wes is pretty handy with a camera so we'll have him take pictures," I add.

"I think I get the newspaper thing, but why no professional photographer?" Tyler asks.

"They all have web sites now where they feature the weddings they've shot. It's just to make sure Layla's name stays out of the system. Luke will take care of changing her name legally, but get her a new social security number so that her old one is still registered to Layla Weston. And we won't change her name with the school since her school records will be attached to her original social."

"I see...I think." Tyler furrows his brow so Will further explains.

"We have to operate as if Layla Weston's moves are being monitored electronically. The only way for Layla to change her name when we get married is if we get her a new social security number."

"Are Layla's moves being monitored?" There's a hint of nervousness and fear in Tyler's voice. It's a lot to take in and understand, so I get it.

"We don't have any evidence of that right now. Wes is tight with all the guys, even the new ones, working for my father. They all hate him for what he's coerced them into doing for him, so they're happy to help Wes by being his eyes and ears on the inside. But, we can never be too safe."

"I just want you guys to be safe, ok?"

"We're taking good care of each other," I say. "It takes a village, you know!"

After quick showers and a review of the movies playing, I tell the boys to go out and have fun doing whatever it is they do for fun, and enjoy the last hours they have before we say goodbye to Tyler tomorrow. They'll see some action flick that I would have seen out of obligation as the good soon-to-be-wife, so when they leave I give Tyler an extra hug for getting me out of it.

Luke and Claire are out to dinner and Wes is still at Eliana's. The house is quiet, which is rarely ever the case, and I'm enjoying it thoroughly.

I've been reading for while in the Great Room and really need to get up and stretch. I find myself walking down the hall to the office. As I creek the door open I'm struck again by the massive amounts of paperwork and stacks upon stacks of files. I can hardly wrap my brain around the fact that all of these files contain evidence against one man's flagrant abuse of the law.

I don't want to disturb the files Luke and Wes have left open in mid-comparison, but there are files on the credenza that are all askew and I can't help but give in to my need to straighten them up. I flip open the top file folder and peruse the documents. It's all legal stuff and I have no idea what I'm looking at.

Shaking my head at the enormity of it all, I close the file and work to create a stack with more stability. *One down, a kabillion to go.* As I move down the row and work on the next stack, I guess I get a bit too animated because I end up knocking the next stack in line, causing the top few files to slide and fall to the floor. *Great!*

They seemed to fall keeping most of their contents close to the file they came from – mostly out, but still hanging on for dear life. As I work to clean up my mess something in one of the files catches my eye. This file isn't filled with legal paperwork. It's filled with black and white photographs, big ones the size of the file folder itself. I've seen enough crime dramas on TV to know that these are surveillance photos.

I flip through the pictures, not recognizing anyone or anything that I'm looking at until I see a photo of Eli's father, Alexander Briggs. *Poor guy. Just doing his job got him killed.* I decide I'll look at just a few more, out of sheer curiosity, when my world stops. At first I think my eyes are fooling me. There's no reason why there should be pictures of the accident the night my parents died. *What?* They're not just of the aftermath. It's the accident in motion. *How?*

I take the stack of photos and sit on the floor, examining each one, tears filling my eyes as I relive the horror. The vantage point is from the sidewalk, far from the side of the intersection where we landed. There's Dad's car, and the one that hit us coming straight for us. It was raining so hard that night, but the pictures are so clear. They obviously were taken from a safe and dry location.

Picture after picture tells the story of the worst night of my life, everything from the moments leading up to the accident to the swarm of police cars and ambulances. There's the fire department using the Jaws of Life to open my father's door…his lifeless body being pulled from the car…me, on a stretcher being wheeled into an ambulance. There's blood all over us. Then there is a series of pictures of the police draping a white sheet over my parents' dead bodies. They're so sequential, if I flipped them in order it would look like a movie. I don't understand who would have taken these pictures and why. Moreover, why are they here? What do they have to do with Gregory Meyer?

"Layla! We're home!" Claire calls out.

I don't answer.

"Layla?" Claire calls again. She repeats my name a few times until she becomes louder in her approach to the office. "There you are! What are you doing in – " Claire stops cold in her tracks seeing what I'm looking at and the tears streaming down my face. "Layla, honey…"

"I don't understand," I choke out as Luke joins Claire in the doorway.

"Oh, Layla." Luke runs his hands through his hair as he strides across the room to join me.

"What…what are these?" I manage in between sobs.

"Layla, I…I know this is difficult…but…you really don't need to know," Luke says softly as he gently takes the pictures from me.

"How could I not need to know why there are real time pictures of the accident that killed my parents?"

"Come, let's get you some tea," Claire says as she pulls me from the floor and escorts me from the room.

As I settle at the kitchen table with freshly made hot tea, I notice the time. It's just 9:00 pm so I know I won't be seeing Will and Tyler stroll in anytime soon. This buys me some time to get some answers from Luke and Claire.

"Thank you for the tea. Can you please tell me what's going on now? And, P.S., I hate having to ask that question all the time. I wish people would just tell me without me finding out and then having to ask." I may be calm, but it doesn't mean I'm not mad.

"Layla, there are things that you don't need to know," Luke says.

"I'll be the judge of that," I retort. There have been only a few times since living with Luke and Claire that I have responded like a bratty teenager. This is one to add to that list.

"No, you won't. Don't push this, Layla."

"If it has to do with my parents' death, I think I have a right to know!" I demand, raising my voice.

"Why? What difference is it going to make?" Luke's temper is rising and I can see that I'm really pushing him on a subject he wants to protect.

"Tell me! Tell me why there are pictures of the night I killed my parents!" I shout.

"Layla! Don't say that!" Claire scolds.

"Then tell me why the hell someone took pictures of that awful night, and why they're in a file in your office among all the incriminating evidence against Gregory Meyer!"

Luke sits down at the table and puts his head in his hands.

"Is this really how we're going to start communicating? After everything we've been through?" Luke says quietly from behind his hands.

"No," I answer after a long beat. "I'm sorry. I was taken off guard by the photos, and seeing them…they captured every moment leading up to and after…I just relived the whole terrifying night."

"I can't tell you, Layla. You don't want to know." Luke's tone is calm, but he's got fear in his eyes. It's the same fear I saw the day Will's father exposed my parents as ecoterrorists and outted Luke as having not come to my father's legal aid.

"How do you know that?"

"Not telling you protects you from more pain. As your *father*, I just can't do that to you. I *won't* do that to you. So…you can be angry with me if you need to be, but I would rather you be angry with me for the rest of your life than tell you something that would break your heart."

"I…I need to take a shower." I can't think straight so I do the only other thing that seems to clear my head outside of sitting at the edge of the dock. I turn the water on as hot as I can stand it and strip down after pulling my hair into a messy bun. As I let the water rush over me I feel my muscles relax and my heart rate calm.

Why on earth would Meyer have photos of that night? Not just photos of the aftermath, but the whole thing. Maybe they're from a traffic camera. No, there are too many sequential pictures and they're all from a human level, not a bird's eye view. Tourist in a restaurant? But even if that were the case, how would *he* have them? *Why* would he have them?

Does it matter? That's the question.

Yes. It matters.

Do I need the answers right now? That's the bigger question.

Maybe not.

I turn the water off after my hands have turned into raisins and wrap a towel around me. As I exit the shower I'm reminded of the night I discovered Marcus' disturbing message on my mirror. I think about how Luke responded to that event and everything Marcus did. He shielded me, came to my rescue, brought Wes into our lives. He did all of that to protect me. I trusted him then, so why am I bucking him on this?

Because this is about the night that changed my life forever.

The night that sent me into five years of hell.

The night that sent me to Luke and Claire.

The night that sent me to Will.

I've struggled with this for so long. How can I be happy in a place I would never be had my parents not died that night? Do I really want to bring it back up again, relive that night over and over?

Regardless of why those pictures exist, Gregory Meyer is behind them. I don't know why or how, but he was involved in some way. That's the only explanation as to why those pictures were in those files. He tried to separate me from the only family I had left, and did everything he could to keep me from Will, my only reason for breathing. Rage begins to boil inside me for the man who has single-handedly worked to destroy my life. I am full of new determination to make sure Gregory Meyer gets taken down.

Regardless of why those pictures exist, Luke has spent the last two years loving and protecting me. He and Claire took me in when I had no one left. He supported my decision to be with Will, despite the looming consequences. He and Claire gave up the lives they built in Davidson to move me to a place where Will and I could be together. He has done nothing but fill the father-shaped hole in my heart and there's no way I can reject his love now.

"I'll make you a deal," I say entering the kitchen where Luke and Claire are still seated at the table. "I'll let you do whatever it is you're doing to nail Meyer's coffin closed…and when it's all over, and he's rotting in prison for the rest of his short life, you tell me about the pictures."

"I don't know how long that's going to take, Layla," Luke says quietly but firmly.

"I know."

"Then, as long as you can be patient, you have a deal." Luke stands and embraces me. "You know I'm only trying to protect you because I love you."

"I know that, too."

Chapter 30

Luke and Wes have spent the last weeks combing through every shred of evidence they've got. It seems that they have uncovered a plethora of evidence that doesn't necessarily point at Luke as being the source and jeopardize his status with the Bar Association. It turns out Alexander Briggs was very good at what he did. The evidence has been solid enough that we've even had a few visits from Agent Croft with the FBI over the last few months. Will and Eliana have had to make themselves scarce, but with fall classes starting up again, that hasn't been so difficult.

"I don't understand why the FBI is involved – no offence Agent Croft." This is the second time this month he's been here. I suppose this isn't exactly the kind of stuff you fax over.

"None taken," he smirks. He's pretty mellow for an FBI agent. "The FBI only gets involved when the subject commits a crime across state lines."

"You mean he's been tormenting people all over the country?" My jaw drops at realizing this man really has no limits.

"Not all over the country. Just in Virginia, Georgia, and New York. North Carolina has reciprocity with them. That means that if you're licensed in North Carolina, and have practiced for so many years, you can practice in those other states as well. So, yes, he's been spreading the love," Agent Croft answers.

"Do you mind if I ask what the charges are?" All I've seen is evidence collecting, but no one has said anything about what they're going to charge him with. "I mean... I know he's broken the law, but I don't know what that means in legal terms."

"She's ok," Luke says, indicating that I can handle it. I appreciate his confidence in me.

"We've been working on a foundational charge of conspiracy because he never is directly involved with what goes down, but conspiracy is hard to prove. There has to be solid evidence, for example, that he provided the tools, means, or information that led to the crime committed."

"Like recorded conversation?" I ask, knowing that Wes, Taylor, and Cline had been recording their dealings with Meyer for quite some time.

"Yes, but we need something other than the recorded conversations between Meyer and his thugs, however useful they may be."

I feel a twinge of offence at Agent Croft's reference to Wes as a thug, but that's how Meyer painted him and the others. They were just muscle, a means to his criminal end. I can't take any more of hearing about all the obstacles to taking Gregory Meyer down so I leave the office to find Claire in the kitchen. She's at the table flipping through some new bridal magazines that I bought the other day. Before she knows I'm there, I hear her actually turn a page and sigh at the gown she's looking at.

"You're such a hopeless romantic," I say kissing the top of her head.

"Guilty!" she says beaming. "Look at this one, Layla. Oh, you would look so beautiful in it!"

"It's a bit much, don't you think? I mean, for a garden wedding?" The dress is a full on ball gown, complete with crystals and a long train. "I want to look beautiful that day, but I draw the line at Disney Princess."

"I know...you want simple. It'll be just lovely...a very Layla wedding. Oh, I called and reserved the Gardens today."

"Already?"

"Layla, you're aware that you're getting married in eight months, right?" Her eyebrows are lifted in surprise.

"No, it's not eight, it's..." I look at my phone to see what today is and then actually count the months on my fingers. "Oh my gosh. I'm getting married in eight months. Mom...I haven't done anything to prepare for this. Should I be doing something? What should I be doing? Oh my gosh, Will is going to flip!"

"Settle down, honey. He's not going to flip. You want a small wedding, so there's not as much to do if you were going the path Will wanted. But we really should jump on this. At least we've got the most important detail out of the way. After the groom, the place was the most important and that's all set! We just need to chat about the location for the reception and what you want to do for food, flowers, music."

"Ok, um...can we have the reception here? There won't be a lot of people, so we'll have plenty of room. It would feel more like a family event to have the reception at home, and the idea of going to some hotel ballroom just sounds too fancy for me."

"If that's what you'd like to do, we can do that. See, that wasn't so hard, was it?" Claire grins from ear to ear. I know she's thrilled and bursting at the seams inside.

"Ladies..." Agent Croft stands just inside the kitchen, with Luke close behind. "I'll be leaving now. Thank you, again, for your hospitality, Claire. Layla, always a pleasure. Keep asking questions...you may make a good FBI agent one day." He smiles at me and nods his head. "Get a good look at me because I won't be back any time soon. Luke and Wes have pulled together enough evidence that, with what we have on Meyer, we'll be ready to file charges soon."

"That's great! When do I get to see him in an orange jumpsuit?" I say partly teasing, but mostly serious.

"You won't see Gregory Meyer in an orange jumpsuit until the jury convicts him, and that'll take a while. It's going to be a long trial. But, while he's under prosecution, he'll be heavily monitored, so he won't be enjoying all the finer things in life that he's become accustomed to having. I hope he likes that mansion of his because his ankle monitor won't get him very far."

"Thank you, Agent Croft," I say.

"It's my pleasure, Layla. Luke told me about what he put you through with Will. I'm sorry for your loss, but am happy that you've found someone. Congratulations on your engagement, by the way. But for all you've been through, I'll consider it a personal triumph to take him down on your behalf."

Luke escorts Agent Croft out and returns within moments. I can't believe they're so close to filing actual charges. Seeing Gregory Meyer pay for what he's done had always been this lofty goal, a dream of sorts that was out there somewhere. But now…it's really going to happen. Strangely, I'm filled with mixed emotions. Regardless of what this man has done, he's the father of the man I love. Without him, Will wouldn't exist. I feel an amount of sadness for him, however small it may be. If all goes as planned, Gregory Meyer will spend the rest of his days rotting in prison.

"Is this really going to happen? I mean, is he really going to pay for everything that he's done?" I ask Luke. I'm overwhelmed with the thought that Meyer has every judge in every county he's ever practiced, in his back pocket. How is this ever going to be a fair trial?

"Well, to be honest Layla, he's going to pay for very little of what he's done. Most of his indiscretions have no trail leading to him. He's guilty as sin, but without evidence, even circumstantial evidence, there's nothing we can do. I need you to prepare yourself for that." Luke is serious and doesn't seem as hopeful as I need him to be in this moment.

"Then what's the point?" I ask, defeated.

"Layla, honey, what Luke is trying to say is that, even though we don't have enough evidence to convict him for everything he's done, the sentence for what we *do* have evidence for will be enough to send him away forever." Claire's tone is more reassuring and I'm immediately put at ease.

"And what happens to Wes? He, along with Taylor and Cline, were the ones who actually committed the crimes. Is Wes going to go to jail?" I can't stand the thought of Wes being punished for what Gregory Meyer coerced him into doing.

"Part of my deal with Agent Croft is that Wes and the others won't face charges if they testify and provide evidence that convicts Meyer. So, don't worry, Wes is safe."

"Once the trial starts, will you have to go back to North Carolina? Oh, my gosh, Dad! Will you have to defend him? You were on retainer!" I'm absolutely freaked out now. How could Luke possibly work in a capacity to defend that demon incarnate!

"Layla, stop worrying! No, I won't be defending him. Yes, I was on retainer, and technically the retainer doesn't run out until the end of the year, but considering the circumstances, I doubt Meyer would even approach me about that anyway. The plan is to live seemingly unaware of the proceedings. There's no reason for me to be involved and Meyer reaching out to me for counsel is unlikely. I'm the only one who knew about his dealings and if the FBI see that he's reached out to me after such a long separation, it'll raise suspicion."

"So, we can watch Gregory Meyer fall from a distance?"

"Yes. It'll get some national attention, so we can watch him come unraveled with commentary and everything." Luke hugs me and I feel better about my concerns.

There's a light at the end of the tunnel. Meyer is going to pay for his years of crushing anyone who opposed him under his thumb. It won't change anything for me now being engaged to John Holland, but at least we'll be able to really relax. Even though I don't know how long it will take, the vision of him in that orange jumpsuit will get me through the days of waiting.

Claire and I spend the next few hours looking through bridal magazines and jotting down ideas for my small but elegant garden wedding. She's calmed my nerves about having not been as on top of things as I should have been and assured me eight months is plenty of time to plan my wedding.

Tyler is back for another visit, which makes me so happy for Will. It was hard saying goodbye to him after Will's birthday weekend so when he called a few days ago and said that he found a great last minute flight, we could hardly refuse. He stayed at Will's last night since Agent Croft was already here, but now that there's no FBI presence, the boys will set up camp here for the next two nights.

By the time Will and Tyler arrive back at the house from their afternoon doing all the things that boys love to do, I have a page of ideas and things to do for the wedding, while Claire has four pages. My list has things like checking on flowers that are in bloom in July, and taking Will cake testing.

"I'm so on board for cake testing? Do you think we can just make our way around town to all the different bakeries?" Will kisses my cheek after reviewing my list.

"I'm sure we can milk it for a couple of months," I say laughing at his cuteness.

"So, Tyler, while you're here," Will begins. "I wanted to ask you something."

"Sure man…what's up?" Tyler grabs a soda from the fridge and plops down on a bar stool at the counter. I love how they have just picked right back up where they left off in their friendship.

"There just never seemed to be a perfect time when you were here for my birthday, but…I wanted to know…will you be my best man?" Will's eyes are soft. It means so much to me that he has the opportunity to even ask Tyler. With the way our lives are now, having someone as important as Tyler in our wedding wasn't a possibility until now. I know Will wants our wedding day to be all about what I want, but it wouldn't be complete without having Tyler stand with Will.

"Wow." Tyler is immediate choked up. They've been best friends since forever so I don't know why it would catch him off guard. But clearly it's as meaningful to Tyler as it is to Will. "Of course! Thank you!" Tyler and Will embrace and now I'm choked up.

When I asked Caroline to be my maid of honor, the water works exploded with both of us. Knowing that our best friends will be able to be a part of our special day is the best wedding gift ever. When Will and I got engaged, I was admittedly sad at times knowing that there will be people missing who should have been an integral part of our day. While Gwen and Chris won't be there, it will still be an amazing day.

The weekend with Tyler passes all too quickly, and as we finally say goodbye it's sadder than I imagined it would be. The ride to the airport is filled with second reminders of what he can and cannot say. This is how it was when Caroline came to visit, too. It'll get easier with each visit.

"Are you ok?" I ask Will as we pull away from the terminal.

"Yeah, actually. I'm great. Thank you so much for bringing him back into our lives. It's been incredible." Will pulls my hand to his lips and kisses my knuckles. "How did things go with Agent Croft. Anything new?"

"Yes! He said that he wouldn't be visiting again because Luke and Wes had given them enough evidence that, combined with what they already had, they'd be ready to file charges soon. Isn't that great?"

Will is silent for a few long moments, contemplating the joy I've just expressed at his father's ultimate demise.

"Honey, are you ok?" I ask.

"Yeah, yeah...I'm fine. I don't know...it's just weird. It's not like we haven't talked a hundred times about him getting what he's due...it's just...so real. When did Croft say they'd be filing the charges? I think I should warn my mother since it'll make national news."

"He didn't say when, exactly. He just said soon. So, I would guess in a month or so. I know it seems a bit surreal right now, but...it's going to be ok. He's not going to be able to hurt anyone ever again."

Chapter 31

My idea of *soon* and the FBI's idea of *soon* are apparently two different things.

It's been three months since Agent Croft stood in our kitchen and told us that they'd be filing charges *soon*. I've tried to let the days go by as normal and uneventful as possible. My job right now is to go to school and plan a wedding. *My* wedding. As consuming as those two things are supposed to be in a young girl's life, I can't help but be constantly distracted by the thought of Gregory Meyer being found guilty on countless charges of crimes against humanity.

I keep waiting for Luke to announce that Agent Croft arrested Gregory Meyer himself and the court proceedings against him are scheduled to begin. I've been waiting and waiting and can wait no more. *That's it! I'm setting up a Google Alert.*

I've been obedient in not doing any searches for Gregory Meyer. Luke and Will both said it would only frustrate me since there are a ridiculous number of glowing reviews of him in publications across the country. But I can't wait any longer! No sooner have I typed in his name than a hundred links appear in the box to the right. *This* is *ridiculous!*

My eyes scan the box of links and lock on the third one from the top:

Gregory Meyer of Meyer, Fincher, and Marks charged with 37 counts of conspiracy...

It's dated six weeks ago.

My temperature begins to rise and I can feel my face start to burn. They didn't tell me. No one said anything. I've been sitting here like an idiot while they've all been privy to the progress being made in taking down the Destroyer of Lives.

"When were you going to tell me that he had been arrested?" I say, marching into the kitchen where Luke and Claire are making dinner.

"What are you talking about?" Claire asks.

"C'mon, Mom, it's really not your style to act dumb! I Googled him and found, like, a dozen articles on his arrest already!"

"You owe me $100!" Luke says to Claire. "I had her at no more than four months...pay up!"

"Alright, alright!" she says laughing. "You just cost me a new pair of shoes!"

"What...what are you talking about?" My face scrunches together out of confusion. "Did you bet on how long it would take me to find out what you were keeping from me?"

"We bet on how long it would take you to take matters into your own hands. And I won! So, thanks! You just bought me an upgraded Roku for the Great Room!" Luke is so blasé. Why is he not taking this seriously?

"Why are you not taking this seriously?" I demand.

"Layla, the trial started last week. You knew he was being arrested. There was nothing to tell you. We literally just have to sit and do nothing but wait. They're not televising the trial but there has been some news coverage." Claire wipes the counter where she was working and puts the remaining ingredients back into the fridge.

"It's late and court is closed, so there's nothing happening. We'll put it on tomorrow and see what they have to say." Luke's tone is a little condescending but I try not to take it personally. He knows more about what this process is like and if he says there's nothing exciting happening, then I believe him.

"Ok...I'm sorry. I just...I just thought you would have told me," I sigh. "Am I really that predictable? You *knew* I would start my own search for information?"

"Yes," they answer in unison.

*****

I've let the weeks go by with barely a search on the internet or news about the trial. I deleted my Google Alert so I'm not bombarded with information either. If we're supposed to be moving forward with our lives, then staying updated on even the demise of Gregory Meyer is stunting that growth.

I am now getting married in four months, which means I'm turning 20 in three. When I set this wedding date it was over a year away. Where has the time gone?

Claire and Eliana have handled most of the arrangements. We're having a sunset ceremony at the gardens where my parents were married. We decided to go ahead and have the reception in the Gardener's Cottage since there's a bridal dressing room and the place holds less than 60 people. Right now our guest list is at 30, and that's only because Will and I invited our professors and told everyone they could bring a date.

Today is the day that I've been most looking forward to in all the planning. Today Claire and I have an appointment with a seamstress. Today I am going to put on my mother's wedding dress. I am hoping with everything in me that she can nip and tuck and adjust it so that it looks just as beautiful on me as it did on my mother 26 years ago.

I emerge from the dressing room with Claire's help and stare at the reflection in the mirror. I'm not sure I know who this person is. The girl in the mirror isn't a girl anymore. She's a woman, and in this wedding dress, she's...beautiful.

"Oh, Layla." Claire pulls a tissue from her purse and dabs the corners of her eyes. "You are stunning."

I don't know what to say. It's all so surreal. I fight the feelings of guilt that emerge for being so happy in my dead mother's wedding dress. I know I'm going to have to put this dress on a few more times before I wear it for the last time, so I pull myself together and decide not to cry...just for today.

The seamstress begins to pull and tug and pin the dress all over. It doesn't seem to take too much effort to get it into a place where it fits me as if it were made for me. Its Grecian design is very forgiving, so even though I'm small to begin with, I don't feel the twinge of fear that many brides do in making sure they starve themselves so they fit into the dress on their wedding day.

When the seamstress is done poking and pulling at me, I take another look at myself in this now perfectly fitted dress. I have to admit, the dress is stunning, and I feel the same way in it. I think about Will and how handsome he'll be in his suit and *this* is what brings the tears. Despite everything that we have been through, in just four short months I am going to be Will's wife. There was a time I thought that would never happen and knowing that it's just on the horizon, it feels like nothing short of a miracle.

"Layla, are you ok?" Claire says as she hands me a tissue.

"Yes, actually. I'm just so happy. I can't believe I'm standing here. When I thought Will was dead, I knew I'd never wear this dress. But here I am, standing in my mother's wedding dress, looking ahead at marrying the most incredible man on the planet in just four months."

"I understand how you feel. I never thought I'd be standing here with my daughter, helping her prepare for the most important day of her life. I'm so happy to be a part of this." Claire speaks softly as she reflects on a day she knew would never come after Penny died. This has turned into a much more meaningful day for us that I had imagined. I knew it would be special, but it has far exceeded my expectations.

When Claire and I return home, she calls me to her bedroom and sits me on the bed.

"I have something I want to give you," she begins. "After Penny was born, I wrote her a series of letters. Some were in response to something she had done. Others I wrote when I had been thinking about her life, what she would become, her future. I want you to have this."

Claire hands me a sealed letter labeled *Wedding Dress* on the front in beautiful script. The cream stationary is thick and feels texturized in my hands.

"Oh, no, I can't…" I try to decline the letter, but Claire won't let me.

"We're mother and daughter, are we not?" she says softly.

"We are." An automatic smile spreads across my face.

"Then let me give this letter to my daughter." She closes my hand around the envelope and smiles. "Read it and know that every word and sentiment in there was meant for my daughter, and that's you."

Claire leaves the room and I'm left with this letter that was meant for another daughter, given to me by a mother I never thought I'd have again. It's amazing to me how our family, all of us, so perfectly meets a need and desire in each person. Luke and Claire are the parents I so desperately needed, and I have become the daughter they never thought they'd have. Wes has shown Eliana what it means to be truly loved by a man, and she has given him the courage to be vulnerable again. Will and I gave each other the strength we needed to break free from the chains of our past and forge a new path to the future we deserve. I'm overwhelmed with how loved and blessed I am.

I wipe the tears from my face and gingerly open the letter and begin to read. At first I don't think I can get through it, but I hear my mother's and Claire's voices together in my head and realize that I have been given a great gift. I get to say that I have two mothers who love me with every fiber of their being. My first mother was taken from me too early, but my second mother came to me just in the nick of time. With this newfound elation, I read.

To my beautiful daughter,

Today we chose your wedding dress. As you stood there, looking more stunning than I ever dream, I couldn't help but well up with pride. You've endured struggles and celebrated joys. You've worked hard for what you've earned, but have also been so blessed by others. And you've chosen a man who your father and I know will love and cherish you all the days of your life.

Today was just the first of many days that I am realizing just how difficult it's going to be to let go of my precious little one. I've watch you grow into a remarkable young woman and beam with joy knowing that you are embarking on an incredible journey filled with ups and downs, trials and errors, but most of all, love and joy.

In a few short months, I'll watch your father walk you down an aisle and place your life into the hands of another. I know that those hands will keep you and protect you. But always know that my hands are never far away. My hands will always be there to applaud you, to embrace you, and whether it be from joy or sorrow, to wipe every tear.

Today we take another step in our journey as well. We're crossing a threshold together, not leaving behind mother and daughter, but adding friend. I'll always be your mother, but now I'm so happy to call you my friend as well.

I love you,
Mom

The tears streaming down face I dart from their bedroom and almost tackle Claire in the Great Room. She doesn't say anything as she wraps her warm arms around me. I hear the sound of her soft sobs mixed with mine and know that we have, indeed, crossed a threshold. I thought I had granted her entry into my heart before, but today it's been taken to a whole new level. I love Claire as dearly as if she had given birth to me herself.

"Oh, Mom! Thank you! Thank you for being here, for not sending me to boarding school, for loving me…thank you for everything!" I can't stop crying long enough to say anything else, not that anything more is needed.

I have a bond with Claire that I always dreamed I'd have with my mother when I grew up. It's a dream that had once died as so much of me did at the hands of my grandmother. But now, that part of me is alive and redeemed.

We release our grasp on each other and look into each other's eyes. Mother and daughter. Lost and found. Our bond solidified forever.

It takes a few moments for me to realize that anyone else is even in the room. When I do I see my family staring at us with wet eyes. All of them. Luke and Will, Wes and Eliana. Before I know it, Luke is joining our embrace and I feel a gush a warmth wash over me. I feel so complete in their arms. No guilt. Just as absolutely complete as any child should feel in the arms of their parents.

"You're happy," Will says, brushing the hair from my face as we assemble ourselves after we break from each other.

"Yes, very. Was I not happy before?"

"You've been happy for a long time. Just…not this kind of happy."

I breathe a sigh of unadulterated happiness and join Will on the Great Room couch. I lay back against Will's side and take the hand draped over my shoulder in mine. I scan the room and see six of the happiest people in the world.

"Layla, you should know we're watching coverage of the trial. There's been…an incident," Luke says warning me.

"What kind of incident?" I sit up, immediately tensed at the idea that something could go wrong and Gregory Meyer would not be made to pay for his transgressions.

"One of the jurors was found dead…a victim of a home invasion." Luke's delivery is of what the news is reporting and not the facts. We all know that the fact is Gregory Meyer gave that directive.

"Wes, I thought you said those guys were on our side?" I'm confused. Wes has told us time and again that we don't have to worry about Meyer's new goons coming after us.

"They are on our side, Layla, but all that means is that *we* are safe. As long as he holds the cards, they're going to play his game."

"Oh, no!" Claire has seen the breaking news alert across the bottom of the screen and we all look up in time to listen to the reporter give more details.

"Thanks, Steve. I'm here in front of the US District Court House in Charlotte where the trial of Gregory Meyer has been underway for several weeks. However the trial had been placed on hold while an alternate juror was selected after the unfortunate death of juror number eight. But a new wrench has been thrown into the trial as a second juror, juror number four, failed to report for duty this morning. At this point in time juror number four's whereabouts are still unknown. If this juror is not located within the next 24-hours, another alternate will have to be selected.

"As you can see, Mr. Meyer doesn't seem to be fazed by the disruption in the proceedings." Will's father and his legal team are sauntering down the steps of the courthouse with prideful grins I'd love to punch right off. There are cameras and reporters circling them, each vying for a quote to skyrocket them to the front page of their journal. "And, as you know, Steve, the defense could definitely use this to their benefit by calling for a mistrial and sending this case back to square one, buying the Meyer defense team more time."

A shot rings out through the television and the reporter and her cameraman instinctively duck. *Bang! Bang!* Another two shots and we're literally all sitting at the edge of our seats. The cameraman regains his footing and the angle is upright now. He gets the reporter into the frame and she begins frantically telling about the situation.

"Uh, Steve…as you've just heard, three shots have been fired into the crowd here on the steps of the US District Court House in Charlotte. It's unclear at this time if anyone has been hurt…wait…I can see…hold on…yes, I can see him now. Gregory Meyer has been shot."

Oh, dear God.

The crowd parts as police gather around Meyer's still body. Eliana stands to her feet and then falls to her knees, with Wes immediately at her side. No matter what he put her through, she never wished this kind of payback on him.

There's another crowd gathering near a half a dozen police officers who look to be restraining someone. The camera zooms in as the reporter describes the scene in further detail. It's hard to see through the people swarming the steps, and I find myself tilting and turning my head to get a better view, even though that's impossible.

Will's arm tightens around my shoulder as we watch the horror of his father having been shot unfold on national television.

As the crowd disperses under the direction of local law enforcement, the country gets a clear picture of the person responsible for shooting Gregory Meyer. We all give a collective gasp as we watch in absolute shock as two Charlotte-Mecklenburg Police officers handcuff Holly Reynolds and take her into custody.

Acknowledgements

I continue to be in awe of the tremendous support my fellow bookworms have given. I'm over the moon with joy that you all have fallen in love with Layla and Will as much as I have. Thank you for your kind words of love and for inviting so many of your friends and family on the journey!

A huge thank you to my amazing editor, Lisa. You have become a dear friend. I'm so thankful for you and all the Bang Bang Shrimp two girls could consume!

To my personal Fab Four: Lisa S., Lisa B., Jenna, and Kelly. What can I say that I haven't already said? You continue to amaze me with your pure love for Layla's story. You have cheered me on, challenged me, and filled me with more positive affirmation than this girl truly deserves. I am humbled by your commitment to seeing this story to the end, and I'm so grateful to have each of you walking with me. Your friendship means the world to me.

To my dear, sweet friend Dana. Your friendship means more to me than you may ever know. Thank you for your listening ears and your words of wisdom. You have been steadfast and I will always treasure you.

Thank you to my writing heroes, of which there are too many to name. To write is one thing. To put your writing out there for the world to see requires a level of bravery not for the faint of heart. You paved the way and gave me the courage to be brave.

Thank you to my attorneys-on-call Joe Lackey and Robert Whitlow. Your legal guidance proved to be so incredibly helpful. I feel blessed to have been connected with both of you!

I truly have the BEST fans in the world! The outpouring of love for the Lake Trilogy has been mind-blowing. Some of you repeatedly posted your excitement for these books and encourage your friends almost daily to follow me (Stephanie!), and others of you moved hell and high water to get your hands on a book (Katrina!). Your devotion is heart-warming and I want you to know just how much you all mean to me. I'm fully aware that my success is due in no small part to all of you. Thank you, from the bottom of my heart.

I'm so thankful for my family. My parents, my brothers and their families, my in-laws…you have done nothing but been completely supportive of this crazy venture of mine and for that I will always be thankful.

I continue to be so grateful to my brother, Derek, for his time and talent in making the cover art for the Lake Trilogy so beautiful. The first quarter of 2013 was incredibly busy for you, yet you made time to gift me with your talent and expertise. Thank you so much!

Because my computer knowledge is lacking, I'm so thankful to my oldest brother, Glenn. You gave me your time and helped walk me through making the web site excellent. Thank you for playing such a big part in making the web presence of the Lake Trilogy look so great!

Truman and Claire, you are my proudest accomplishment. You grow so much every day, showing me your brilliance and making me so excited for what God has in store for you.

To my amazing husband: your belief in me over these last few years has been astonishing. Every time I told you what Will and Layla were up to, how their story was unfolding, you encouraged me, telling me how awesome the story line was, or how you were so impressed with what I was accomplishing. If I sell a kabillion books or have as many fans, none of it will mean as much to me as the love and support you have always given me. I love you and would be so completely lost without you.

*Layla's journey comes to a
conclusion in the Lake Trilogy's*

Safe Harbor

Coming June 2013!

For more information, visit:
AnnaLisaGrant.com
Facebook.com/AuthorAnnalisaGrant

Author photo by Charlotte Photography
CharlottePhotography.com

Cover art by Derek Wesley Selby/Divine Spark Creative Services
dwselby@gmail.com

Made in the USA
Middletown, DE
26 February 2015